DIVINE MEAT

'Who are you?' the priest Ti-Charles whispered under the pounding of the drums, his voice throaty with fear and desire.

'Baron Samedi,' the other man answered in a hoarse, nasal voice. He reached out with strong fingers and gripped one of Ti-Charles's bullet-shaped nipples brazenly. 'The Spirits sent me, so I come. And I want you.'

'Are you mocking me?' Ti-Charles asked.

'No, man. I do not mock you. I give you what you want.' Baron Samedi slid a hand down the back of Ti-Charles's tight white shorts, pressing a long finger against Ti-Charles's sphincter. 'Though I want to mount you, human-wise. Tonight, man, tonight I must ride.'

The heat of the other man's body, the scent of cocoa butter on his skin mingling with the cooler night smells, the background scent of the offerings of food, of oil lamps and candles, all intertwined sensually in Ti-Charles's nose. 'Then ride me, Baron,' he whispered.

DIVINE MEAT

An Idol short-story collection

Edited by David MacMillan

First published in Great Britain in 2001 by
Idol
Thames Wharf Studios,
Rainville Road, London W6 9HA

Myth	© Alan Mills
High On a Hill	© Jay Rennie
Angelic Decision	© Louis Carr
Islands in the Stream	© Barry Alexander
Pact With the Devil	© Michael Gouda
Night and Day	© Philip Markham
Divine Lover	© David MacMillan
Into the Fog	© Jordan Baker
Song of the Sea	© Bill Crimmin
Taming Loki	© Jon Thomas
Ridden by the Ghedes	© Johnny T Malice
The New Recruit	© John Patrick
The Flame Within	© Caleb Knight
The People of the Empty Places	© JD Ryan
Changing Death	© Shane D Yorston
The Gift of Eros	© Dominic Santi

'Islands in the Stream' was previously published in a shorter version
as 'Islands' in *In Touch* magazine # 27 in April 1998 and in
Skinflicks, Companion Press 1999
'Myth' was previously published in *In Touch* magazine in 1998
'The Gift of Eros' was previously published in *First Hand*
magazine, June 1999
'The New Recruit' was adapted to fit this anthology from an original
story that was first published in *Dreamboys* (Starbooks, 1998)

ISBN 0 352 33587 4

Typeset by SetSystems Ltd, Saffron Walden, Essex
Printed and bound in Great Britain by
Mackays of Chatham PLC

Contents

CONTENTS

SAFER SEX GUIDELINES

We include safer sex guidelines in every Idol book. However, while our policy is always to show safer sex in contemporary stories, we don't insist on safer sex practices in stories with historical settings – as this would be anachronistic. These books are sexual fantasies – in real life, everyone needs to think about safe sex.

While there have been major advances in the drug treatments for people with HIV and AIDS, there is still no cure for AIDS or a vaccine against HIV. Safe sex is still the only way of being sure of avoiding HIV sexually.
   HIV can only be transmitted through blood, come and vaginal fluids (but no other body fluids) passing from one person (with HIV) into another person's bloodstream. It cannot get through healthy, undamaged skin. The only real risk of HIV is through anal sex without a condom – this accounts for almost all HIV transmissions between men.

Being safe
Even if you don't come inside someone, there is still a risk to both partners from blood (tiny cuts in the arse) and pre-come. Using strong condoms and water-based lubricant greatly reduces the risk of HIV. However, condoms can break or slip off, so:
* Make sure that condoms are stored away from hot or damp places.
* Check the expiry date – condoms have a limited life.
* Gently squeeze the air out of the tip.
* Check the condom is put on the right way up and unroll it down the erect cock.
* Use plenty of water-based lubricant (lube), up the arse and on the condom.
* While fucking, check occasionally to see the condom is still in one piece (you could also add more lube).

* When you withdraw, hold the condom tight to your cock as you pull out.
* Never re-use a condom or use the same condom with more than one person.
* If you're not used to condoms you might practise putting them on.
* Sex toys like dildos and plugs are safe. But if you're sharing them use a new condom each time or wash the toys well.

For the safest sex, make sure you use the strongest condoms, such as Durex Ultra Strong, Mates Super Strong, HT Specials and Rubberstuffers packs. Condoms are free in many STD (Sexually Transmitted Disease) clinics (sometimes called GUM clinics) and from many gay bars. It's also essential to use lots of water-based lube such as KY, Wet Stuff, Slik or Liquid Silk. Never use come as a lubricant.

Oral sex
Compared with fucking, sucking someone's cock is far safer. Swallowing come does not necessarily mean that HIV gets absorbed into the bloodstream. While a tiny fraction of cases of HIV infection have been linked to sucking, we know the risk is minimal. But certain factors increase the risk:
* Letting someone come in your mouth
* Throat infections such as gonorrhoea
* If you have cuts, sores or infections in your mouth and throat

So what is safe?
There are so many things you can do which are absolutely safe: wanking each other; rubbing your cocks against one another; kissing, sucking and licking all over the body; rimming – to name but a few.

If you're finding safe sex difficult, call a helpline or speak to someone you feel you can trust for support. The Terrence Higgins Trust Helpline, which is open from noon to 10pm every day, can be reached on 020 7242 1010.

Or, if you're in the United States, you can ring the Center for Disease Control toll free on 1 800 458 5231.

Introduction

A Collection of Mythologically Skewered Tales

Man's gods have always held an erotic flavour for me – since I found Greek mythology when I was nine. After Zeus with all his women and nymphs took young Ganymede as well, I found that sweet young David had been in love with Prince Jonathan in the Old Testament (which probably went a long way towards explaining why King Saul tried to kill young David several times). Long before I understood the word or its concept, I intuitively knew that man's basic nature was bisexual, even though I couldn't ask a priest or a doctor for comment on my observation.

Unfortunately, homosexuality was still a crime and a sin in those days. It took me until near the end of secondary school before I found Masters and Johnson, who were kind enough to give me the psychological and physiological underpinnings to my intuitive awareness of human sexual nature.

Curiosity aroused, my sexual orientation well set, and a university library near at hand, I indulged my horniness for things godly. Of course, the old scribes didn't get into the specifics of divine buggery, but I had an active imagination. Gilgamesh even entered the land of the dead to win his love back to the land of the living, and he and Enkidu lived happily ever after in the city states of Sumer. The temples of several Sumerian deities even offered up male prostitutes. Seth was the first male to give birth when he gave Egypt Horus's son to worship. I already knew that the Greeks and Romans had their gods pleasuring themselves with male flesh, both divine and human.

I soon found that homoeroticism had been a part of Norse and Celtic mythology as well. Not as much as among the Mediterraneans, of course; but it was there. It was blatantly obvious that all the forebears of Western civilisation had homoeroticism as an integral part of their lives.

These were the halcyon days of the 1970s, however – and the sexual revolution was well under way. Daydreams of having Zeus between my legs changed to visions of having Ganymede's legs around me. But daydreaming and wanking soon surrendered to the real thing. Hawk-faced Horus with the body of a god ploughing my nether regions gave way to my ploughing a beautiful body attached to a bird brain behind a pretty face. It didn't matter then: we were in the middle of a revolution, and the future was the touch of flesh on flesh. But I never completely forgot my fascination with gods and their lusts.

After I'd enjoyed a bit of success in America with erotic anthologies, I submitted a proposal to Idol. I had watched their publishing programme grow and knew they were going to require far more than just a collection about porn stars shagging each other.

The idea of man and god together began to take shape. With a lot more fortitude than I would ever have shown, Kathleen Bryson, Commissioning Editor at Idol, liked my idea and helped me shape it into something Idol – and I – could be proud of. It became a labour of love – one that consciously bound the two sides of the Atlantic.

There are sixteen first-rate stories in this collection – stories that are just as good as fiction as they are as gay male erotica. Two stories define this collection more completely than I have ever seen stories in other collections do. Alan Mills's 'Myth' has a thoroughly modern Eros finally getting his heart's desire only to learn that Ganymede is a bit more than he'd expected. Dominic Santi's 'Gift Of Eros' wraps up what our dream has become in this Age of the Disease.

Barry Alexander and JD Ryan give the gods a sense of humour – even when the humans aren't laughing. Divine whimsy is inherent in all the religions of mankind. These two writers portray it so warmly but with – oh! – such finality.

But even divine whimsy can backfire on the deity, as it does the human. Michael Gouda paints that so very well as he depicts a Satan gloating before he should in 'Pact With the Devil'. Even so, some of us might be tempted to try that pact. What a hell of a way to go.

Idol's own Philip Markham is just so – well – powerful. I won't say any more, except that I wouldn't mind an Egyptian eternity if I could have what his protagonist got.

I have a soft spot in my heart for warm, gentle, sweet stories. Bill Crimmin and Jay Rennie provide that with their stories set in Britain's own Celtic past.

I've mentioned only eight of the sixteen stories in this anthology. There are eight more that are just as good, just as strong, and just as commanding. All sixteen are stories you'll go back and reread over the years. They'll possess you anew each time with their strong characters and with their sexiness.

I can only hope you'll enjoy them as much as I have. I think you will.

Dave MacMillan
Atlanta, GA, 2001

Myth

Alan Mills

I

I know from Narcissus not to love myself too much, but I find that difficult to do as I stare at my reflection in the mirror. Even I have to admit that I've grown up well. I comb my black hair and stare at the way I fill my jock. I never thought I'd go out like this, in just a strap and boots, but – what the hell! – tonight, everyone will look this way.

OK, that was the hook. Every story has one. I put it there so you'd keep reading. I realise how improbable fiction is, especially fantasy or erotica, but I want you to keep reading anyway.

I'm still playing with my fringe when my mother walks in. 'Holy shit!' she says.

I only answer with, 'Don't you ever knock?'

Of course, she's being attended by a handful of nymphs, and two of them immediately start messing with my hair.

'Don't be so hostile, Eros. It isn't becoming,' she says in her melodic and inappropriately coy voice.

'Yeah, OK, whatever,' seems to be a good enough answer. Naturally, the two nymphs working on my hair take every opportunity to stroke my chest and biceps. One even slyly feels up my arse.

'What are you doing in a jockstrap, sweetie?' my mother says.

'Underwear party at the Inferno.'

'Oh, in that case, girls, make his fringe just a little messy. And, Eros, did you clean behind your wings?'

'Mother! Can't I just get ready on my own!' Of course, she never listens. She just walks up and starts sniffing my neck.

'Oh, girls, he needs a little scent –'

'Nothing fruity!' I should probably just move out.

'Something citrus –'

'Damnit! Nothing fruity!' I think I will move out.

'OK, something fresh – clean maybe.'

Thankfully, it doesn't take long for her to get what she wants. It never does. She even gives me a spiked leather strap for my wrist. 'To beat the boys away,' she says.

This scene is typical of my life ever since I moved back home. You see, Psyche and I broke up back when Nietzsche said that God was dead. I supposed that meant that 'love' had left the 'soul'. I don't know. Sure, it's fucked, but sometimes that's just the way things are. Face it, man, you've been screwed again. At least my mother Aphrodite finally got her way.

OK, so I'm a bit resentful. Who wouldn't be? Before stepping off the balcony, I tell her that, if she shows up, I'll never speak to her again. She laughs, so I threaten to make her mortal boyfriend fall in love with Howard Stern. That seems to do the trick.

II

I have to say I like the 1990s, despite the faults. Olympus is bigger than it used to be. It rises to the sky. It's darker, too. What you might call pre-apocalyptic. I guess the whole world is more cynical these days.

I remember when Olympus was all green fields with a group of temples gathered on the hill. Now, that's downtown, and I think they levelled the hill decades ago, as they once did in the mortal city called LA.

Anyway, it's a short flight to the Inferno, Olympus's biggest queer nightclub. Once again, I think how terrific it would be to leave my mother's temple in the clouds and live in this seedy part of town. I had a really fierce temple of my own – before – but that belongs to Psyche now. When it ended, Athena handed Psyche everything. I have no doubt that she deserved it all. After time, my other love for men finally broke her heart.

III

When I land, there's already a queue outside Inferno that stretches down the block, all the way to Café Styx. All the regulars are here tonight, but I walk straight towards the door. After all, I'm not just some lowly demigod. The two centaurs at the entrance part to let me through. I've always liked their kind, and I'm glad that someone finally brought them back.

Inside, the club is a steamy sea of men. The place smells like sweat cologne. The beat burrows deep into my chest. I see skin everywhere and smile from liberated joy until I feel a sting when someone snaps my jock. I recognise the snigger and slug the god's chest when I turn around. 'Fuck you, Hymen!'

'Fuckin' relax, Cupid.'

'Don't call me that!'

'What's wrong, Cupid? Got parasites in your wings?'

'Shut up, Hymen! At least I'm not named after some chick's cherry!'

'Oh, you arsehole! You know that it's the other way around!'

We laugh and hug. It's always this way with us: the queer god of weddings and the queer god of love. Oh, well, blame it on the modern age.

I look down. 'Silk boxers, huh? How Victoria's Secret.'

IV

It isn't often that gods write stories. There's a lot of stuff out there that people claim some god has said, but it's usually a lie. Deities typically have better things to do. Once, while in Chicago – I think – I read a poem. The guy who wrote it said that every word in it was handed down by 'God'. I looked at it, laughed and said, 'Well, clearly, "God" can't spell.'

Anyway, I don't know why I decided to write this. I just felt the need – a very natural thing. Who knows, maybe I might even start my own 'zine. That'll definitely upset the three leeching Ps: preachers, poets, politicians. I think I'll call it 'I'm Moral Love'.

V

'Where's Apollo?'

'Oh, you know him. He's causing havoc in New York. He loves me to death, but you know how gods are.'

'Well, that sucks. Fuck! Gods can be such pigs. You know, I could always –'

'But, look who is here.' He always cuts me off whenever I start talking about arrows.

Hymen points to a table on the other side of the dancing pit. 'Zeus,' I gasp. I stare as the god of gods spills wine down a young warrior's back, making a river of his sculpted arse.

'And, look who's with him.' He moves his pointing finger to the nearby bar.

'Ganymede.' I'm utterly stunned.

Hymen grins. 'Girl, now's your chance.'

VI

I do my best to catch up to him. On the way, I knock one satyr over with one of my wings, but I still manage to get to Ganymede before he leaves the bar.

'Um, hi, Ganymede,' I say as the barman hands him his drinks.

Ganymede lifts the golden cups and turns to face me. He smiles and I feel like I've just shot myself. He looks perfect in his white Calvins, his hair like gold, his eyes a pure Elysium green. 'Hi, Eros,' he says and turns to the barman. 'One more for my friend.'

'Thanks, Ganymede.'

'You're welcome, Eros.'

I feel lost. In front of me is a boy so beautiful that even Zeus could not resist giving him eternity. If I could offer more, I would.

He hands me one of the cups and takes another from the bar. 'Well, Eros, I have to be going now. Your grandfather is waiting.'

'Yeah. See ya, I guess.'

'Yeah.' He walks off, leaving me alone. I look down at my crotch. Just looking at his face, his smooth flawless chest, has made me hard like rock. I adjust my cock. There's a wet spot in the fabric.

VII

I spend the next hour watching Ganymede from across the bar. 'You've got it bad,' says Hymen.

'Fuck you. Don't you have a wedding to go and bless?'

'Most weddings are cursed from the start these days. Why bother?'

'That's a fucked-up thing to say.'

'Oooh, what's up your arse?'

'Lots of shit,' I say and stare down into the dancing crowd. Below me, two guys grind against each other. They're young, passionate, eager to enjoy the night. I open my palm and let the arrows fly. At least, I figure, someone should know what it feels like to be in love.

VIII

I've spent centuries fantasising about Ganymede. I've wasted whole decades in my temple stroking my cock and spilling scalding come while the image of the universe's most perfect boy teases and taunts me from the shadows of my memory. I've spent millennia just trying to be near him, close enough to share his breath, smell his immortal skin. There've been other men, nymphs, satyrs, gods, goddesses – Psyche, of course – but never once a soul like him. Every moment with him has been a treasure. Each moment brief. Each moment stolen quickly by a jealous Zeus, who fears my arrow and how it might make Ganymede fall in love with someone else. I suppose I should be grateful. At least Prometheus has never given Zeus any hints about my true intentions.

IX

That's when it happens. The unexpected. I watch the boys kiss with even greater fever. Their need for each other is a flame, and it burns through them, through the crowd, and everyone feels it, knows it to be real as it moves through them like a wave. Even Zeus can feel it. Across the club, he looks at me and smiles while naked boys dance in circles before his throne. Zeus quietly applauds, but it's not for them. Instead, he stares at me.

I step up, on to the rail, spread my wings, float above the writhing, almost naked, floor, and come to a graceful, gentle stop before the greatest god. Ganymede stands next to him, with Zeus's cup held firmly in his hand. I keep my glance away from him for fear. Zeus looks down, straight through my eyes, and speaks with a soft and caring voice. 'You always bring such joy and passion to every place you bless. Why is it that you, Eros, always seem so sad, so totally devoid of love?'

I hesitate to speak, to try to lie, but his eyes are turquoise like the summer sky. In them, white clouds float slowly. Calm, he is the breeze. The only storm is the water in my eyes. 'I'm sorry, Grandfather,' I say with a cracked voice, 'but the only man I love belongs to you.'

I lower my head and expect thunder, but it doesn't come. Afraid, I still look down. It's not Zeus I fear so much right now. It's Ganymede and the apathetic countenance, the cold and perfect face of heaven he probably wears right now.

'This is bad,' says Zeus. 'The world has become a sad and lonely place. Eros, you're supposed to be the source of love, true love itself, the undeniable force of attraction that first caused the universe to form before there were men even to know your name. But look at you; look at the countless shards that might have been your heart. To heal this, to spread your gift of love across creation, I would give you anything that's mine. Just speak his name.'

'I can't. It would be wrong even to say it.'

'No, Eros, there is no love that cannot speak its name.' He reaches down to stroke my cheek and combs his large fingers through my hair. 'Ganymede, my dear, set down my cup. Your job is done.'

X

I know I've laid the romance on a little thick. I sincerely thank you for your patience. It's just that I think sex is such a sacred thing that I don't feel it right to just tell you about how quickly or how violently I could get Ganymede into bed. The truth is, when I looked up, I saw his smile,

Ganymede's smile, so warm and tender. No love I had ever made could look so sweet. Without a word, he sets down the cup and places a gentle kiss on Zeus's cheek. It makes Zeus cry. And then Ganymede says it. He says, 'Thank you,' as if I had been a gift to him. I know that sex is what this story is supposed to be about, but some moments, some feelings, are too important not to be given fully to your needy world.

XI

Ganymede grins and leads me by the hand. The club becomes a fading blur as we slip away and float down towards the Earth. I hold him tight and let winds play gently off my wings as we descend towards the ground. 'I've always wanted this,' he says and places a kiss softly on my neck. It feels like gold – you know, the way that something indefinable inside begins to swell when diamonds are draped across your skin. It feels like that, and he kisses my lips, once, again, another time before opening his lips and mine so that our tongues touch, taste, commingle in the sweet nectar passed between us.

Around us is a line of trees and thick grass is crushed beneath our boots. I'm too occupied to envisage where we are. I think it's France. The climate's nice, the season warm. Ganymede kisses my neck again and nibbles on my ear. Above us is a clear night sky. The stars are endless. There definitely aren't any cities nearby. I bite softly into his silky shoulder as he begins to whisper.

XII

This is where the story gets injected with a sudden change of tone. What Ganymede whispers is a very stern: 'Now, boy, get on your knees!' And, needless to say, I am as shocked as you.

But I do as I'm told – I worship him. I lower myself slowly and kiss his honey-toned chest and taste his nipples, running my hands gently up his sides as I go down. Without warning, he pushes me back. I fall on my arse, one of my wings becoming painfully pinned behind my back. 'I didn't tell you to do that!' he shouts, and I think I understand. He's been an immortal's toy for several thousand years, and now it's his chance to be on top. 'Now, get up on your knees – and keep your hands behind your back!'

I do as he says, but I can't help but plead, 'I just wanted to –'

'To what, boy?'

I hesitate. 'To finally touch you.' He slaps my face. It stings. He slaps again. The same spot. It hurts like love.

'All I want is for you to behave,' he says – kindly.

I nod.

'Say, "Yes, sir".'

'Yes, sir.'

He rubs a thumb across my cheek as the stinging begins to go away. 'Good,' he says and kisses me. I feel like I could give him anything.

'Now, keep your hands clasped behind your back. If I want you to touch me, boy, I'll let you know.'

'Yes, sir.'

'Good.'

'Thank you, sir.' I lower my head.

XIII

He stands over me and starts lowering the waistband of his Calvins. 'I want to show you something, boy.'

My breath is heavy as he pushes the front of his underwear down and exposes his perfectly shaped cock. 'Look at this cock, boy. Do you like this cock?' Fuckin' A I do, but I can't exactly say that.

'It's a beautiful cock, sir,' I whisper – all my strength having been stripped away by lust.

He lifts out his smooth, rosy nuts. His scrotum is shaved, unlike my own dark and hairy sac. 'You like my nuts, boy?'

'Yes, sir.'

He strokes his cock slowly. 'Come here and smell them.'

I move closer, bury my nose in the groove between his sac and thigh. He smells pungent, the way men smell: not dirty, but slightly sweaty even though he's totally clean. I stick my tongue out and lick at the soft flesh as he strokes his thick cock next to my face – his knuckles grazing my tender cheek. I taste his salty warmth, and he rubs the top of his leather boot against my swollen groin, pressing his knee against my heaving chest, pushing me back, away from his heavenly crotch.

'I didn't tell you to lick!'

'Sorry, sir.'

'Just smell.'

He grabs the back of my head and buries my face in his pliable nuts. 'Yeah, boy, smell those nuts! Oh, yeah, breathe deep.'

I do.

'Inhale my smelly nuts!'

I do – I do.

His fingers twist in my dark hair, and he pulls my head back. He strokes his cock right in front of my eyes. 'You love my cock, huh?'

It's beautiful. Just the right length. Nice and fat. Totally solid. I can't even speak.

'Open your mouth.' I do, and he rubs his cock against my lips, my tongue. 'Oh, fuck,' he says, 'look how hard you're making me.'

XIV

'I want to see you naked,' he says. I reach for my jock and he shouts, 'What the fuck do you think you're doing, boy?' He grabs the back of my neck and pushes me down on to my hands and knees, stepping on to my back with his heavy booted foot to push my body the rest of the way down until blades of grass stab against my chest and stomach.

He walks to my feet and roughly pulls one of my boots off. My leg falls when he's done, and I feel cool grass sink between my toes. He pulls the other boot off and slaps my arse. I groan, and he slaps my arse again before grabbing it firmly in his hand. He runs his thumb along the deep crack between my cheeks, sliding the digit right against my hot arsehole. Right at that moment, I feel a thick glob of pre-come leak from my cock and soak in the jock. His thumb finally stops at my pelvis as his fingers close around the tight, elastic band. With one hard pull, he rips the jock off my waist and down my legs, my cock getting scratched by the grass-stained fabric as it's torn away.

He sinks his thumb deep into my arsehole, snagging the sensitive flesh as he pushes in. His other fingers close firmly around my balls, and he starts to pull. I push my arse back as his thumb invades me deeper, and I sit up on my knees to avoid getting my nuts torn off. He's kneeling right behind me. I feel his prick against my flank. My cock sticks straight up into the night. It's covered with dirt – more so than the rest of me. Ganymede reaches around to slap it. It hurts, but the attention feels good, and clear drops of pre-come are hurled through the air when he slaps my cock again, snapping it hard against my belly.

'You've got a nice cock, too, boy.'

'Thank you, sir.'

He pulls his thumb out of my arse. 'Here, taste this.' He rams his thumb deep into my mouth. 'How do you like yourself, boy? Do you taste good? Do you taste good enough for me?'

Fuck yeah! I'm a fucking god! Of course I do!

XV

He wraps an arm around my neck and bites my ear – just hard enough to hurt. His hand grips my jaw as he licks my shoulders and back, stroking my flank roughly with his other hand. Suddenly, I feel a sharp stab in one of my wings, and Ganymede laughs as he reaches his hidden hand around to show me one of my own feathers in between his perfect fingers. 'Look what I found,' he says as he strokes the white feather against my cheek. 'What do you think I should do with this, boy?'

'I don't know, sir.'

He laughs again, running it down my neck and chest, tickling a nipple, my sides, and my thigh and balls.

XVI

Holy shit, I think, this is really starting to get warped. Perverse, even.

XVII

He pushes me back on to my hands and knees. 'Let me see that arse.' His fingers push into my crack as he pries my cheeks apart. Both of his thumbs play with my sphincter as his knuckles keep my hairy hole exposed. 'Reach back and hold your arse open for me!' I lower my chest to the ground, turn my face to the side – the grass almost icy against my skin – and reach my hands back, prying my arse cheeks completely open for this god that I love.

'That's good,' he says.

'Thank you, sir.'

He runs a finger along my arsehole and gently slaps my come-swollen nuts. I feel his firm grip on my rock-hard cock. It feels amazing as he strokes me slowly. I moan. He chuckles.

'You like that, don't you?'

'Yes, sir.'

'You like getting your cock stroked, don't you, boy?'

'Yes, sir. I like it when you stroke my cock, sir.'

'Do you like it when I slap your arse, boy?'

'Yes, sir.'

'Do you like it when I cause you pain?'

'Yes, sir. I love everything you do, sir.'

'Good boy.' He gives my cock a nice squeeze, and I can feel the pre-come dripping out.

XVIII

I keep holding my arse open for him, but he stops touching me. Instead, I feel his stare. 'You've got such a beautiful little hole. I wonder if it's as tight and warm as it looks.'

'It's really tight, sir.'

'And hot?'

'And hot, sir.'

'You want me to play with it, boy?'

'Yes, sir. I love it when you play with me, sir.'

Then I feel it. It's unbelievable. He takes my own soft feather and runs it along my held-open crack. It feels so amazing that I almost lose my grip on my cheeks.

'Oh, fuck!' I groan.

A hard slap falls on my arse. 'What did you say?' The tip of my feather returns to my convulsing sphincter.

'Oh, fuck! Sir!' He tickles my arse and nuts, goes down to the tip of my cock and back up to my burning hole. I hump my arse, wagging my cock between my spread thighs. 'Oh, shit, sir, oh, fuck! Sir, I can't handle it, sir! Oh, fuck! Sir!'

He pulls back the feather, and his warm, wet tongue slaps against my arsehole.

'Oh my Gawd – fuck, sir!' His tongue licks at me, pushes into me. I push out, open up my hole for him. His tongue invades the rim. My whole body is on fire. Thick pre-come clings to the head of my cock. His tongue feels like a fiery serpent, burrowing up my vulnerable arse, and when he finally takes it away I don't even have time to consider what's coming next.

XIX

His thick, immortal cock violates my arse without any issued warning. The overwhelming girth opens my inflamed hole violently. I feel like one big stretched-out circle. The immense length spears deep into my guts like a huge metal spike. I scream out, '*Fuck me, sir! Fuck Me!*' so loud that I think everyone on Earth and in Heaven can hear me roar.

XX

Ganymede's cock fills me entirely and then pulls out to leave me void. He bucks his hornlike cock into me wildly, his strong hands pushing down on my back. I keep my arse held open to give him total access, my face and chest pounding against the ground. I slide forwards a few inches with each thrust until my head starts tearing up the cold, wet soil.

He pounds into me and pounds into me for hours, all night long. My cock tingles and itches like I'm about to shoot. It goes on for ever. His cock head rivets my prostate like a machine tearing up a street. I stay on the very brink of orgasm while the moon falls from the sky. My prostate is on fire. My arse becomes a gushy hole that his cock falls into. He fucks me and fucks me, never once saying a single word. The sky turns silver and then the sun falls on our glistening skin. Ganymede starts tugging on my feathers without actually pulling any out. My arse clamps down on his cock every time the engrossing pain explodes from my wings and shoots down my spine. The sun rises to the vertex of Earth's glowing dome, and still Ganymede's cock sends thunder through my body.

It's afternoon when his cock explodes inside me. I feel it. He has the burning come of a god. The hot liquid fills my bowels. No mortal could handle come like this. We both scream out. My prostate feels like it will either explode or melt. My pain-filled cock aches angrily for release.

Ganymede pumps a few more times and slowly pulls his still hard prick from my throbbing arse. When his dick escapes, some of his burning come spills out and seeps down to scald my clenched-up balls. He pulls me up to my knees and kisses my neck. 'Oh, fuck, Eros, that was so hot. Thank you.' I reach down to give my wagging cock that one last squeeze it needs, but he grabs my hand before I get there. 'Don't even think about it, boy! I don't want you coming until tomorrow, when you see me again.'

XXI

Well, that was my story. I hope I spelled all the words correctly. After all, it isn't often that gods decide to do this kind of thing.

Let's see. Ganymede and I spent the rest of the day just lying in the grove, watching Apollo's lovely sun take its own sweet time to descend into Poseidon's sea. Zeus kept the heavens clear for us, and when the stars came out I could feel my mother's gentle influence working on our swelling hearts. I looked at Ganymede's perfect form and quietly planned tomorrow's revenge. He spent the evening talking about how he'd decorate our temple. Of course, for now, we both knew that we'd settle for another date, maybe a little dancing inside Inferno. After all, we'd met only a few millennia ago, and everyone knows that even the most perfect lovers shouldn't rush towards their freedom's end.

It may please you to know that two young men soon found the feather lying on the ground, where we had left it. Needless to say, their love turned pure. Hymen blessed their wedding, and, when they died a joyous lifetime later, Zeus honoured them with a constellation so that they might live eternally in human memory, my feather for ever gripped between their entwined hands.

High On a Hill

Jay Rennie

Brian had come to this little place in Dorset called Cerne
Abbas, and he really didn't know why. 'It's a lark, lad. Just a
lark,' he'd told himself more than once as he decided to make the
trip. He'd told himself that several times on the train out. But he
still felt quite stupid. Coming to Cerne Abbas was probably the
dumbest thing he'd ever done. He was a city boy, born and bred
within the sound of the Bow Bells of east London. He'd never
been particularly interested in history or archaeology. The quaint
little town of Cerne Abbas didn't mean anything to him, nor did
the picturesque Dorset countryside.

But what made Cerne Abbas special was the one-hundred-and-
eighty-foot-tall figure of a naked man etched into the long sloping
hillside overlooking the town.

According to historians, the ancient Celts had spent months,
perhaps years, cutting out and hauling away tons of grass and soil
to reveal the white chalk rock below, slowly defining the huge
nude figure, which had subsequently lain emblazoned on the
hillside in rampant splendour for more than four millennia.

Brian had first seen a picture of the naked giant of Cerne Abbas
when he was sitting at his computer, surfing the Internet, looking
for the more usual naked sights. At first sight, he'd thought,

Blimey! That's not the kind of naked guy I'm searching for! But then, something about the picture had attracted him. Had kept attracting him.

It wasn't the giant's cock. At least it wasn't *just* the cock. There was something about the way the figure was drawn, strong and sturdy, standing with its legs apart, its arms spread wide, and waving a huge cudgel in its right hand that made Brian feel that he was looking at a friend from the distant past.

Brian didn't have all that many friends − not real friends. He'd never had a lover. Tall, good-looking and easy-going, with a wicked sense of humour, he was never short of sex partners. But real, deep, true friendship had always somehow eluded him. At parties and in crowded pubs, he always felt somehow apart from the others, adrift in a sea of people, but somehow never quite connecting with them.

The only way Brian could ever get close to another person was through sex. In his early adolescence, he'd thought that boys had to go for girls, and so that was what he did. But it was never satisfying. There was always an empty loneliness.

Then he'd discovered men. Or at least men had discovered him. At the age of eighteen, his tall, well-muscled body, his intense brown eyes, his charm, his wit and, not least, his sturdy, ever-ready cock had made him very popular and he had happily plunged into an orgy of male sex. But that hadn't fully satisfied him either. When all the rolling and the writhing were over; when he lay side by side in bed with his partner, instead of a warm glow of satisfaction, he still felt separate and alone; he still felt like an alien in a world to which he didn't quite belong.

Gradually he had stopped looking for a real friend, for that one true friend that only a lover can be. He began to make do with casual one-night stands and, more and more, with remote sex, over the Internet; typing one-handed as he exchanged fantasies with men who were hundreds or even thousands of miles away.

Searching for something new to titillate him, he'd opened the website that revealed the Cerne Abbas giant. According to the text that accompanied the picture, the outline figure was that of an ancient Celtic god called Cernunnos and, apart from the late nineteenth century when the highly moral Victorians had filled in part of the trenching and allowed the grass to grow over his massive genitals, Cernunnos had been rampant across the hillside in all his male glory for century after century.

So, now, Brian stood at the foot of the rise gazing up at the Cerne Abbas giant. A naked giant with his cock highly visible and fully erect. He felt a sense of kinship with the ancient Celt. Like the giant, Brian too stood alone and apart and, he suddenly realised, he too was developing a rigid erection. On an impulse, after carefully adjusting his cock for maximum concealment, he began to climb the hill. Vivid and exciting and sexy images chased across his fertile mind, and he was oblivious of the oncoming evening.

The further Brian climbed up the grassy slope, the more the shape of the giant became lost to him. Pretty soon he was simply climbing up alongside a channel cut in the springy turf to reveal the dirty-white chalk below. This channel was, in fact, the inside line of the giant's leg and, as Brian veered more and more to the left, up the thigh, he came eventually to the giant's crotch. Now he could clearly see that he was standing between the swelling curves of the giant's massive balls and that rising ahead of him was the upright stretch of that enormous cock.

On impulse, Brian climbed on into the area of grass that formed the cock and then turned to face down the hillside, his strong well-muscled arms half raised in the same attitude as that of the giant. Far below him, the picturesque village looked small and toylike. Tiny cars buzzed along the road, the sound of their engines faint and distant.

The sun was beginning to set on the far horizon and, in its dying rays, Brian felt a surge of sexuality burn through his body. He felt his cock stir again and, after looking all round to confirm that he was truly alone, he began to strip.

The T-shirt came off with a well-practised flowing movement, revealing a powerful, tanned and well-muscled chest. Next he flipped open the brass buckle of his belt and pulled the zip down over the growing bulge. Then with both hands to his slim waist, he slipped jeans and pants to the ground and stepped out of them. Finally he took off his trainers and socks and stood once again in the posture of the giant, but this time in the same naked magnificence.

His cock, which had softened somewhat during the long climb, slowly began to unfurl again, climbing ever higher up his belly, the rising force pulling a pair of fully proportioned balls up tight below it. Like a man in a dream, Brian lowered his arms and, cupping his balls in one hand, began to masturbate his huge cock with the other.

He felt that something primitive and powerful was driving him. It was an animal force, far beyond his control, coursing through his body. He could feel the blood pulsing through every vein and artery and already he was aware of copious pre-come leaking from the head of his circumcised cock and lubricating the rhythmic motion of his hand.

Initially, Brian's masturbation action was slow and sensuous. First his thumb and forefinger circled the base of the pillar of pink flesh and began to rise slowly, up the entire length of the cock. As they rose, the other fingers of his hand circled the cock too, rising up the turgid tube and raising the already high and tight balls even tighter. When the upper ring of his fist reached the bright red head, glistening in the rosy glow of the lowering sun, he paused for a moment before his hand slid down again, taking with it further gleaming lubrication and at the same time causing the eye of his cock to wink open and release yet more delicious juice.

Very gradually the speed of movement began to increase and each time, on the upstroke, as the rim of his cock head was rubbed, Brian began to make low moaning sounds.

A long time seemed to pass; lights began to appear in the windows of the small town below him; headlights appeared on the cars; the sun sank even lower and Brian continued his purposeful masturbation. He was approaching his climax very gradually. He could feel it building and growing: rivers of sensation surging through the muscles of his thighs, burning up into his groin and delivering white-hot sensations each time his encircling hand flowed over the burning head of his cock.

Then, from behind him, a deep male voice said quietly, 'What a lovely tight arse!'

Brian released his cock and turned with a gasp to see a tall, deeply tanned and naked man standing behind him. He said, 'What the hell?'

The man seemed almost as shocked as Brian. He said, 'Can you see me, then, lad?'

'Too right I can see you. What did you want to creep up on me like that for? You gave me a right fright!'

The tall, naked man gave a throaty chuckle. 'Well, it may seem strange to you, but I'm just not used to lads seeing me. Lasses, yes, at least in times gone by. Many a lass used to open her legs to her lad for the first time simply because she'd had a glimpse of my jolly todger to warm her up first.'

To demonstrate what he meant by his 'jolly todger' the man put his hand down to his huge dangling, uncut cock, and, grasping it by the base, twirled it several times in a clockwise rotation. The circle it made spanned the region from below the centre of his hairy thighs to just above his dark and deep navel.

'Now that,' said Brian, 'is a sight that would warm anybody up.'

The man said, 'Thank you kindly, young sir.'

Hardly believing what he was saying, yet knowing instinctively it was true, Brian said, 'You're him, aren't you? The Giant?'

'Oh yes,' the man said, 'the very same. Although not quite as large in real life as they drew me on the hillside.'

'My name's Brian. And your name is – is –' Brian struggled to remember what he had read in the guidebook.

'Cernunnos is my true name, Brian' said the giant. 'But you can call me Cer.'

'Well, hello then, Cer,' said Brian. 'Let's have a good look at you.' He took a step back to get a better view of this tall figure and to allow the warm light of sunset to illuminate him. Then slowly he scanned the god from head to toe.

Brian himself was tall – six foot two in his bare feet. But Cer towered above him by almost another foot. His hair was dark and unruly. His face was at once handsome and rugged, with the suspicion of a friendly grin lurking at the corners of his mouth. The god's torso was massive and well defined and, like every other inch of him, was tanned a light walnut colour. There was some dark and wiry chest hair and a huge dark bush of hair at the base of the cock.

The cock itself was massive. Even hanging, as it was now, Brian estimated it to be at least nine inches and he felt his arse cheeks twitch again at the thought of accommodating such a monster when it was on full stretch. Below the cock the balls hung close to the body, each one clearly outlined in their tight, light-brown, hairy bag. Cer's arms and legs were well muscled and shapely; his feet stood broad and firm.

Brian allowed his gaze to return to the face. 'I'd judge,' said Cer, 'from the time you spent looking down there, that you've taken a bit of a fancy to my todger, then.'

'It's very – big, isn't it?'

'Big enough, I fancy,' said Cer, giving his cock another twirl and making Brian wish that it could have been *his* hand that was doing it.

'And you're a god?'

'Yes. What they call "a minor Celtic god". We don't have the influence we used to have. But we still manage to have a bit of fun from time to time.'

'You mean sex?' said Brian.

'Of course.'

'With men?'

'Ah. Well, now,' said Cer, 'that's what I wanted to talk to you about.'

'It is?'

'It is. Will you sit beside me on the grass while I tell you all about it?'

'OK.'

The two handsome, naked men settled themselves down on the still-warm grass.

'Now then,' said Cer, 'the thing of it is that in the early centuries I had quite a few women.' He paused for a moment to think. 'Quite a few *hundred* women, come to think of it.' He turned to look at Brian. 'You know how it is.'

'Well, not exactly,' said Brian, 'but I know the general idea. Go on.'

'Well, in the years after the Romans had been and gone, people just seemed to stop seeing me. I'd display myself to a woman I fancied, wave my old todger at her, all friendly-like, and she'd just look straight through me.'

'You mean she just couldn't see you?'

'Nobody could. For a few hundred years now I've just had to watch and – well, rumble my own todger. You know what I mean?'

'Oh, yes, I know. We call it having a wank these days.'

'I've heard it called that. But, anyway, as you can well imagine, over the long, long years I've seen all sorts on this hillside, doing all sorts of things to each other. And just lately, in the last six or seven hundred years or so, I've been beginning to wonder what it would be like if – well, let's just say I've been getting a little curious about what men do together. You understand me?'

'Perfectly,' said Brian. 'When you say you're curious, I suppose you've seen men together?'

'Oh yes, Brian, many's the time I've watched the ways of men with men.' Cer paused for a moment with a reflective look in his eyes and then he went on: 'And very strange ways they seemed at first, too.' He paused again and absent-mindedly fondled his thickening cock.

'You mean . . .?' asked Brian, his eyes riveted on the growing pillar of nut-brown flesh.

'I mean the whole thing. I mean, a man with a man, that seemed strange to me at first. And then there was what they did to each other. First off kissing and playing with each other's todgers. Then putting their todgers in their mouths and kissing all over the place. Then, most times, they'd end up doing – you know –' Now Cer's eyes were gazing at Brian's massive dick.

'You mean arse-fucking?'

'That's right. Fair brought tears to my eyes just to watch it.'

'It does, at first, when you do it, too,' said Brian. 'But once you get used to it –'

'Took me long enough to get used to just watching it,' said Cer, slowly stroking the full length of his cock. 'But over the years I must confess that took me to wondering. I mean, they all seemed to enjoy it so – and I naturally fell to considering what it might be like.'

'Do you mean taking cock or giving it?' asked Brian, feeling an almost irresistible urge to reach over and touch Cer's now rigid tool.

'Oh, to take it, definitely to take it. I always reckoned that giving cock must be much the same, whoever you give it to.'

'Not always,' said Brian, reaching for the giant man's giant cock.

As his hand clasped the brown, gnarled pillar of flesh, Cer uttered a gasp of pure relief. 'You can touch me,' he breathed, his voice full of wonder.

'Thank you,' said Brian, his fist sliding slowly up Cer's massive organ.

'I wasn't giving you permission to touch me,' said Cer. Brian stopped. 'No, no,' said Cer. 'Don't you stop. I'm enjoying it. I just meant I was surprised that you actually can touch me as well as see me. I've not known a mortal soul able to touch me these thousand years or more.'

Brian began the movement of his hand again and, as he began the downward stroke, he was rewarded by the appearance, at the emerging tip of Cer's cock, of a single drop of clear liquid which gleamed rosy in the dying rays of the sun. Unable to resist it, Brian leaned forward and delicately touched the drop with the tip of his tongue. It collapsed and ran into his mouth.

'Whhoooo!' said Cer, and his whole body shook with delight. Then he said, 'I see you're leaking, too. Can I taste?' Without waiting for a reply Cer leaned across and began to lick avidly at the head of Brian's own cock. His tongue was hot and rasping and his breath felt unusually warm. 'Mmm,' he said. 'I've often wondered what it tasted like.'

Brian said, 'Have you ever tried this?' And he manoeuvred himself and Cer into the classic 69 position.

Cer said, 'Are you going to –'

'Yes I am.'

'And do you want me to –'

'That's up to you,' said Brian and, pulling down Cer's brown and wrinkled foreskin to reveal the blood-red head, he closed his lips around it and began to tease the tip with his tongue. It smelled of woodsmoke and tasted of sea salt.

Almost immediately, Cer said, 'Whhoooo!' again. Then his body began to shake and he said, 'Oh! Oh! Oh!' Three massive jets of come burst into Brian's mouth. Again he had the tang of woodsmoke, this time with the added richness of roast oats. The young cockney man sucked every last drop of the Celtic giant's come, impressed by the fact that Cer's rigid tool showed no sign of deflating.

Cer said, 'That was a surprise.'

'For me, too,' said Brian. 'I never thought a geezer like you would come that quick.'

'Well, it was very exciting.'

'Never thought you'd come so much, either!' Brian grinned wickedly.

'Well,' Cer said again, 'it was very, very exciting.' Then he added, 'And you are very good at it!' Cer's grin was as wide and as wicked as Brian's, his gleaming, even white teeth contrasting with his dark skin and the deep red of his lips.

Brian fondled his own heavily veined and rigid tool and pointed it at the dark god. 'I bet you'd be good at sucking, too.'

Cer considered the idea for a moment and, in the brief pause, Brian found himself filled with an immense longing to feel those teeth grazing the head of his cock and to see those lips pistoning down his shaft.

Then Cer said, 'I don't know about being good at it right away. But I wouldn't mind learning.' Then he leaned forward and took the head of Brian's cock into his mouth.

The shock to Brian's nervous system was almost electric. Cer's mouth was warm; it was wet; it was wonderful! The god spent some time licking and sucking at the head of the younger man's cock, pausing for a moment now and then to savour the taste. Then, having withdrawn for a moment to say, 'Here I go, then,' his head powered down on Brian's cock until every last inch of that not inconsiderable pillar of flesh was totally consumed.

Even then Cer was not fully satisfied. He pushed, pushed and pushed again, grunting at each push. Brian sensed the compression on the head of his cock, felt the rough stubble of Cer's chin graze his scrotum, and knew that quite soon his balls would erupt.

Slowly Cer withdrew, each fraction of an inch of movement

generating lightning flashes in the whole length of Brian's cock. Again Cer paused with his lips at the head, licking, sucking and savouring the salty dew that was now flowing freely. Then, the god took a deep breath and the mass of dark curls dived down over the massive cock once more, driving it even further into the warm and constricting channel of Cer's throat.

Encouraged by Cer's fearless dive, Brian lifted up his hips to thrust himself even deeper into the Celtic god. He was rewarded by a deep grunt of satisfaction from Cer and a fiery thrill that ran through the whole of his body.

Now Cer's muscular hands clutched hard at Brian's buttocks and he began to rise and fall on the young man's cock with increasing power and speed. Each dive of Cer's head brought new rivers of excitement coursing through Brian and, with each withdrawal, he knew that he was getting ever closer to exploding.

Eventually he did explode, just as Cer was at the end of an upstroke. The god held his position with his lips circling the bursting cock head as it pumped out an almost continuous stream of thick white come, which overflowed from Cer's mouth and fell in huge white splashes on to his dark chest hair.

For a while, the two naked figures lay on the grassy hillside, in the warm darkness. By now the moon had risen, a soft wind blew and, down below, the lights of Cerne Abbas seemed to flicker and dim. For practically the first time in his life, Brian felt relaxed and at peace.

Cer was the first to break the silence. 'I enjoyed that, lad,' he said.

'So did I. I feel great.'

Cer turned towards Brian, leaning on one elbow, and gazed at him for a moment. 'You're not exactly a happy lad, are you?' he asked finally. 'Not normally?'

'I manage,' said Brian. 'I get by.'

'But you are troubled.'

'Sometimes.'

'So – do you want to do the next thing now?' asked Cer.

Lying back on the grass, Brian looked from one to the other of the two thick, upright cocks, silhouetted in the moonglow – one with a proud, defined head and the other hooded. 'Looks to me like we're both ready for it,' he said. 'Who goes first?'

'You mean who rogers whom first?'

'If that's what you want to call it, yes. Who puts their dick in whose bum first? You or me?'

'I think it would be good if you do me and then, if you still want it, I will do you,' said Cer.

'If I still want it? Try and stop me!'

'How shall I lie for you, then?'

'On your back, legs in the air, would be good.'

'Like this?' Cer lay back and, grasping his thighs with his huge hands, pulled them back and apart. In the pale moonlight, Brian could see the darker centre in the midst of the dark thicket of hair. It looked very small and tight. 'Come on, then, lad,' said Cer. 'Let me have it.'

Brian spat copiously into his hand and coated the head of his cock with saliva. Then he knelt between Cer's open legs and carefully aimed the red and glistening missile at its target.

'Here goes,' he said and thrust hard.

Cer drew in his breath sharply as the young man's knob entered his virgin arse. There was a moment's pause, then Brian pressed forward again, feeling the constriction of the sphincter travel down the length of his dick. He looked down to see Cer's balls squashed between their two bodies, with the man's nut-brown cock jutting straight upwards.

Cer gave a long, drawn-out moan of sheer pleasure. Then he said, 'I knew it would be good. But I never knew –' He paused and wriggled his torso slightly, pressing Brian's throbbing cock even deeper in. 'You can start moving now, lad.'

Gently at first, Brian began to fuck the tall brown body. Then, as the fire built within him, his thrusting became deeper, faster, harder. As he felt his climax approaching he reached a hand down to masturbate Cer's rigid cock. Instantly he felt Cer take his wrist in an iron grip. 'No, lad,' he said, 'that's for you. I want that inside of you!'

'OK,' Brian panted. 'Yeah.' Cer released his hand and Brian resumed his relentless fucking action. Soon the two were grunting and groaning in unison, the sweat on both naked bodies gleaming in the moonlight.

Brian's climax began deep inside, the fire within him spreading and glowing, burning and flaring, until finally a white-hot flame flashed through his body and he released a flood of boiling come deep inside the writhing body of Cer.

It was a minute or more before Brian withdrew from Cer. Now was the time when he would normally have felt at his most alien, most alone and most abandoned. Yet this time he felt nothing but love and warmth. Wordlessly he lay on his back and, like Cer before him, pulled his thighs apart.

The head of Cer's cock was already well lubricated. It felt huge, but not impossible, as it slid straight into Brian's tight sheath. Cer said, 'I am hot. This will be quick.' And he began to move – hard, deep and fast. Brian felt a strange joy as the nut-brown cock penetrated him more deeply than he'd ever known before. He felt the fire begin again, even more intense this time than before. It started even deeper within him and burned with a greater intensity, as the god's cock drove into him again and again.

Then, with a great roar of pleasure, Cer released a torrent of come, which, as it entered into Brian's body, seemed to him as though it exploded in a white-hot flash that consumed his entire being. Cer collapsed on to Brian with a huge sigh of relief and they clung to each other silently.

'Do you know what?' whispered Brian, as he recovered his senses.

'I think so,' Cer whispered back.

'For the first time in my life I feel as though I belong.'

'You do,' said Cer quietly, 'you do.'

At the foot of the hill, the lights of Cerne Abbas faded, one by one, into history. The sound of distant traffic was replaced by the eerie cry of a wolf, baying at the moon. High on the hill, the two lovers clung to each other, at home, together, at last.

Angelic Decision

Louis Carr

When Ken's uncle vanished, he figured he was going crazy. Uncle Matt's visit and lecture had come as an expected result of the latest message Ken had left on the old man's phone.

'What do you mean, you need tuition for another semester?' Uncle Matt had begun his tirade before Ken could even shut the door of his basement apartment. 'You're twenty-six years old, for God's sake! How much longer do you plan on hiding in graduate school?'

'I told you,' Ken answered. 'I just need one more semester to finish my thesis, then I'll have the MFA. Don't worry, you'll get rid of me soon enough.'

Uncle Matt snorted like the bulldog his thick frame and double chin suggested. 'Thesis? One of your crappy novels, you mean. Master of Fine Arts? What kind of stupid title is that? How do you ever expect to make it in life with a degree in writing horror stories? Name one man who ever made a decent living with that trash.'

'Stephen King.'

Uncle Matt forged on along his usual track. 'When the hell are you going to get a real job?'

With a long sigh, Ken plopped down on the sagging couch.

'You don't consider thirty-five hours a week in the bookstore, on top of school, a real job?'

'You want to spend the rest of your life clerking in a chain store in a mall?'

Wearily, Ken ran a hand through his dishevelled, blond hair. 'It's not for ever, just until I start selling. My first novel is being read by an agent now.'

Another snort. 'I promised my little brother I'd take care of you, God rest his soul. Your father must be –'

'I know. Turning over in his grave, with a son who's a slacker and a faggot, too.' Ken sprang to his feet. 'Damn it, Uncle Matt, I'm doing my best. Why can't you just leave me alone?'

That was when the old man had vanished like a switched-off TV image.

Ken's vision went grey. He felt his knees buckle.

A pair of arms scooped him on to the couch. Violet light flooded his eyes.

He squinted against the brightness. The glare contracted into a gently glowing nimbus that surrounded the shape of a man. Or something manlike.

The being loomed over Ken, at least six and a half feet tall. It had feathered wings of glossy purple-black that trailed almost to the floor like a cloak. Flame-coloured hair curled to its shoulders. A translucent robe that shimmered in rainbow hues draped its body.

Not 'it'. He. Patches of the robe kept thinning to transparency in random order, exposing ruddy skin on a broad but not overdeveloped chest, taut abdomen, muscular thighs and an appendage worthy of a stallion. Ken noticed that there was no body hair.

'Oh, my God!' He groaned.

The light flickered. A bell-like voice said, 'No, far from that.'

'What happened to Uncle Matt?'

'I answered your wish. He is gone.'

Ken's stomach lurched. 'Good God, did you kill him?'

The creature's serene expression, smoothly blank except for a faint smile, didn't change. 'Certainly not. You wished that he would leave you alone, so I simply removed him.'

'Where the hell is he, then?'

'Not in Hell, merely in an interdimensional pocket, a corner of Limbo. He is not conscious or being harmed in any way.'

Ken bowed his head in his hands, then looked up again. The – angel maybe – was still there. 'Look, you don't understand. I can't spend more than two minutes in the same room with Uncle Matt, but he's still my father's brother. I don't really want him *gone*.'

'Very well, I will remove him to his own dwelling place. He will remember travelling there by his customary means.'

'Yeah, great.' Ken couldn't believe he was thinking so clearly. 'With his car still parked out front?'

'His –' The angel's features dimmed for a second, then re-formed. 'Ah, I see it in your thoughts.' He closed his eyes briefly. 'There, I have transported both your uncle and his vehicle to their proper place.'

'What are you, anyway? My guardian angel?'

'I do not have that honour, Kenneth.' The facial expression didn't change, but the creature's voice turned a shade more sombre. 'I am Zothiel, one of the angelic host who were cast out of Heaven.'

'Now, wait just a minute!' Ken cried and slid further down the sofa from the creature. 'You're a demon? I'm not interested in selling my soul.' The being didn't look demonic. At least, Ken's stereotypical image of the diabolical didn't include anything this beautiful. He couldn't keep his eyes off the tantalising glimpses of the angel's loins. To his dismay, his prick stirred at the sight.

'Why would I want to purchase your soul? I am here to serve you.'

'I'm not sure I want help from a demon.'

'That word.' The creature slowly shook his head. 'Have you never heard of the spirits of the air? We lesser members of the heavenly host who rebelled but took no active part in the Great War are not condemned to Hell. We are exiled from the celestial realm to this terrestrial sphere. I spend most of my existence in ethereal form in your upper atmosphere. When I choose to interact with humanity, I clothe myself in earthly matter.'

'I still don't get it – Zothiel? What are you doing here?'

'As I wandered to and fro upon the Earth, the urgency of your need called to me. I came to serve you.'

'Whoa! You can read minds?' Ken felt his face grow hot and he caught his eyes drifting below the angel's waist yet again.

'Only strong emotions and surface thoughts, unless I deliberately choose to probe deeper.'

That assurance wasn't much comfort, since Ken's fantasies about Zothiel were right on the surface, despite the strangeness of the situation. He hadn't been laid in almost two years: he'd been too busy with work and school to seek relationships. It was almost impossible not to indulge in a random fantasy. 'Why would you want to serve me?'

Sweeping his wings behind him, Zothiel settled on the armchair opposite. 'I have grown to regret my rebellion. I want to re-enter Heaven. To demonstrate true penitence, I must perform a valuable service for a mortal.'

'There's a homeless shelter a few blocks away, full of lots more needy people than me.'

The angel shrugged, scattering sparks from his wings. 'Your thoughts called to me first. No condition was decreed about the nature of the mortal I must serve. Now, what need or desire can I fulfil for you?'

Ken dragged his eyes away from the curve of the angel's penis under the translucent robe. 'What? You're here to grant my wishes like some kind of genie?'

'The wish uppermost in your mind,' Zothiel said, 'is to be free of asking your uncle for money. Strange, how your species spends so much effort on acquiring wealth. A wish easily fulfilled.' A leather pouch appeared in his hand. He tossed it to Ken, who automatically caught it, startled by the weight.

Opening the drawstring, Ken peeked into the bag and saw a dull gleam. He plunged a hand into the contents – coins. Gold. Real, he'd be willing to bet.

'Where did this come from? Out of thin air?'

'No, I have no power to create matter *ex nihilo*. I fetched these sovereigns from a merchant's hoard in England in your seventeenth century.'

'Nice try, but it won't work.' Ken regretfully dropped the coin in his hand back into the bag. 'We have this institution called the IRS. How am I supposed to explain a fortune in gold to the government? Not to mention Uncle Matt and my mother?'

The bag vanished. Zothiel's glow ebbed and brightened for a few seconds. Finally he said, 'Now I perceive how wealth functions in your place and time. Activate your image box – your computer.'

In a daze, still half convinced he was dreaming, Ken stumbled over to the army-surplus desk in the corner and booted up the computer.

'Now access your . . . what is the term? Ah, yes, bank account. Your mind tells me that the numbers on the screen are what truly matter.'

When Ken brought up his balance, it read one million dollars. 'Come on,' he groaned. 'Don't you understand?' He exited the program and flicked off the monitor with an angry jab. 'That would just get me in a world of trouble.'

'Then how can I serve you? Perhaps some object you can sell to acquire wealth?' Zothiel blinked out of existence.

So he was a hallucination after all. Ken felt a twinge of regret that he hadn't acted out his fantasy while the dream lasted.

Zothiel reappeared, once again standing in the middle of the room. He handed Ken a book.

Ken collapsed on the couch, turning the volume over in his hands. *The Outside and Others*. 'Oh, damn, this is an Arkham House first edition, worth a couple of thousand dollars, maybe more. And in mint condition. What the hell did you do now?'

'I travelled back to the time when these books were printed and appropriated one.'

Ken ran his fingers over the binding. With a deep sigh, he handed the book back to the angel. 'Nobody would believe it's genuine. It looks too new. And even if you magically aged it, I couldn't keep it. That would be stealing.' The book disappeared. 'Look, all I want to do is make a career as a writer. Once I find an agent or editor who likes my work –'

Zothiel's nimbus brightened. 'Yes, that is what I can do for you. I can ensure that every person who reads your writings, agent, editor or common folk, will be enthralled by them. You will receive wealth and fame beyond your wildest dreams.'

For a second, Ken basked in the daydream of his name on the bestseller list. But only for a second. 'Hold it, that's not what I want. It wouldn't be real. I want to make it with my own talent – if any.'

The angel glided closer. His breath smelled like spiced wine. 'Then how can I serve you? I am trapped here in this terrestrial realm until I perform a deed showing true repentance.'

Ken's own breath quickened. His heartbeat accelerated. Zothiel's wings curled around him, brushing his shoulders. 'Better go find a homeless guy, I guess. All I really want is for Uncle Matt to get off my case.'

Zothiel snapped his fingers. 'Done! Your uncle now appreciates your efforts and will supply the funds you need without argument.' His fixed half-smile shaded to something like wistfulness. 'Surely you will not force me to undo this deed?'

'No, I guess not.' After years of fighting with his uncle over his career choice and lifestyle, Ken couldn't resist the idea of a cease-fire. 'Uh – thanks.'

Zothiel's light coruscated, flickered, darkened to a smoky cloud, and finally returned to its normal intensity. A single silver drop slid from one of his violet eyes down his cheek. 'My deed is not accepted. Because I interfered with a mortal's free will, the act is not pure.'

'Hey, I'm sorry.' Forgetting the bizarre context, Ken got up from the sofa, crossed the room, and placed a hand on Zothiel's shoulder. The flesh felt fever-hot. 'Would it help to undo it?'

Zothiel shook his head, setting off a shimmer in the air around him. 'I must do something else for you, something that harms no one. You wish –' He stared into Ken's eyes. 'You want to view my body unclad.' The robe vanished.

Ken felt a warm blush spreading over his face. 'I thought celestial spirits were sexless.'

'We are,' said the angel. 'But not without gender. When we become incarnate, our corporeal forms reflect our essential nature.'

Ken let his gaze roam freely over Zothiel's firm, reddish-bronze body. The angel's wing feathers still grazed Ken's shoulders and upper arms through his short-sleeved T-shirt. Inside his cut-offs, Ken felt himself hardening. Zothiel's cock stood up, rampant – a foot long. It was all Ken could do to keep his hand away from his own crotch.

The angel raised one hand to stroke Ken's hair and run a finger along his jawline in a painlessly burning track down to the pulse point in his throat. 'You have a strong desire to touch my genitals. Please do so.'

Reaching for the smooth scrotum, Ken savoured the weight of the angel's balls in the palm of his hand. Meanwhile, Zothiel's fingernails seared down his chest and skimmed over the front of his shirt. His nipples pebbled up. Ken wrapped his hand around Zothiel's shaft and squeezed. He went to his knees, mesmerised by the foot-long cock in front of him.

'An interesting sensation,' the angel said. 'Many of my fellow spirits exiled to your world have shared the pleasures of the flesh with the sons and daughters of humankind. I have never tried this sport before.'

Ken's fist pumped up and down the hard, hot column. His own cock stiffened further. To keep his free hand from wandering into his lap, he reached around to knead Zothiel's buttocks.

The angel rocked his hips, thrusting into Ken's strokes. 'Most intriguing. Please continue.'

Ken pumped faster and harder, still massaging Zothiel's buns, while the glossy wings enfolded him and the angel's nails flicked his nipples through the T-shirt.

Zothiel let out an elongated cry, his back arching. Searing ropes of angel jizz spurted forth in a prismatic gush of glittering droplets. They evaporated the instant they spattered on Ken's arm.

'Fascinating,' the angel said. His breathing remained even, the tone of his voice still the clear resonance of a steeple bell. He ran his open palm down Ken's chest, past the waistline, to his groin.

Ken felt his prick twitch. Zothiel removed his hand, and Ken's clothes disappeared. With a gasp, Ken snatched his hand away from the creature's still-rigid shaft.

Zothiel swept his eyes up and down Ken's body. 'Your sexual organ is engorged.'

'Oh, man, is it ever!' He moaned. His prick was sticking straight up from his lap. There was no use in denying it.

Zothiel drew him to his feet, encircling him with quivering wings. The feathers tickled the base of Ken's spine and the crack of his buttocks. His gluteal muscles involuntarily tightened. He tasted the angel's spicy breath as Zothiel tongued the corners of his mouth and rubbed his erect cock against Ken's own. Ken groaned aloud at the mounting pressure inside him.

The angel's voice vibrated against the side of his neck. 'You desire the same experience you just bestowed on me. Would that be a valuable service?'

'To me it would! God, I need to shoot off in the worst way!'

The angel's hot, dry hand clasped Ken's prick. Long fingers rolled his balls from side to side, pressed the sensitive spot just behind them, and skimmed up and down the shaft, pausing to encircle the head. Dizzy, Ken grabbed Zothiel's shoulders to keep from falling.

'You want another form of stimulation?' Zothiel took a seat on the couch and turned Ken to face him, his lips level with Ken's groin. A sinuous tongue emerged to lap around the head of Ken's penis. It teased the opening at the tip, while fingers crept between his spread legs to probe his crack. One finger plunged deep inside. He thrust forward, silently begging for relief.

The tongue, impossibly long, wrapped around his shaft and stroked up and down. His prick ached and throbbed, ready to explode. Zothiel sucked the organ into the hot, wet cavern of his mouth, all the way to the root. His inserted finger pressed on the trigger point within.

The pressure built to bursting point. Heat boiled up along Ken's shaft and shot forth in ecstatic convulsions. They went on and on, while the caressing tongue licked him until he collapsed in exhaustion.

Zothiel pulled him down on to the couch. When his breathing slowed, Ken opened his eyes. The violet light around the angel dimmed and went out. A second later, it began to glow again, but now transformed to pure silver.

A radiant smile spread across the angel's lips. 'My deed has been accepted.'

'Wow, that's great. So you can go back to Heaven.'

Zothiel wrapped an arm around Ken and kissed him lightly on the lips. 'Not yet. I find that this world has delights I have not fully explored. I would prefer to remain here a while longer – your guardian angel, as it were.' He looked into Ken's face hopefully and wiggled his finger still in the man's ass. 'Surely, there will be many other occasions when I can serve you.'

Islands in the Stream

Barry Alexander

Someone gave me a push. 'Hurry up, you're next. Keep the line moving.' I stumbled into a small boat floating on the choppy water of a river. The boat swung away from a shore lined with more people than the crowd at a Red Hot Chilli Peppers concert, but no one waved or threw confetti like they do when the Love Boat sets out.

An old geezer wearing a funny-looking dress stood in the front of the boat. He jabbed a long, battered pole into the water and pushed. The current caught us and we started down the river. I didn't like the looks of that dark, oily water. It gave me the creeps. I didn't much like the looks of the boatman, either. Where in the hell was I?

I must be dreaming. Or maybe that last trick slipped me something. Must have been damned good stuff. Everything seemed so real. I could even smell the noxious odour of the river. I pinched myself, trying to shake myself out of the dream, but the boat and the guy in the dress were still there. Great, wherever I was conked out, I probably wasn't going to make it to the shoot on time tomorrow. And I sure didn't want someone else stunt-dicking for me, not with that cute little German boy waiting for me, so eager to take it for the first time from Rod Cruise.

'Keep your arms and legs inside the boat at all times until the ride stops.'

I looked around to see who the boatman was talking to, forgetting that I seemed to be the only one on board. 'What about all those other people?'

'This is a voyage each man must take alone. Now take your seat, shut up, and listen. You won't be coming back this way, so you might as well enjoy the scenery, but, whatever you do, don't put your hands in the water.'

I wasn't the least bit tempted to touch the filthy-looking water, but I couldn't help asking. 'Why not?'

'You might not like the local fauna: sharks, piranha, giant swamp rats, creatures from the black lagoon, alligators people flushed down the toilet.'

Great, the guy was a loony as well as a cross-dresser. I had to be stoned – I never had dreams like this.

'Now on the left bank we have Jersey, but only the worst offenders are sent there. Coming up on the right . . .'

'OK, I'll play along. Who're you and why're you wearing a dress?'

'It's not a dress, damn it. It's a Greek Ionic chiton – Classical Period. You really don't know? That doesn't say much for the educational standards of your state school system.'

'Wait a minute – I think we covered this in English class – you're supposed to be that Styx guy and this is the river Sharon. Hey, did you know they named a group after you?'

'Gods, why do I even try? No, you plebeian ignoramus. I'm Charon and we're out on the Styx.'

'So what am I doing here?'

'You haven't figured that out? You're dead.'

Something about the way he said that made me believe him. It all began to make a weird kind of sense. Oh, God, maybe I *was* dead. But I couldn't be. I seemed to be dressed in my working clothes, skin-tight jeans with a few strategic rips and soft-as-butter leather shirt unlaced to show off the hard plateaux of my chest. I still had my body. Didn't I?

Frantically, I took a quick inventory. Handsome, clean-cut face, check. Hair, gold as honey, thick and silky, and all of it still there, check. Pumped-up pecs, check. Gorgeous ass, check. But what about . . .? I grabbed the front of my jeans and groped.

The boatman chuckled. 'Yes, that is still there, too.'

I sighed with relief. I could get by with an average face. A less than perfect ass didn't really matter in my case: I never let anyone near it – although I did enjoy watching guys drool over it. And I supposed I could make out with slightly less muscle.

But I absolutely, positively would not want to live without my cock. It was perfect, beautifully shaped, straight and veiny with a fat, rosy crown, and so thick guys squealed when I shoved it in. Those ten inches of hard fuck muscle had brought me where I was today. One look at this baby and every guy I met wanted to play doggie chew on my bone or roll over – and most were willing to pay for the privilege. I had money in the bank, a hot car, a great apartment and any man I wanted. And I had all of them, at least the good-looking ones – no fems, fats or ugos for me. I may have been for sale, but only to an exclusive clientele. The rest had to settle for drooling over my videos. I made more as an escort, but the videos were a public service. At least the pathetic little bastards got to look and dream of what they could never have. But I didn't really feel sorry for them. A gorgeous body takes upkeep. If they weren't willing to work out at the gym every day as I did or invest in some plastic surgery they deserved to sit home alone jerking off. Anybody that touched this bod had to deserve it.

And now some asshole was telling me I was dead and it was all over. Well, I didn't buy it. OK, maybe I was dead, but he wasn't taking me up the river without a fight. No way was I going to give all that up to strum on some harp.

The boat passed a pretty island where contented cows grazed on green pastures and where the sun shone on amber waves of grain.

'Is that heaven?'

'No, it's Iowa. Common mistake.'

'So when do we get to heaven and the pearly gates?'

Sharon or Charon or whatever the hell his name was made a strange sputtering noise. He doubled over his pole and roared with laughter. 'Boy, are you on the wrong boat. That's the deluxe package. This is the economy three-hour cruise.'

'So is this hell?'

'Which one? People try to put things into neat little boxes. Things blur together. One man's heaven is another man's hell. Consider the next island. Hell for obnoxious teenagers. You know the type: driving around with their car stereos thumping out rap at two in the morning. Paradise for the other residents – senior citizens with state of the art boom boxes. Nothing but Lawrence Welk and Mitch Miller round the clock.'

'But that's fiendish.'

'That's nothing compared with the island of Penile Impostors – gorgeous, horny men chained for eternity. They can see each other. They can even touch fingers, but every time they even try to touch themselves, they get a huge shock.'

'What was their crime?'

'False advertising. They claimed they had huge cocks. The gods aren't fond of deceit.'

'Serves them right. So where am I going – a good place or a bad place?' I was starting to get a little nervous.

'I can't tell you. But don't worry. Whichever it is, a great deal of planning went into creating the perfect place.'

Up ahead, a thick bank of fog covered the river. Charon handed me a breathing mask. 'Put this on. We're passing the smoker's paradise. Please keep your oxygen mask on until we clear the island.'

And then I thought of something else. 'How did I die?'

Charon shrugged. 'What's the difference? Dead is dead. It's how you lived that's important. We've heard about you, Rod Cruise.'

OK, so it was nice to be recognised, even here, but I didn't want to be dead. There had to be a way back. I couldn't disappoint all my fans, especially the German virgin waiting for me. 'Look, just turn this boat around. I'll give you anything you ask.'

'Half of your kingdom and all of your bank account. What would I do with it? Look around. You see any malls?'

As we came out of the smog, the river narrowed, passing

between high river bluffs. Tall pines on the peak leaned over the water towards each other, almost forming a dark tunnel. Up ahead I could see a faint blue glow. I took off my oxygen mask.

'What's that up ahead – that glowing blue light. I've heard about that! First we go through a tunnel and then we reach the blue light. We are going to heaven!'

'No, that's just the shopaholics paradise – a giant K Mart where everything is on blue-light special. Some people are so easy to please.'

Farther up the river, I could hear pitiful moans and sighs. 'Those poor souls – what fiendish torture are they being subjected to?'

'That is the hell for gluttons. Every night a sumptuous banquet is spread for them. Pheasant under glass, Big Mac and Super Size fries – whatever they fancy. They can't resist. But as soon as they take a bite, it turns to low-cal, low-fat, high-fibre health food.'

'How awful.' I was a little partial to Big Macs myself.

'That's not the worse of it. They have to spend all of eternity listening to Richard Simmons and *Sweating to the Oldies Two*.'

OK, so money and fame weren't going to help me out of this. But if he thought I was going to go along with this crazy afterlife stuff, he was nuts. I wasn't out of options – the guy was Greek after all; I had to be able to do something with that. I knew what those Greek guys liked. I'd seen statues of naked Greek guys. Those guys didn't have any dick worth bragging about. If I had a toy dick, I'd hide it under a fig leaf, too. I was pretty sure I knew how to tempt this guy. Charon probably hadn't seen a dick since he was alive. When he got a look at my meat he was going to bend over, open wide, and say, 'Aaaaah!'

I looked at the boatman again. He wasn't as old as I'd thought, but he had to be at least forty. His black curly hair was heavily streaked with grey. He was in pretty good shape for an old guy: I could see his chest swell every time he used the pole to guide us back into the main current. That dress really threw me, though – he didn't have the legs for it. His knees were knobby and his calves ropy. A heavy brooch shaped like the face of a very ugly woman having a really bad-hair day gathered the loose folds of fabric at his left shoulder and held it in place. His chest was half exposed, showing a thick mat of grizzled hair. I was really going to have to use my imagination for this one.

I tucked my hand in my jeans and jostled my equipment to the best position. I gave it a couple of strokes to get it started and thought about hot men. OK, so this guy wasn't hot, but I knew he sure must be hungry after all this time. I love watching guys get into my cock. I love that hungry look, when they just start to drool, but aren't sure they're going to get it. I like hearing men beg. Sometimes that's better than getting sucked. Seeing those pretty boys down on their knees begging for a taste of my meat.

I spread my legs and pushed my hands deep into my pockets to give him the best view. The bulge snaking down my leg was obscenely large, and it wasn't even close to hard yet. My jeans were so thin my cock head was clearly outlined.

Charon continued with his little travelogue.

'Next we have the island of the queens. Vanity is also something the gods don't favour. After all, what do humans really have to be vain about? The island is filled with ageing drag queens, who refused to admit they were over twenty-five. The entire island is a maze of mirrors, each one slightly more distorted than the next. TV cameras ring the island, each one adding twenty pounds . . .'

When I didn't comment, he turned around and stopped in mid-sentence. Yeah, he was interested. His jaw dropped open and his eyes glazed as he stared at my basket. My hand was cupped near my crotch, framing the huge bulge. I slowly stroked the shaft with one finger. My cock squirmed.

'Let's make a deal, Sharon,' I said softly. 'You got something I want. I have something you want.'

The old boy had to have been hungry: he didn't even correct me. It wasn't every day a gorgeous guy like me put out for someone like him. I hoped he appreciated how lucky he was.

I knew that look. I'd seen it in the faces of hundreds of guys as they kneeled before me. Hunger, awe, worship – and rightly so. It was a privilege to touch my meat. So what if they had to pay for the privilege? When you have a perfect cock, it's only right lesser men worship what they can never hope to possess. I should be used to the look by now, but it never failed to send a fresh surge of blood to my cock. This was going to be so easy.

My cock jumped another fraction of an inch. He stared – totally mesmerised, unable to move. He was actually quivering, he wanted it so badly.

I took my time, unbuttoning my shirt slowly to give him the full effect. My chest was bronzed and buff, not a hair on it. I didn't want anything hiding the definition I'd worked so hard to achieve. My nipples stood out like little pink erasers on my squared pecs. I'd charged guys a thousand bucks for the show he was getting for free. It wasn't fair, wasting all this on someone like him. Hell, would he even be able to get it up? Did guys really have sex after forty – it seemed obscene somehow. I tried to avoid looking at him. All that grey hair and those wrinkles around his eyes were a major turnoff. You'd think the guy would at least use some moisturiser.

I had to keep thinking of hot men to keep my erection. I was a pro, sure. But even a pro has to have something to work with. I thought of what I was going to do with that hunky little German. Eighteen years old. Pretty little bubble butt. I loved popping cherries. I couldn't wait to hear him squeal as he squirmed on my meat.

I unpopped my jeans and let them slide down my legs. His eyes lit up like a kid's on Christmas morning as I opened my package for him. My cock sprang out, but it was too heavy to stand straight up. It bobbed a few times, then levelled, thrusting from my crotch like a weapon, thick and hard and powerful.

He started to drool. Yeah, best one you've seen in a while. I peeled my jeans all the way off and flashed him a glimpse of my snow-white ass. No way was he getting in there, but I couldn't resist teasing him. Rod Cruise didn't bottom for anyone. And I sure as hell wasn't going to start now, letting some old guy core me.

I ran my hands over my body. I loved the feel of my own skin, smooth and golden and perfect. My fingers glided over the hard ripples of my stomach, trailed up the deep cleft between my pecs, and spiralled around my nipples. I tweaked the meaty points and felt a jolt of pleasure/pain tingle right down through my cock.

God, I had a gorgeous body. Every time I touched myself, I felt awed by its perfection. Married guys turned around in the street to watch me pass. Directors fought over me. Porn stars who only topped took one look at my hard, tight body and giant cock, rolled over on their bellies and begged me to fuck them. And now I was going to waste it all on a dotty old guy in a dress. I was a pro, but I needed a little inspiration to keep it hard.

I closed my eyes for a second and thought of the cute young stud I'd ploughed in my last video. He was supposed to be a virgin. Maybe he was: he was damned tight and he hollered like one when I speared all ten inches right through his little pink rosebud. He sure wasn't now, I thought with a grin. I'd fucked him so long and so hard he couldn't walk straight when he left the set. After that session with my horse cock, he could probably take a Mac truck up there.

I was getting hot thinking about it. The first drippings of pre-come bubbled up in my slit and I scooped them out with my finger. The boatman's nose twitched at the scent, hot and pungent. I glossed his lips with it and he looked like he'd died and gone to heaven. The tip of his tongue leaped out and flicked over his wet lips. He carefully licked every bit, then washed my finger, sucking it into his mouth and scouring every possible trace from my skin. I do like enthusiasm. Something was definitely stirring under his dress.

'Show me how much you want it: lick my balls.'

He dropped his pole and crouched lower, bracing his hands on my hips to steady himself. He lapped my balls so hard they swung between my thighs. He took one between his lips and sucked. It sure wasn't his first time: the old guy knew how to do this. He kept just the right amount of suction and swirled his tongue all over my captured ball. He let it plop out and gobbled down the second one.

'You might as well take that dress off.'

He spat out my ball and stood up. 'I told you, it's a chiton, not a dress.'

'Whatever.'

He grabbed the hem and pulled the weird garment over his head. I guess he had a nice enough body for an old guy. His arms

47

and shoulders were in pretty good shape from poling the raft around. But he was soft in the middle. He sure didn't look like any of the statues of Greek gods I'd seen. The hair on his chest was mingled with grey.

He unwrapped some kind of cloth twisted around his hips, but there was no need. His cock stabbed the air, already slipped free of the swaddling undergarment. The pointed head was draped with a long foreskin, dangling a thread of pre-come. His cock was nothing to brag about, but it was hard and the dark skin on his shaft was exotic. His balls were swollen and purple under their grizzled fur, pulled up tight to his cock. I pushed my finger inside the pouch of skin and pulled it out, dripping with his pungent juices. I wiped it off on my chest. 'Ugh, you got me all sticky. I think you better clean up your mess.'

I grabbed him by the back of the neck and pulled his face close. Eagerly, he went to work, licking his own juices off my sweat-dampened skin. As I explored the firm muscles of his back and shoulders, his lips found the point of my nipple and sucked it in. He bit it lightly and rubbed his tongue over the rubbery peak. I loved having my nipples worked. When they were both hard and tingly, I raised my arm and shoved his head over to my pit. He tried to come up for air; I do tend to sweat a bit, but I yanked him back in place. He must have got used to it, because his talented tongue went to work, lapping my sweaty pit and sucking on the tangled hairs, grooming them with his mouth. I locked my fingers in his curly hair and held him in place. When I was satisfied, I released my grip. His lips trailed down my stomach, licking and kissing. He dropped to his knees, hypnotised by the swaying cock inches from his mouth.

Honey oozed from my slit; he was good at this. My stomach muscles tightened in anticipation when he leaned close and breathed on the glistening cock-head. But I wasn't ready to let him have it yet: I wanted to see him beg. I smacked him on the face with my rock-hard cock. It must have stung: he yelped.

'I didn't say you could have it. I'm not convinced you really want it. Tell me how much you want it.'

He moaned in frustration. 'I want it. I want that big cock. Let me suck it. Please. Oh, gods, don't do this to me.'

I liked driving a guy almost to tears before I let him touch my cock. I'd have held out for more, but the sample I'd already had of his skills made me ache for more. 'OK.'

He didn't need a second invitation. He teased me with huffs of warm breath over my hypersensitive dick and tiny flicks of his tongue – a taste here, a nip there – driving me insane with need. My hips bucked upwards, trying to force my turgid cock into his mouth. He just laughed at me. 'Now you know what it feels like.'

I squirmed helplessly under his exquisite torment, but I wouldn't ask him for it, I wouldn't. I felt like crying from frustration. My cock poked futilely at the empty air, aching for contact, but I refused to beg. His head hovered over me, his hot mouth inches away. The tip of his tongue poked between his lips, a drop of saliva suspended above my dick, a millimetre from contact. He caught it on his thumb. I shivered in anticipation, eager to be touched. Then the bastard rubbed it over his own cock.

'Suck me, damn you,' I groaned. 'Please.'

It must have been what the sadistic bastard wanted to hear. He opened wide and swallowed my cock. He sucked my cock down so fast I had to check to make sure it was still attached. It glided over his tongue, thumped the back of his palate and coasted right down.

I still wanted to throttle him, but I soon forgot everything but the feeling of my cock in his hot, slick mouth. He pulled back and flicked his tongue over my cock head, swirling his tongue across the silken skin. I couldn't help moaning when he dipped his tongue in the gaping slit of my cock head and lapped the abundant fluid. With a growl, I drove my hips forward, slamming my cock down his throat. His lips pressed tightly against my groin, as his tongue slithered and stroked the veins along my shaft. He wrapped his callused hand around my balls and rolled them around in their sac. My balls shifted under his hand, trying to rise against his grip. I was close to blasting his tonsils, when he pulled off.

'What the hell?'

'I want to feel that big cock sliding up my guts.'

That was fine by me. There wasn't a hell of a lot of room in the boat, but we managed. He spread himself over the seat, hands and feet on the floor and ass propped up nicely for me. He spread his legs and the forest in his cleft parted, revealing his secret portal. I swear the damned thing winked at me.

I kneeled behind him and pushed the head of my throbbing cock against his wrinkled hole. The heat kissed my dripping crown and invited me inside. He turned around and looked at me.

'That thing's pretty big and we don't have any oil. Take it easy.'

'Don't worry. Once you feel a real cock inside you, you won't want it to ever leave.' Jeesh, what a baby. It can't hurt that much.

His wasn't the first butt I'd ploughed dry. I meant to take it easy, but, when I saw his cheeks spread and that little hole quiver at me, I couldn't resist. He wanted it, that's for sure, and I was going to give it to him – the whole ten inches. I spat on the end of my cock and smeared it around. It wouldn't help him much, but what the hell! At least I wouldn't be getting butt-burn on my dick head.

I bullseyed my spear against his target. Damn, he was hot. His dark eye fluttered against my knob, as soft and warm as a kiss. I gave a steady push and he opened around me, but not enough. He grunted as I pushed harder. I got in maybe a quarter-inch and pushed again. Another quarter-inch. The hell with this, I thought: it's going to take for ever to get in there. I grabbed his hips and plunged.

'Awwwh!' he screamed.

Oh, yeah! Heat enveloped me as half my length forced its way inside him. I loved fucking guys – feeling that tight embrace around my cock, the little quivers that rippled along my shaft. There was nothing like it. And I liked seeing guys on their faces sticking up their butts for me – just begging to be plugged with my gorgeous cock.

I gave another lunge and shoved every inch up his ass. He screamed again in pleasure – he was getting used to it. They all did. I ground my pubic hair against him, sanding his butt cheeks.

I pumped him as hard as I could. Power driving my cock into his ass. He finally stopped hollering and started to push back. He had a tight hole and started clamping down on my dick every time I thrust inside. I didn't have to hold back so I could pull out for the cameras, so I started giving him everything I had. The boat rocked back and forth so much we were probably in danger of capsizing, but I was too damned horny to care. His ass was as well trained as his mouth. I loved those little squeezes he gave me each time I thrust.

I knew he was getting close, from all the groaning. I reached down and strangled his cock for him a few times. It didn't take much. His guts spasmed around my cock and he shot his spunk all over my hand.

I hammered his ass with my cock, shoving every inch as far inside him as I could. My hips went into hyperdrive, pummelling him as I blasted his guts with volleys of white-hot come. I collapsed against him, crushing him against the hard wooden seat.

When my heart stopped hammering and my breathing steadied, I rolled off him. Not too bad for an old guy.

'That was great.' Charon stood up and pulled his chiton over his head.

'Glad you liked it. Now turn this damned boat around.'

'I can't. Time is a one-way stream.'

I picked up the pole and thought about cracking it over his head, but I poked it into the river instead. There was no bottom, nothing to push against.

'You damned old bastard. I went through all that for nothing? That's not fair.'

'Whoever said death was fair? Besides, you enjoyed yourself, didn't you?' He took the pole from me and pulled a small knife out of his clothing. I stepped back, but he calmly started to cut a notch in the battered pole. That's when I noticed it wasn't really battered. It was scored with thousands of notches.

'You think you're the first pretty boy on this boat? Don't flatter yourself. You're not even that big. There's a spot here where all the guys have fourteen-inch cocks. Nine and a half is nothing.'

'It's ten.'

'It's nine and a half; you can't lie here. Hell, everybody wants to go back. I can have anyone I want. It's one of the perks of the job. That and seeing people get what they deserve. No one can turn the boat around, so stop whining. Now sit down and enjoy the rest of the tour. We're getting close.'

I sat down and started thinking. OK, so I couldn't go back in the boat, maybe I had to accept that. But there was no reason I had to go to whatever god-awful place they had planned for me, not when there were alternatives all along the river. I'd wait until we got close to one that sounded promising and jump overboard. The old guy would never be able to stop me.

Charon started his damn travelogue again as if nothing had happened. Graceland for Elvis Impersonators? I didn't think so. He was still chattering on about the airport terminal for lax Hari Krishna guys and erring Jehovah's Witnesses when the current pushed us close to a different island.

Giant stone arches ringed the island, like Stone Age McDonald's. Within each hung the naked body of a man. Perfect! The one he had told me about – dozens of gorgeous guys chained for eternity. Thank you, Lord! I'd never get a better chance. I jumped.

'No, don't!' Charon yelled.

I landed waist deep in the river. Remembering all of its nasty inhabitants, I quickly waded to shore. I couldn't help laughing with delight as I approached the first hanging figure. His body was sleek and golden. His tight buns slightly spread by the chains that held his feet apart. Some kind of harness secured his shoulders, leaving his arms free and his ass fully accessible. As Charon had said, the men could touch hands but that was about it.

I looked along the row of arches, each body more luscious than the next. They looked like they'd spent half their life in the gym. I'd never seen such hard, gorgeous bodies. And they were all mine. It was going to be a hard job keeping all those hungry holes satisfied, but I was up to it. Too bad I didn't have any lube, but hey, how bad could it hurt? My cock was already hard and aching, and I suddenly realised I hadn't bothered putting on my clothes again. Just as well, I thought, as I walked behind the row admiring each of the gorgeous asses that I was going to plough for eternity. I grinned. This may not be Iowa, but it sure was heaven.

I heard Charon call one last time as the boat drifted away. 'You should have waited for the gangplank. This was your stop.'

Well, the joke was on me. I should have trusted that whoever was in charge of things certainly knew what he was doing. This was paradise!

Where to begin?

The polite thing to do would be to introduce myself. I ducked between the spread legs attached to a particularly cute butt.

'Hi, I'm Rod . . .'

And that was when I knew there was a terrible mistake. Each of the men sprouted a huge fourteen-inch cock, thick as my arm with a swollen head as big as a baseball. And every single one of them was pointed right at me.

The guy clamped a giant hand on my shoulder. I tried to twist away but he was too strong. He slapped my cock with his meaty hand. 'That little thing? That's not a rod.'

His hands slipped down to my waist and he hoisted me into the air, suspending me above a battering ram of a cock. I felt his heat against my tightly clamped hole. 'What you're going to feel is a rod.'

The man crowed with delight. 'I got him, guys!'

A cheer echoed around the circle. 'Hurry up and fuck him. Pass him down.'

'Wait!' I screamed. 'What are you doing? I thought this was paradise.'

'It is now.'

And then he started to push.

I could have sworn I heard Charon laughing as pain roared out of my ass and seared through me. It hurt like hell. I was being ripped apart. I thought of all the guys I'd dicked. How had they taken it?

The guy tweaked my nipples. The pleasure-pain shot down through my balls. My hole fluttered around the head of the big cock still trying to force its way inside me. And then the head was in.

It still hurt, but not quite so much. It was almost bearable as he forced inch after inch inside. He pinched my nipples again and I opened even more. He slammed in another few inches and suddenly hit something that felt damn good. Oh, yeah, I thought as he slid the rest of that giant cock over my prostate. I could get to like this.

By the third guy, I was beginning to think I'd been right all along – this was heaven.

Pact With the Devil

Michael Gouda

I t was all his Great Aunt Marion's fault . . .

If she hadn't had a birthday and Adrian hadn't felt pressured into buying her a present . . .

If she hadn't made pointed remarks about liking old books and how the back streets of the town were full of second-hand bookshops . . .

If her birthday hadn't fallen on the 25th of the month and his payday wasn't until the 28th . . .

If he could just have ignored that birthday without incurring her displeasure, which might have meant being left out of her will – and she was after all pushing eighty . . .

And all those 'ifs' meant that Adrian was wandering down the High Street when it was at its hottest and grubbiest, the air feeling close and sticky and the sky a heavy uniform grey. He had just finished his morning shift in the local Burger Bar and had hoped that the air outside would be less clogged than the greasy atmosphere of his workplace.

Sundry homeless people sat against the walls and spread their legs and feet out on to the pavements, begging. Adrian passed one who was young, perhaps twenty, and quite attractive with curly dark hair and wide eyes who looked open and appealing. He was dressed in a pullover – must be hot, thought Adrian – and some tight jeans, which, as the man sprawled his legs out on to the pavement, wrapped and emphasised the shape of his genitals in a very stimulating way. Surely intentionally.

Adrian tried to catch his eye but the young man seemed to be looking into the middle distance, his eyes glazed and unfocused. Maybe he was on drugs, Adrian thought.

The spa town had once – perhaps some two hundred years earlier (Adrian was not all that good at history) – been the height of fashion when gentlemen in silk hose and ladies in crinolines came to take the water at the Pump Room, but Time and the corrosive effects of sulphur dioxide had not dealt kindly with the elegant stonework, which was now pitted and marked so that it looked as if it was eaten away by a disease. Nor had the economic recession helped, for almost every other shop front was now boarded up, the graffiti and advertising posters making a patch-work of cluttered disorder.

But Great Aunt Marion had been right in one thing – there were second-hand bookshops in abundance especially in the little side streets that branched off the main thoroughfare every twenty yards or so. Adrian wondered how they could possibly make any sort of profit, there being so many of them and so few apparent customers. Some of them had tried to attract sales by putting a box of dog-eared paperbacks and old remaindered hardbacks in the front with a sign saying 'ONLY 50P EACH', but it was hardly an unrefusable inducement to buy.

Adrian, though, was out for just such a bargain so he stooped down and rummaged through the contents of one such box. Now would Great Aunt Marion appreciate a grubby, torn, 'bodice-bursting' Mills and Boone? He thought not. Right at the bottom of the box was a yellowed book which, at first sight, appeared as unsuitable as the first. Its print was crabbed and blurred and the paper was thick. The pages seemed almost torn rather than cut to size, their edges rough and uneven. It had no front cover and Adrian was about to toss it back in disgust when his eye caught a date in Roman numerals at the bottom of the title page – MDCLXXV.

It took him a little while to work out but eventually he

deciphered it as 1675. The title seemed to be in Latin, *Compendium Rerum Malorum*, and the author someone called Thomas Weir of Edinburgh. None of this meant very much to Adrian – a compendium, he thought, meant a collection – but certainly the book looked old and, if he had worked out the date correctly, could be quite valuable. It would do for Great Aunt Marion. He wondered if perhaps the book had got into the box by mistake and the bookseller would make a fuss about selling it to him for 50p so he picked out three other books and took them into the shop.

'Four from your bargain box,' he called out cheerfully to the little man, crouched like a gnome behind the counter, and looking as dusty as most of the stock on his shelves. He waved them in front of the man's face and then plonked two one-pound coins on the surface.

The man grunted and seemed to want to look at the titles but Adrian swiftly turned and made for the door, and the man picked up the coins and examined them closely as if he thought they might be counterfeit.

Outside it had started raining. Large drops the size of penny pieces splashed on to the dusty pavement. The grey sky looked as if it was going to burst. Shit! He and the books were going to get wet and he hadn't got anywhere to put them. He needed some shelter. The public library, though, was just round the corner and Adrian broke into a run to make the steps leading up to the pseudo-Gothic front just before the heavens opened and the rain came down in torrents. He wondered whether the attractive young man he had seen earlier had got some shelter.

He stood in the covered entrance hall and stared out at the sleeting rain. What to do now? Glancing at his watch, he found he still had half an hour before his lunch break was up. He looked at the books in his hand, three thrillers that might be worth reading and the old volume, which appeared even more tattered and miserable on closer inspection. Could he give this to his great aunt?

He turned over the first page and tried to make out the writing. If it was all in Latin then there did not seem much hope, but, to his surprise, it was apparently written in English – or at least a sort of English. 'A fpell for gaining the heart's defires.' What on earth did that mean?

Suddenly he realised that he was probably in the right place to ask questions and he took the book into the reference library where, behind a wooden counter, a bespectacled woman was doing something academic with a large tome. Her grey hair was scraped back from her face into a bun at the back. She looked up as Adrian approached and smiled, immediately looking less severe.

'Excuse me,' said Adrian politely. 'I've just bought this book and I wondered if you could tell me something about it.'

The woman took the book and looked at it. 'Interesting,' she said. '*Compendium Rerum Malorum* – Collection of Evil Things.' She turned over the pages. 'It appears to be an anthology of spells.' She turned back to the title page. 'Sixteen fifty-seven. Thomas Weir. Don't know the name. Let's see what the encyclopedia has to say,' she said to herself and turned aside to a shelf from which she chose and took down a large volume. She rifled through the pages and eventually found an entry. 'Here we are.' She read out aloud, 'Weir, Thomas: Born in 1600. After having led an apparently normal life as a religious man, he confessed in 1670 to sorcery and horrible debauchery. He was burned at the stake near Edinburgh in April 1670 along with his sister, Jane, who was accused of incest with him.'

'Is it valuable?' asked Adrian, crossing his fingers.

'Well,' said the woman, 'I'm no expert and the book's obviously not in good condition – but an enthusiast of demonology might pay a couple of hundred pounds for it.'

Adrian breathed again. That wasn't a bad profit. 'Is it written in English?' he asked. 'Some words seem very odd.' He pointed to the entry he had read on the first page. 'Fpell – defires?'

'Oh, that's just the long "s". Printers in those days used a long form for the letter "s" if it was anywhere but at the end of a word. Yes, it's in English. That reads, "A spell for gaining your heart's desires". Pretty marvellous that would be – if it worked.'

Adrian agreed, thanked her, and went back out to the entrance hall. He sat down on one of the benches that ran round the inside. The rain seemed to be easing. Soon he would be able to go out again. While he waited he opened the book and read the first spell. It was difficult to make out and he found that the easiest way was to mouth the words just under his breath.

'I conjure you,' he read, 'Prince Lucifer, dark Angel of Light, to procure for me what my Heart most defires – no, desires – in the name of your lieutenants Mammon, Asmodeus, Satan, Beelzebub, Leviathan and Belphegor.'

He got to the end, the names causing him the most difficulty, and suddenly had the feeling that he was being watched. He looked up and saw the young man he had noticed earlier in the High Street. He was standing just inside the doorway and staring at him but had obviously not been as lucky as Adrian in escaping the rain for his hair was plastered to his scalp while his jeans and pullover looked soaked.

Adrian gave him a sympathetic smile and, as if this encouraged him, the guy approached. 'Pissing weather,' he said.

'Got caught in the rain, did you?' said Adrian, though the answer was obvious. 'Haven't you got anywhere to go?' As he said it, Adrian realised that the question could be seriously misconstrued.

The boy gave Adrian a shrewd look, seemed to make a decision and said, 'Yeah, I got a place. Just couldn't get back there in time. Want to see it?'

Adrian realised that he would be late back for work but he nodded anyway and the guy turned and led the way briskly through the now gradually decreasing raindrops across the road and down a side lane, much like the ones Adrian himself had explored in his search for the bookshops earlier.

They did not say much, the young man limiting his remarks to a brief introduction, Steven, and Adrian responding with his own name. Halfway down the street Steven stopped and turned left to where a flight of stone steps led down to a basement. At the bottom there was a scuffed painted door which had once been blue. A window with bars was set in the wall. Steven unlocked the door and the two young men went in. Inside, lit by the subdued light from the window, was a single room which contained a bed, a small table and two chairs and, in the corner, a gas ring and sink. In the furthest corner a plastic curtain hid probably what was a shower. A greasy-looking rug – once red – covered the centre of the floor.

'Gotta get out of these clothes,' said Steven, pulling the jumper over his head. His body was slim, his chest hairless, his stomach flat. He kicked off his trainers, unzipped and pulled off his jeans without the least trace of embarrassment. He was wearing a pair of dark-blue jockey shorts. He took a towel from beside the sink and rubbed his hair until it was dry and tousled. Then he wiped his body and legs.

Adrian watched, expecting him to put some dry clothes on, but instead he leaned back, half lying on the bed, his hips thrust forward. The vigorous towelling had disturbed his jockey shorts, pushing the leg open so that Adrian could see his balls and the root of his cock. Steven looked across the room at him, his expression telling nothing.

Adrian took a step forward, then another. He was standing over Steven, his hand only inches away from his groin, the young man looking up at him, his eyes wide open. Then Steven's hand was on his thigh and moving upwards over the material of his trousers. Adrian could feel his penis hardening even before the guy's hand reached his balls. He put his own hand over Steven's dick and could feel it growing through the blue underwear.

The man's eyes flickered. He whispered, 'A tenner.'

Adrian froze. 'You want money?' he asked, snatching his hand away.

Steven's eyes fell. 'I've got no job,' he said slowly. 'What sort of life do you think I can have on social security? I have to make it any way I can. I'm sorry.'

Adrian said, 'I haven't got any money either. I only have a part-time job and probably don't get much more than you.'

There was a pause and Adrian was about to turn and leave when Steven suddenly smiled. It made his face look beautiful. 'What the hell,' he said. 'I make a rotten rent boy, anyway.' He grabbed at Adrian and pulled him down on top of him, their groins pressed together.

The man's naked flesh was again under Adrian's hands, soft and silky, though the underlying muscle was hard. 'Let me take my clothes off,' he said and Steven let him go, pulling off his own underpants and socks.

Swiftly Adrian stripped off his shoes and socks, jacket, trousers and underpants until he stood in just his shirt, having trouble with the buttons. They both shivered with the damp chill of the basement room and the excitement. Steven couldn't wait for Adrian to get his shirt off. He grabbed him again and pulled him down. They held each other, their tongues and hands exploring each other's body.

Adrian, on top, slowly inched down Steven's body, kissing and licking. He paused and sucked at the nipples, then went down and put his tongue in Steven's navel, smelling his scent, a mixture of soap and sweat. Steven giggled and wriggled, so Adrian went even lower so that he could reach the fuzz of pubic hair around that sprouting cock.

'Turn round,' said Steven's voice, high with arousal, 'so I can do the same to you. Adrian needed no second urging and soon both boys' faces were buried in each other's groin. Adrian ran his tongue up and down the erect shaft facing him and then licked the firm young balls, taking each one into his mouth and gently mouthing them one at a time. Then he moved back and enclosed Steven's prick as far as he could into his mouth. He could feel his own erection being taken into Steven's warm mouth and knew ecstasy.

He put one arm over Steven's legs and gently explored his arse. He found the puckered hole and inserted his finger. He heard Steven gasp and then felt him doing the same. He pushed harder, at the same time sucking and wanking with his free hand.

Steven gasped, 'I'm coming,' and then clamped his mouth down again.

There was a warm, salty spurt filling Adrian's mouth and spilling down his chin but all he felt was his whole being centred in his own groin as a source of pleasure, exploding and pulsing again and again.

Afterwards, they lay together stickily and Adrian told him about the book of spells and how, just before Steven had turned up, Adrian had said the spell for granting his heart's desire. Steven laughed. 'Am I your heart's desire?' he asked.

'Well, I was thinking of you at the time. I did rather fancy you,' he admitted. 'I'm not sure I believe that it really happened because of the spell, though.'

'Can I have a go?' asked Steven. 'If I ask for something and get it, that'll prove it.'

'OK,' said Adrian, 'but you've got to say what you want first.'

'That's easy,' said Steven. 'I need money more than anything.'

'Go on, then,' said Adrian and watched while Steven ploughed through the words of the spell. For a moment they waited and then, when nothing happened, Steven sighed.

'Well,' said Adrian defensively, 'it doesn't say it'll happen immediately.'

He got up and dressed while Steven lay in bed suddenly depressed.

As he was leaving, Adrian said, 'Will I see you again?'

Steven didn't answer.

Adrian lived with his mother in a small two-up-two-down on the outskirts of the spa town. His home was constricting to Adrian. He could not take anyone back in the evenings – not for sex, anyway – and he had worried about the few that he had met and invited back in his off-duty periods during the day in case nosy neighbours enquired of his mother who they were. These encounters, anyway, had seemed unsatisfactory to Adrian and provided only temporary sexual relief, which otherwise would have to be gratified by solitary and manual methods.

The meeting with Steven the day before, though brief and ending so disastrously, had been different, Adrian thought. The phrase 'heart's desire' sprang again into his mind and Steven's mocking remark, 'Am I your heart's desire?' He wasn't sure about that but, try as he may, he could not get Steven's face out of his mind – those large eyes, so apparently trusting and confident, the way his dark hair curled over his forehead, the sensuous mouth that had smiled so bewitchingly and had fastened on to his cock like a lamprey. At the memory, his penis hardened. He knew he wanted to see Steven again. But did Steven feel the same? If he did, there was no way Steven could get in touch with him. He did not even know his full name – but Adrian knew where he lived. Did he dare to call round? Their parting had hardly been propitious. Steven hadn't even answered his tentative question as to whether they would see each other again. But Adrian had rushed off so quickly and Steven couldn't have followed immediately for when he had left he had been lying naked on the bed.

'Heart's desire!' Adrian had asked it from the Book, and the Book had produced Steven – but hadn't apparently granted Steven's request for money!

Adrian leaned out of bed and picked up the Book, which was on the table beside it, and again flicked through the pages. It seemed not to have been put together in a very organised way: there were spells, recipes, instructions for the gathering and processing of herbs, all apparently jumbled together. And there was no index, either.

Then something at the top of a page caught his attention.

'For the gaining of one's true love's affection,' he read. Then the book flipped shut and he had lost it. It took a while to find it again. 'For the satisfactory performance of this spell,' he read, 'it is necessary to have some hairs or clippings of the nails or article of clothing of the beloved or other appurtenance.' Shit, that was no use. He had nothing like that. What the hell was an 'appurtenance' anyway? You had to make a wax image and include the hair or whatever, say the spell over it and then carry it next to your heart until you next saw your beloved. It also advised the shared eating of periwinkle leaves – whatever they were. As it said, 'Venus owns this Herb, and sayeth that the Leaves eaten by man and his beloved together causeth love between them to grow and prosper.'

He studied the book, then went downstairs to find a dictionary. He looked up 'appurtenance' and found it meant 'anything belonging to someone or something'. He sighed. That didn't help at all.

Back in his room he dressed, feeling despondent. His shirt lying on the floor was crumpled. He was working in the afternoon this Thursday and they wanted you to look smart though he couldn't imagine why as no customer even looked at you. Perhaps the shirt would do for one more day. He was about to put it on when he noticed some obvious marks down the front.

Shit! Now he couldn't wear it. What were they, though? It looked like dry toothpaste – or . . . He remembered yesterday's tussle on the bed, which had started before he had even managed to take off his shirt. The discharge of Steven's come into his mouth and the dribbling down his chin. It must be Steven's – an 'appurtenance' if ever there was one. If the police could get a DNA profile from bodily fluids then surely he could use it in a love spell.

Suddenly cheerful, he looked for what else he needed. 'Take some wax – the common sort will do – and soften it in the hand.' Where could he find wax? Candles, that was it. There were some in the cupboard under the sink downstairs, waiting for an emergency such as a power cut. He raced down and found one. The white cylinder was hard and wouldn't soften – not in his hand at any rate – just like something else, he remembered. Then he thought of lighting the gas and holding it over it. He nearly burned his hand but at least the candle softened and he was able to mould it. Should it just be the face or the whole body? Shit! He'd left the book upstairs – and the shirt.

Carefully he scraped the precious stains with his fingernail on to a piece of paper. The instruction didn't make it clear whether the image had to be the whole body or not, but it was easier to make a figurine rather than attempt an accurate representation of the face, so he modelled the wax into a human shape, carefully incorporating the powder with it. Then he carved, with his mother's nail file, a face and a cock and balls between the legs – he felt this to be important. It wasn't easy and the result didn't have the lissom grace of the original, but hopefully it would do. Feeling slightly foolish, he said the threefold spell over it, kissing it on the lips, genitals and feet after each sentence. 'Bind Steven to me in this the image of his person. Cleave Steven to me in this the likeness of his being. Secure his love for me through this the figure of his body.'

Well, that was it. The spell was cast. Now all he had to do was carry the image in his inside jacket pocket, left side where his heart was, until he saw Steven again. If only he had some periwinkle leaves. He read the description of the plant again:

'The common sort hereof hath many Branches trayling, or

running upon the ground. At the Joynts of these Branches stand two small dark green shining Leaves, and with them come forth also the Flowers of a pale blue colour.'

To be honest it didn't mean much to him. OK blue flowers, dark leaves and growing along the ground, but unless it was as large as a sunflower Adrian didn't think he would have noticed. After all, flowers were not really his strong point.

Well, he'd just have to rely on the wax image.

He finished dressing and, feeling quite cheerful, ate some breakfast, brushed his teeth – after all, you never knew – and set out for town.

After yesterday's rain, the air smelled fresh and washed, and the sun, though shining warmly, didn't have the enervating heat of the past weeks when every exertion seemed to bring on a sweat. He smiled happily to himself and even managed to greet his next-door neighbour with a 'Good morning, Miss Davis.' She was a dowdy little sparrow of a woman with glasses who was energetically digging into her flower border with a small fork.

'Oh, oh,' she said seemingly startled. 'Good morning, Adrian.'

He went on down the road when a thought suddenly struck him. He turned and walked back. 'Miss Davis,' he said.

She bobbed up from her patch as if on a spring and looked terrified, almost as if he were about to mug her.

'I just wondered if you knew what a periwinkle was,' he said.

'Oh,' she said, and then cleared her throat. 'If you mean the plant, it's that one over there.' She pointed to something with trailing stems and blue flowers.

'Yes,' said Adrian, feeling like punching the air. 'That's it. I wonder. Could I pick a few leaves?'

Miss Davis looked puzzled. 'Well, yes,' she said.

'Thanks, Miss Davis,' said Adrian, and then, feeling mischievous, added, 'It causeth love to grow and prosper, you know.'

'Er, no, I didn't,' said Miss Davis and watched him with bewilderment as he hopped over the low wall into her garden, picked off half a dozen of the dark, shiny leaves and continued on his way, whistling.

Steven was not where he had seen him yesterday at his pitch on the High Street. Adrian felt slightly disappointed, because, if they had met there, he could have pretended it was a chance meeting. Calling personally at his basement flat could hardly be construed as such.

On the way to Steven's flat he rehearsed what he would say when he got there. 'Oh, hello, Steve.' No, 'Hi, Steve. I was just passing so I thought I'd pop in' – pop in! – '. . . thought I'd call and see how you were. But it had been only yesterday – Steven would know he was after him. May ignore him completely – ask him for money again. What if the spell didn't work? He felt the image in his inside jacket pocket – was it next to his heart? Stuffing hell! What was the matter with him? He was acting like someone with his first boyfriend. So, if he was rejected, he could face rejection. If he thought he would be so embarrassed, he might not even bother to call. It wouldn't be the end of –

'Hi, Adrian,' said a voice. It was Steven, smiling, looking genuinely pleased to see him. 'I was wondering how to get in touch. You left yesterday so quick. Got time for a coffee?' He was everything Adrian had remembered. Beautiful – in what looked like some really expensive new clothes.

'Steven, you look as if you've come into a fortune,' said Adrian.

'Thanks to you,' said Steven and turned to him, there in the High Street, with people all around them, and kissed him, full on the mouth. 'Come on,' he said, 'first one to get home gets to fuck.' He turned and raced up the street, Adrian, after a second's surprised hesitation, in pursuit.

They arrived at the top of the basement steps together, laughing and clutching at each other.

'Dead heat,' said Adrian.

'OK, OK,' said Steven, 'we'll have to decide some other way.' His eyes glinted with mischief.

Once inside the flat they looked at each other. Adrian could scarcely believe that he had met the young man who was smiling at him only the day before. He felt that he had known him for half his life. He put his hand over his left breast and felt the outline of the wax image through the material of his jacket. 'Secure Steven's love for me through this the figure of his body,' he mouthed silently.

'Where did the fancy clobber come from?' he asked.

'Your spell. It was your spell that did it. After you left I went out and bought a scratch card. I won a thousand pounds.'

'Told you it would work,' said Adrian. He touched the other man on the cheek with the palm of his hand and then cupped it round the back of his neck, drawing him forward so that lips met lips in a long kiss. He felt Steven's tongue probing at his mouth and let it in, the muscle, slick and smooth, twining with his own. He tasted a sweetness and wondered what Steven had been eating.

Their hips came together, groin pressed against groin, both cocks erect and that irresistible urge to copulate spreading through their entire bodies. Adrian's hand went to the zip in the young man's trousers but he drew back.

'Wait, wait. I need a shower,' said Steven.

'Prick teaser,' Adrian growled. 'Let's have one together.'

They jostled into the tiny cubicle, scarcely big enough for the two of them, laughing and pushing. Steven turned on the water so that it was hot and they soaped each other. As they got to each other's groin, they got excited, the lather slithering over erect cocks and balls.

'Turn round,' said Steven in a breathy whisper into his ear.

'Tenner,' said Adrian, teasing, and kissed him on the mouth. He turned his back on Steven and felt soapy hands rubbing the cleft of his arse. He relaxed his muscles and a finger was inserted, then two. He bent over, spreading his buttocks to allow even further access.

'Shall I put my cock in?'

Adrian wanted him to, wanted to feel Steven inside him, becoming part of him, but was worried. 'I've never done it before,' he said.

'I'll be gentle. Do you want me to?'

'Yes,' Adrian said.

'Hang on, then.' Steven stepped out of the shower and disappeared behind the curtain. A little while passed before he returned, still dripping.

'Where have you been?' asked Adrian.

'Condom,' said the other man and Adrian, for the first time, knew the reality behind all that talk there was about AIDS and

HIV. But he had no time to think about it further, for he felt the tip of Steven's penis nuzzling his hole, then pushing. He tried to relax but gasped when it actually pierced the sphincter. But it was inside. He could feel it in him and the thought that it was Steven made him excited again, overriding the pain. Added to that, Steven's hands came round and held his cock, rubbing it with the lather so that they slipped deliciously up and down the shaft. He pressed back to get the man even further in and then started pushing in and out, getting quicker and quicker as he approached his climax.

'Adrian, I love you, I love you,' Steven groaned against his ear and Adrian felt the spurt inside him and at the same time came himself so that he jetted a stream of come on to the floor.

Afterwards, they lay naked together on the narrow single bed, Steven on his back, his arms around Adrian, who nuzzled his head into the space under his lover's chin.

'What's your name?' asked Adrian.

It was a time for shared confidences and the telling and receiving of personal details, the beginning of a relationship. Steven told him of the rows with his family and the final one where unforgivable things had been said and he had left to live on the streets for a while until begging and some petty stealing got him enough to put a deposit down on the damp single basement room. 'You can make a bit on the streets,' he admitted.

Then Adrian explained about Great Aunt Marion and her birthday present, and finally – the Book.

'So two spells worked,' said Steven. 'You got me and I got the money.'

'Three,' said Adrian. He reached over to where his jacket lay on the floor and fumbled in the breast pocket for the wax image. 'I did another one this morning.'

'What's that?' asked Steven.

'It's to keep you, to secure my true love's affection,' said Adrian. 'Then there's periwinkle leaves. Eating them causes love to grow and prosper.'

Steven looked at the image carefully. 'Is that me? Well, at least you've given me a cock and balls.' And he snuggled up to Adrian, their bodies close together, and began to play with Adrian's prick, which immediately responded.

Adrian sighed contentedly. 'So that's all right, then.'

'The money won't last for ever,' said Steven. 'I've already spent quite a bit.'

Adrian sat up, serious. 'There is a way,' he said, 'according to the Book, by which unlimited wealth and desires can be obtained.'

'Sounds good. What is it? Another spell?'

'The signing of a Pact with the Devil.'

There was a silence while the words seemed to hang in the air between them.

Eventually Steven said in a quiet voice, 'I don't think I like the sound of that. Adrian, don't get into this too deep.'

At home that evening, Adrian turned to the Book again. On the last few pages were the instructions for making a Pact with the Devil. It was complicated and there seemed to be three parts. There was a potion that had to be made and drunk – but the instructions were there, as was also the recipe for making the drink. Then there was a spell for the conjuring up of the Devil – with suitable precautions for protection – and finally there was the Pact itself, which had to be written with the left hand and signed in blood.

Adrian sighed. It was going to be difficult and he was a bit squeamish about the blood, but it had to be done – and done quickly – for tomorrow was Great Aunt Marion's birthday and, if he was going to give her the book, now would be his last chance.

He looked at the list of ingredients for the potion: aconite (wolfsbane), digitalis, hellebore and hemlock. He sighed again. Even more difficult than he thought. He had never heard of any of them.

Of course, Miss Davis. Why hadn't he thought of her? 'I'll just call round,' he said aloud to himself. 'Won't be a moment.'

It was still quite light but Miss Davis wasn't in her garden, so Adrian knocked at her front door. There was a long pause and he wondered whether she was out, but eventually he heard the rattle of a chain and the sound of bolts being pulled back. The door opened a crack and her timid face peered out. It cleared when she saw who it was, though she still didn't open the door wide.

'Adrian,' she said. 'I wondered who was calling so late.' Late! It couldn't be much more than half past seven and it wouldn't get dark for another couple of hours. Still when you're old . . . 'What can I do for you? Not more periwinkle leaves?'

Adrian started. He had forgotten all about them when he was with Steven. They should have eaten them together.

'No,' he said. 'It's something else this time.' He looked at the piece of paper on which he had jotted down the names. 'I'm looking for some aconite, digitalis, hellebore and hemlock. I think they're plants.'

At the mention of plants, Miss Davis looked suddenly interested. 'My!' she said. 'That's quite a collection. Dangerous, though!'

'Dangerous?' echoed Adrian. 'In what way?'

'Oh yes,' said Miss Davis. 'They're all deadly poisonous – if you eat enough of them.'

'So you wouldn't have them in your garden, then?'

'Oh yes,' said Miss Davis happily. 'I don't have children or pets, so there's no need to worry – and I wouldn't be silly enough to eat them myself. Why do you want to know?'

Adrian paused, his mind racing. He hadn't been prepared for the question. Then he fell back on the old excuse from school. 'It's a project.'

But Miss Davis was brighter than she looked. 'You're not at school now,' she said.

'Oh no,' said Adrian. 'College. I've started a course at college.'

'Have you? Your mother never said. What is the course?' The woman was becoming too curious, thought Adrian. 'Comparative religion?' She smiled. Was this a joke?

Adrian laughed as if he understood. 'No,' he said, thinking it best to keep as near to the truth as possible. 'We're looking at some seventeenth-century herbalists and trying out some of their recipes. Not to really drink them of course.'

'Interesting,' said Miss Davis, then briskly, 'Well, come on, while there's light.' She opened the door and they both went into the garden, where the evening sun lit up the banks of flowers that hours of tender care had produced. 'Now by aconite, I assume you mean *Aconitum vulparia*, wolfsbane or monk's hood.'

'That's right,' said Adrian, 'wolfsbane.'

'Well, there you are,' she said pointing to a tall plant with frondy leaves and purple bell-shaped flowers. 'Called monk's hood because of the shape of the flowers of course – very poisonous. Now digitalis is the Latin name for foxglove over there. It's still used as a heart stimulant.' She pointed to some plants with even taller spikes down which purple and white flowers grew. 'Foxgloves. Nothing to do with foxes of course,' she explained. '"Fox" is a corruption of "folk's", the little folk, the fairies. The hellebores are here, in the shade, which they love.' And she showed him some more dark-leaved plants which looked rather unhealthy. 'Not at their best at this time of year,' she said. 'They're winter and early-spring flowers.' She paused while Adrian consulted his list.

'Hemlock,' he reminded her.

'Can't help you there,' she said. 'That's the poison Socrates used to commit suicide with.' Adrian nodded, though he had no idea who Socrates was. 'Hemlock's a wild flower. You'll find some up on the hill.' She waved her hand at the hill, which reared up behind the houses. 'It's an umbellifer with purple splotches on the stem.' Adrian looked blank. 'I'll show you. I've got a book.'

'Can I take some leaves of what you do have?' he asked.

'Wait a minute,' she said and she went into the house, not inviting him in, and came back with the book. She also had a pair of secateurs and a newspaper. She showed him a picture of a tall plant with thick stalks and a head of umbrella-shaped white flowers.

'It's like an umbrella,' said Adrian.

'Yes. That's what "umbellifer" means. You can find them alongside the road that leads up to Lonley Farm, on the right-hand side. There's a whole clump of them. Very poisonous. Remember the purple blotches on the stems.' She took the book back as if she feared he might run off with it. Then she went into the garden and cut off some stalks with leaves from the various plants, carefully wrapping them in the newspaper.

'There you are,' she said, giving him the package. 'And do

make sure you wash your hands after touching them.' She went into the house and shut the door. A second later, and before Adrian had had time to turn away, it opened again. 'Good luck with the project,' she said and added, with a smile, 'Sounds like witchcraft to me.'

He set off at a steady run towards the hill, his trainers slapping on the dry surface of the tarmac. Soon this gave on to a track with a ditch at either side and started climbing. Adrian was out of breath now but he forced himself onwards. Surely Miss Davis was not the kind of woman who would go for long walks – just a gentle stroll. Then he saw them: tall, elegant plants with thin spiky leaves and masses of white flowers formed into umbrella shapes. He noticed the rather sinister purple splotches on the stems, which otherwise looked like bamboo. He pulled off a stem and some liquid oozed out on to his hand. After a little while it started to irritate and he wiped it on his jeans.

He turned for home. He was late and he knew his mother would nag, but she would get over it. And he now had everything for the potion.

He read the instructions:

Juyces are to be pressed out of Herbs when they are yong and tender and tender tops of Herbs and Plants, and also out of some Flowers. Having gathered your Herb you would bruise it very well in a stone Mortar with a wooden Pestle, then having put the Herb into a Canvas Bag press it hard in a press, then take the Juyce and put it in a Vessel which can be diluted up to ten times.

He had no pestle and mortar. He would have to improvise. After all, the main object was to get the juices out of the leaves and collect them in some sort of container. Eventually he wrapped them in a clean tea towel and used his mother's rolling pin. A little liquid oozed out, which he squeezed into a glass. It was greenish in colour and did not smell very nice. Perhaps diluted it would not be so bad. He took it upstairs with him.

He got a clean piece of writing paper and made a copy of the

Pact as recommended by the Book. Written with his left hand, it looked amateurish and strange.

> *Pacta cum daemonibus.* Lucifer, Angel of Light and Darkness, Lord and Master, I recognise you as my God and promise to serve You while I live. I promise to adore your Body and to pay Homage to you at least three times a day, to do Evil, and to cause as many people as possible to do Evil. I give you my Body, my Soul and my Life and, having given them, I never wish to repent. In exchange for this you will grant me all that I desire in things both Material and Immaterial. Thus signed in my own blood . . .

Now came the difficult part. He found a sharp knife in the kitchen and made a faint stab at the thumb of his left hand. It didn't seem to want to pierce the skin. He tried again and gasped as a little drop of blood appeared. It was hardly enough to sign his name. Shutting his eyes he plunged the knife in and, though the sharp pain caused his eyes to water, he was gratified to see a much greater quantity of blood. Quickly he dripped it into the only container he could lay his hands on – the glass that held the toothbrushes in the bathroom. It may be contaminated a little with toothpaste but that would hardly matter. Now, what could he write with? Really, he could do with one of those old-fashioned fountain pens, but who had one of those nowadays? He would have to find something soon for blood clotted quickly and already the wound in his hand had stopped bleeding. He did not want to have to stab himself again. Eventually he found a matchstick, and carved it into a point with the knife.

Then, after dipping it into his blood again and again and, with his left hand, he shakily signed his name at the bottom – Adrian Pritchard.

There – that was done. He put a piece of Elastoplast on the cut. Now the final thing was to drink the potion and say the spell. Adrian, though, did have a little sense of the dramatic. He went downstairs again and collected two candles, which he lit and put on his bedside table, first moving it into the middle of his room.

Then he placed the Pact between the two and switched out the light.

He had the glass with the potion, diluted to the right consistency, and the spell, which he had copied out to make it easier to read.

He wished he had Steven with him for moral – and physical – support but that could not be helped. He was not on the telephone and lived too far away to go and fetch. He would have to do it alone.

Adrian took a deep breath and drank the potion. It tasted foul, as bitter as gall, so that his throat gagged and for a moment he wondered whether he would choke it all up again. But after another breath he managed to control the instinctive rejection and focused on the spell.

Seated in a chair and in the wavering light of the two candles, he read out loud: 'Emperor Lucifer, Master of all rebel Spirits, I pray you to look on me with Favour in the Name which I give to your great Minister, Lucifuge Rafacale; I beg you also, Prince Beelzebub, to protect me in my Enterprise; O Count Astaroth be favourable to me and grant that tonight the great Lucifer may appear to me in human Form and give me all that I ask, according to the Pact that I shall present to him.'

Suddenly everything blurred in front of him. He felt a tingling in his fingertips which gradually spread up his arms. He tried to lift them but they seemed paralysed. A dreadful feeling of panic rushed over him. He remembered Miss Davis's warning: 'They're all deadly poisonous – if you eat enough of them.' And he had drunk the juices of all of them! There was a buzzing in his ears and for a moment he could see nothing – even the light of the two candles disappeared. He experienced a dizzying feeling of lightness, of floating, of drifting.

Then everything cleared.

Standing in front of him was the figure of a man. Even by the fitful light of the candles, Adrian could make out his features clearly. It was a handsome face but cold and cruel with a sallow complexion. His dark stubble formed the suggestion of a moustache and little pointed beard. His eyebrows flared upwards at the sides (Adrian was irresistibly reminded of Mr Spock from *Star*

Trek) and his eyes were penetrating and had a yellowish colour, though the pupils were elliptical like a cat's.

He was naked and his phallus stood erect and proud from a bushy nest of pubic hair.

For a while there was a silence as each stared at the other, the stranger with a sardonic half-smile on his face.

'Hi,' said Adrian not quite knowing what to say.

'"Most High" would be more appropriate,' said the man. His voice was low and vibrant and sent a shiver down Adrian's spine. 'You have summoned me.'

Adrian found his voice – just – and stuttered. 'I would like t-to make a P-pact,' he said and pointed to the paper that lay on the table between them.

Lucifer – if it was he – picked up the paper and looked at it. 'You want all things material and immaterial.' It was a statement rather than a question. 'And what are you prepared to give in exchange?'

'It's all there,' said Adrian. 'I'll serve you, er – adore your body, pay homage, get others to do wrong et cetera, et cetera. Isn't that enough?'

'You will also give me your body,' said Lucifer, reading from the paper. Then he looked up and gazed at Adrian speculatively. He seemed to like what he saw, for he said, 'I am mindful to try the pleasures of the flesh.'

Adrian was not quite sure what he meant, though he thought he knew. 'And then you will agree to the Pact?' he asked.

'It is customary to seal it with a kiss,' said Lucifer. 'Remove your clothing.'

Adrian hesitated. Did he really want this? And yet – 'all things material and immaterial'. All he ever wanted: enough money to buy everything, a house, a car, clothes, a computer, a helicopter – his head whirled. He ripped off his shirt and unzipped his jeans, pulling off his trainers and socks so that he could get the jeans over his feet. He drew down his shorts and stood there naked in front of his Lord.

Lucifer held out his hand and Adrian stepped towards him. They touched and Adrian felt the other's flesh against his. It was dry and warm, though it had a rough texture which was strange but not unpleasant. Lucifer drew him close and his head dropped to Adrian's left breast, nuzzling him with his lips. Then he felt a sudden sharp bite just above the nipple and started away with a cry. For a moment the pain was intense, spreading outwards to fill his whole body. Then it faded, becoming an ache before finally disappearing. Where Lucifer had bitten him, there was a blue scar.

'You have my mark,' said Lucifer. 'Now you are mine.' He clasped him and now his embraces were tender and ardent. Adrian felt himself becoming stimulated, imprisoned as he was between the other's thighs and with that prick, which had never lost its hardness all the time, pressed into him and jousting with his own erection.

Lucifer stooped and picked Adrian up in his arms. He did it with no trace of effort or exertion, the muscles in his arms scarcely tightening, and carried him over to the bed. He laid him down gently on his back, lifting his legs so that his arse was exposed and vulnerable. Adrian knew what was coming and tensed himself for the assault, but, instead of a steel-hard rod, he felt a tongue, slightly rough like a cat's, licking under the base of his scrotum and then along the perineum, that sensitive area between the anus and the balls which is the centre of sexual being.

He could scarcely bear the delight and arched his body upwards so that his arse was even more open and into which the catlike tongue probed and licked. He could not stop himself making animal-like noises, being almost out of his mind with the desire to come and be fucked.

Then Lucifer's cock plunged in, searing him with a pain that was both ice-cold and red-hot, exquisite agony and delight. It filled him and at the same time fulfilled him. Adrian had enjoyed it with Steven because it was Steven whose cock was inside him, but Lucifer's member was giving him the most acute physical pleasure, the frenzied ecstasy spreading out through his whole body in wave upon wave of anguished delight. He had never felt anything like this before and he wanted the cock to remain inside for ever, going deeper and deeper until it merged with his very being.

He felt it being withdrawn and then plunging in again until the movement was regular – and at each stroke he knew delight and physical satisfaction.

Then the cock inside him pulsed and he knew that Lucifer was coming. He reared his own body up, clutching the other's haunches and pulling him, if possible, even closer, even further inside. His own cock twitched and jerked, seemingly stimulated from behind, from some central core in his bowels. He came and came again and could not stop, the throbbing pulses feeling as if they were emptying out his very entrails.

He collapsed backwards on the bed, utterly spent, gasping and panting, his limbs trembling uncontrollably. Dimly, through the mists of that aching post-coitum he heard Lucifer's voice.

'The Pact is sealed. What is your wish?'

'Money,' mumbled Adrian, scarcely aware of what he was saying. 'I need money.'

'Granted,' came the sound of that low, vibrant voice – and then he was gone, leaving Adrian to a night of tossing restlessness and turbulent dreams.

The following morning Adrian awoke feeling as if he had the flu. His limbs ached and he felt alternately flushed and then shivery. From outside the door, he heard his mother coming upstairs and then knocking on the door.

She opened the door and came in carrying a mug of tea. 'And what on earth have you been doing in here?'

Adrian focused his eyes on his room. The table with the candles he had used last night had been overturned. Luckily the Pact had disappeared but he wondered whether the evidence of the debauchery was noticeable on the bed.

'I'll clear it up,' he promised.

Fortunately his mother was in a hurry to get to work so, apart from grumbling a little, she did no more than pick up the table, restore it to its place beside his bed and put the tea on it. 'Don't lie there all day,' she said and went out.

A couple of minutes later he heard her go downstairs. He drank his tea. It made him feel slightly better. Suddenly there was a call from downstairs, urgent, excited.

'Adrian, Adrian.' He got up, groaned, pulled on underpants

and jeans and went downstairs. His mother was standing in the hall at the bottom of the stairs. She had an official-looking letter in her hands. 'It's Aunt Marion. She's dead. This is from the solicitors. They say you and me are her "heirs and beneficiaries". That means we get some money, doesn't it?'

Adrian felt slightly dizzy. It was the money he had asked for – but he hadn't really wanted Great Aunt Marion to die. She was a dry old stick but she had as much right as he did to live.

'Odd,' said his mother. 'She wasn't ill when I last saw her. Must have been sudden – heart attack, I suppose.'

'When did she die?' asked Adrian.

His mother looked at the letter. 'Doesn't say – oh yes it does. Day before yesterday.'

Adrian felt a bit better. She had died before he had asked for the money. So Lucifer hadn't actually killed her. Still, it was a coincidence. The thought of Lucifer reminded him of last night and he suddenly felt a twitch of excitement in his groin. It had been such bliss that he wanted it again.

His mother looked up. 'What's that mark on your chest?' she asked.

Instinctively he covered it with his hand. 'Just a bruise,' he said. 'I must get dressed.'

In the bathroom mirror he examined the blue-black bruise mark in the mirror. Adrian remembered seeing a similar shape in the sheep fields around – a cloven hoof, the mark of the Devil. He stepped under the shower and turned the water on, then squeezed some gel into the palm of his hands and rubbed it into a lather on his body. As he soaped his genitals, his cock rose; though, in an attempt to re-create the pleasure of the previous night, he found he was transferring the focus of his attention to his arse, inserting first one finger, then two, into the hole. But they wouldn't go in far enough to give him the ecstasy of the night before and, thinking of the satisfaction he had obtained from Lucifer's cock, he murmured his name, over and over again. 'Lucifer . . . Lucifer . . . Lucifer . . .'

Instantly he was there, standing beside him, ithyphallic as last night, echoing the words of the Pact: 'I promise to adore your

Body and to pay Homage to you at least three times a day.' He took him in his arms, wet and slick as he was, and their skin glided together sensually. 'Bow to me, Adrian. Pay Homage as you have agreed.'

Adrian stooped in compliance towards him, thinking perhaps that he wanted him to suck his cock, but Lucifer stayed him. 'When you bow to Lucifer,' he said, 'you bow away from him.' And Adrian knew he had to present his buttocks, open and ready, slippery with the gel so that Lucifer's cock could slide in as far as it could go. Adrian sighed, willing to accept and be fulfilled.

Gradually the momentum built up; the ecstasy was repeated and, as Lucifer came inside him, his own orgasm spattered the wall of the bathroom, leaving him, as before, drained and exhausted. As he staggered to stay upright, he felt Lucifer's cock leave him and he cried out at the empty void it had left. Then there was no one with him in the shower. On shaky legs he dried himself and put on some clothes. He did not feel well but could not bear to stay in the empty house, so he went into town.

He was fortunate to catch a bus that dropped him in the street at the top of Steven's, as his legs would not have carried him any distance, and even the short walk tired him so that he was weak and shaky by the time he reached the basement. He knocked on the door and Steven opened it.

He smiled when he saw who it was, then looked concerned as he saw the state Adrian was in.

'What's the matter with you?' he asked. He grabbed hold of him as he staggered and nearly fell, helping him over to the bed, on which Adrian collapsed.

'I'll be all right. Just need a bit of a rest.'

After a while, during which Steven made some coffee and forced Adrian to drink it, he seemed to get a bit stronger and sat up.

'You see,' he said with a smile and sounding more like his old self. 'I told you I'd be OK.'

He went on to tell his new lover about the Pact and Lucifer's appearance. Then there was Great Aunt Marion's death and the inheritance.

'We've got money coming, Steve,' he said. 'Real money.'

Steven listened to the story with amazement and some disbelief, but Adrian's obvious sincerity convinced him. 'OK. So what do we do now?'

Adrian looked at him and smiled invitingly. 'Guess,' he said, undoing the zip in his jeans.

'Randy bugger,' Steven said, joining him on the bed, though he wasn't expecting the passion with which Adrian approached their sex, nor the near animal ferocity with which he demanded to be fucked, almost raping him, forcing him to lie on his back and then sitting on his hurriedly covered prick so that it was driven hard up into his arse.

Even then he wasn't satisfied and hadn't come. He wouldn't let him withdraw, shouting, 'Leave it there. I want to feel it there. Please don't let me be empty.'

Steven felt worried. He knew something wasn't right. This was completely different behaviour from the previous two times that they had had sex, when Adrian had been tentative and inexperienced. Gently, he pulled out and tried to finish off Adrian with his hand, but he would not let him.

'What's the matter, Adrian?' he asked but the other man couldn't or wouldn't tell him and just lay beside him, his head buried in his shoulder, while an occasional shiver ran through his body. Steven held him.

Suddenly Adrian sat up and said he must go. Steven watched him put on his pants and jeans, which were all that he had taken off.

'Won't you stay?' he asked.

'Can't, mate. Gotta get home. I'll be in touch.' He got up and made for the door. Then he stopped, turned and kissed Steven on the lips. 'And remember Auntie's millions.'

Steven watched him go.

Adrian did not get in contact the next day, nor the next, nor the next – and Steven became more and more worried. Eventually he decided to go round to Adrian's house and find out, if he could, what the hell was going on.

He knocked at the door and waited but there was no answer. He was about to knock again when a voice said, 'I don't think there's anyone at home.' A little grey-haired woman with glasses was standing on the next-door steps. 'Mrs Pritchard's at work and Adrian's left.'

'Left? How do you mean "left"?'

'He and his mother had a row. She was telling me how much he'd changed. Got moody and depressed, would flare up – and then he just left. He hasn't been in touch for two days and she doesn't know where he went.'

Steven had more than an idea where homeless people congregated in town. If it was warm they would go to the patch of grass around the church, where there were seats to lie on, and shelter in the porches if it should rain.

But Adrian wasn't there. He asked around but no one admitted seeing anyone answering to his description: fresh-faced, straight, black, glossy hair, tall, slim.

When Steven actually saw him, hobbling along the gutter beside the road, he was nothing like that description. He could scarcely believe it was the same person. The dirt on his face would certainly have obscured the freshness but the bloom of his skin was also gone. It looked taut and grey, pulled tightly over the bones of his face. There was a spattering of angry red pustules around his nose and mouth. His hair was matted and lacklustre, the eyes staring.

He met Steven's horrified greeting with a blank gaze, one that almost denied recognition. Steven gently took him by the arm and they went back to his flat, Adrian allowing himself to be led unprotestingly. Once there, Steven stripped him of his rancid-smelling clothes, the front and back of his jeans stiff with dried semen, and gently bathed him with warm water. The skin of his body looked wrinkled and old, as if it had been submerged in water for a long time. It was covered with scratches as if he had clawed himself with his fingernails – and so thin that his ribs stood out above the sunken flesh.

All this time, Adrian said nothing, but at last, when Steven had put on some of his own clean clothes, and prepared a cup of sweet coffee, he let out a deep sigh. Only then did Steven ask him, 'What has happened to you?'

Again the answer came. 'It's the Pact. I must have congress with Lucifer three times a day.'

'But why?' asked Steven.

'You don't know what happens if it's denied,' said Adrian, and, as if talking about it brought back the memory, his body was shaken with racking tremors. 'Itching, dreadful itching, stomach cramps, hallucinations. You can't believe the agony.'

'I'll get a doctor,' said Steven.

'And tell him what? That I have to get fucked by the Devil?' He lay back on the bed wearily and closed his eyes.

'You need some food,' said Steven, 'to get your strength up. When did you last eat?'

Adrian's answer was so low that Steven could barely hear him. 'I can't remember.'

'Look,' said Steven. 'I'll go out and get a pizza or something. There's a takeaway on the corner. Will you be all right for ten minutes? Does this Lucifer just turn up?'

'I have to call him,' said Adrian. 'I'll try not to.'

'Stick it out, kid. There's two of us together now. I won't be long.' He covered Adrian's body with the duvet before he left.

But there was a queue at the takeaway and they took an unconscionable time heating it up, so it was a good half-hour before Steven returned. Anxiously he unlocked the door and went in. He breathed a sigh of relief when he saw the mound on the bed.

At first he thought he was asleep and decided that rest would be good for him, but, when he bent over to look at him, he saw that Adrian's eyes were wide open. He was shaking with uncontrollable shivering and his fingers were raking the skin of his body to try to stop the irritation. He lay beside him, holding him, trying to keep him still and, at the same time to warm him up. His breathing was laboured and smelled rank.

He muttered consoling words. 'It's all right, Adrian. Keep fighting. I'm here with you.' But he saw no signs of recognition in Adrian's staring eyes, and the gasps were turning into words. Steven at last could make them out.

'Lucifer . . . Lucifer . . . Lucifer . . .'

Suddenly Steven sensed a presence behind him and, turning his head, he saw a figure standing beside the bed, between him and the window so that it was just a dark silhouette against the light. The shape was that of a man and at first Steven thought that he had left the door open and someone, perhaps even a friend, had wandered in. He sat up and then saw that the man was stark naked. From the fork between his legs a monstrous phallus projected, erect and demanding.

He heard a voice, low but with a timbre that reverberated through his whole body. 'Stand aside, boy. He is mine – and needs my attention.'

Steven stood up to face him. 'No! He doesn't want you any more. Cancel the Pact.'

Lucifer laughed and the sound was terrible. 'The Pact is irrevocable.'

Behind him Steven heard Adrian sit up and give a low moan. He stretched back his hand and groped blindly for Adrian's, found it and squeezed to give him a little reassurance. Adrian's hand was cold and damp.

'Your Homage is due,' said Lucifer and took a step forward.

Adrian whimpered and started to babble, almost as if he were two people arguing with each other. 'No . . . please . . . no more . . . yes . . . fuck me . . . I want you in me . . . it hurts . . . I want to come.'

Steven looked at him. He was twisting and turning, wrenching at his clothes, pulling at his jeans to bare his arse while at the same time trying to turn away from that erect phallus that was advancing towards him. The expression on his face was one of terrified loathing mixed with a dreadful anticipation. Saliva dribbled from the corner of his mouth, which was now uttering no more than subhuman grunts.

Lucifer's cock was almost touching Steven and Adrian had turned himself so that he was on his knees facing away from him, his bared arse raised in anticipation of the entry.

'No,' screamed Steven. 'Get away from him.'

Lucifer raised his hand and struck him a sweeping blow. It did not seem to have much power but Steven was hurled across the room, hitting the wall at the foot of the bed with the back of his head and, for the moment, too dazed to move. Dimly, as if through a haze, he saw the huge cock plunge into the waiting hole and bury its full length inside. Adrian let out a scream of delight. Then all Steven could see were the haunches of the intruder as he ploughed into the defenceless arse.

It was all over very quickly. There was one last terrible lunge and Adrian's cock exploded, spurting come over the bed in an unbelievable stream. His head bent back in a rictus of agonised pleasure. Lucifer withdrew violently and Adrian collapsed on the bed and lay still.

Lucifer turned to Steven, his eyes shining yellow with lust and victory. 'He is mine and will always be mine,' he said.

Steven shook his head to clear it. 'You are killing him,' he said.

Lucifer shrugged his shoulders as if that had very little consequence.

'Then he will be mine all the time.'

'Can you not spare him for a while?' asked Steven. 'I love him.'

'He agreed to it in the Pact.'

Steven turned to look at the prostrate figure on the bed and then turned to Lucifer.

'Release him from the Pact, please.'

Lucifer's refusal was apparent in the look of contempt he gave him.

'Than take me instead,' said Steven. 'Let him go and take me.'

'What do you want in exchange?'

'Nothing. Just let him go.'

'You want nothing in exchange?' Lucifer's tone was incredulous.

'Just set my friend free.'

The figure on the bed stirred. 'No,' said Adrian in a weak voice.

Lucifer laughed. 'You see, he wants it all for himself.' He glanced down to his cock, which had remained erect even after his orgasm and now twitched obscenely.

Adrian's voice strengthened. 'I do not want it. I do not want my friend to have to go through this hell.'

A sudden change seemed to go through Lucifer's face. A spasm twisted one side making it go lopsided so that the words he said were indistinct, almost as if forced out of him against his will, some words giving him greater difficulty than others.

'Greater . . . love . . . hath no man than this,' he mumbled, 'that a man lay down his life for his . . . friends.' He paused and then ground out between his clenched teeth. 'I find this mutual self-sacrifice . . . obscene!'

His once handsome face twisted even more and a stink of corruption, of long-dead flesh, filled the air. Lucifer's apparently invincible erection drooped and the penis hung flaccid and ineffective. He gave a scream and grabbed hold of himself, jerking at his member in a vain effort to revitalise it.

'Anyway it doesn't change the situation,' he panted, so great was his exertion. 'You signed the Pact – in your blood. You get the money. I get *you*!' He finished in a scream and dropped his cock, which swung as if lifeless.

Steven realised there was nothing else to be done.

Then there was a weak comment from Adrian. It was as if he were suddenly realising what had happened – and what it meant. 'But you didn't . . . You have given me nothing . . . She died before I signed the Pact. I would have got the money anyway. You haven't kept the Pact.'

Lucifer suddenly looked as if he had shrunk, his whole body diminishing.

'You can have anything you want,' he said despairingly. 'What do you desire?'

'Nothing,' said Adrian. 'I want nothing further from you.'

The scream that issued from Lucifer's open mouth had an almost tangible quality. It bounced around the room, growing louder and more anguished as it was forced out of him. Then, just as it reached the level when the two mortals feared their eardrums must burst, it and he vanished.

The silence that followed was almost as loud.

Neither Steven nor Adrian dared break it.

They huddled together on the bed, holding each other for their mutual comfort rather than in any sexual need.

Eventually Adrian whispered, 'I love you. I will always love you.'

In answer Steven planted a gentle kiss on Adrian's lips. 'Where are those periwinkle leaves?' he asked. 'Would they go well on a cold pizza?'

Night And Day

Philip Markham

My cock rises with the sun.

'OK,' you might say, 'that's not at all unusual.' And in some respects you'd be right: if you have a dick, it's going to get hard sometime – and first thing in the morning is as good a time as any. I have often lain there with the soft, downy feel of the cotton bedsheet brushing against my erection, tempting it upwards to reward the head of my cock with its light kiss. Sometimes I squeeze my nipples between my finger and thumb – gently at first; I get a feeling of spreading emotion throughout my whole body when I do it. Emotion and sexual fire are one and the same to me.

Getting a hard-on first thing in the morning is a fact of nature that I share with most of the males on this planet. However, what I have, which they don't, is absolute, guaranteed satisfaction every morning and it's totally problem-free. You might have a naïve notion that sex is sex and, as long as he's not covered in warts, there isn't a great deal to choose between one man or another. Wrong! I have better sex than any you could even dream of and – I'm sorry to gloat – I don't even have to make him breakfast afterwards. His very reason for existence is to give, give, give and he accepts that mine is to bask in his warmth. I have no sense of building up bad karma. How can there be a price to pay when I am following the laws of the universe?

It's happening now. He is rising from his sleep, throwing his light over the world from his throne in the sky. At least, I know he's there, even if he's not exactly visible to the rest of you. On mornings like this, he uses the London skies as a veil to cover his lovely face. He is my secret whore, my angel of the day, my Ra.

I realise, of course, you've got me down as a hopeless case: completely barmy; ripe for the funny farm. You may have a point. Before all this, if I had met me, I would have been the first to agree with you. In fact, months have gone by when I've questioned my right to call myself sane. Now I just have to accept the fact that I'm having a love affair with a god. Not just any old god, either: I like to think of him as being one of the special ones, one of the essentials. After all, without him, none of us would be here at all. The ancients saw him as a hawk-headed man, or a bull, or a ram. The modern, scientific world thinks he is so much exploding gas. I know he's all and none of these things. He is Ra, Lord of the Sun.

Gods don't work like the rest of us. Because he's a spirit, he can assume any shape I care to give him. I have therefore decided the following:

He looks as though he's round about my age – I'm twenty-five and intend to stay that way – but of course he's as old as the universe itself; it's just that he doesn't age in a physical way. To say he's bigger than most men would be misleading: he's of exactly the same proportions but on a larger scale – as though he'd been enlarged on a giant photocopier. When I stand next to him I feel like a child next to my big, protective, grown-up brother.

Whereas I'm dark, he's all gold and shining. (I suppose that's a cliché but, at the end of the day, he is the Sun God so I suppose he's entitled to be a bit more radiant than the rest of us.) He has a massive chest – I mean, really massive – powerful and impossibly wide at his pectorals, but tapering down to a sexy, narrow, dainty sort of waist. Clichés again, but I don't care. At first I wondered a lot about whether he would have a navel. Is a god born with an umbilical cord like the rest of us? I didn't know and I decided I liked navels so he was going to have one of those really cute little button ones, the sort you can get your tongue into and then lick around the rim as though it were the inside of a thimble. Needless to say, he has gorgeous nipples: like mine, they're large, brown and really sensitive. I know this because he always closes his eyes when I grip them, ever so carefully, between my teeth . . .

Yes, where was I? His eyes: well, guess what. They're blue: absolute blue, clear, sky-blue . . . (I know – and I don't care!) And, yes, the hair of his head is all blond curls and the hair on his legs is soft and golden and he has really, really, strong muscles (biceps to die for) and wrists (I love a man's wrists) – they're strong, thick and, oh yes, hirsute: dense with wiry, blond growth.

Actually, I think I must have taken that last detail from a young man who used to live next door to my parents when I was a teenager. He always wore those crisp, white, cotton shirts with his sleeves rolled up to the elbow; his whole forearm was enough to make me weak at the knees. Why should my Ra be less perfect than the boy next door?

I can curl up on top of him. He puts his arms around me and I am wholly and completely safe. When I'm with him I feel so much in need of his protection, not because I'm afraid of anything, but because it's so comforting to have. He doesn't just help me forget my aches and pains, the detritus of modern city life: his powerful, masculine gentleness removes every insignificant, niggling worry I have ever had in my life. When he's near, I cease to be a brain and become a heart.

I'm being poetic and I must try to be more precise.

It's not in my heart that I feel the bond: it's in my stomach. That's where the beautiful feeling seems to well up. From there it radiates throughout my body. Not only my stomach, though: my cock is another, smaller, but no less significant centre of this love. It's tingling now, as I speak about him – it burns at its head with an enigmatic fire which surges down its length to a bristling tightness in my balls. I want so much to feel his mouth around it.

Let me tell you about the very first time.

It was at the point in the year when summer is just around the corner. It was one of those mornings when everything around looks good – even this dreary room I inhabit. I'd never noticed before how the sun could stream into my life and transform everything it touched, if not into a thing of beauty, at least into something I could bear to look at.

I was naked – I was in bed in fact. I pulled back the covers and let the light play over my body. I'm not a bad specimen – I work out and, though not exactly Mr Universe, I have enough shape to justify my habit of removing my shirt whenever possible. I have brown, soft hair which flops over my forehead in a disarmingly boyish manner and large brown eyes under thick, artistically arched brows. People have called me cute and I won't disagree.

On this occasion, as I lay there, I found myself thinking, Hey! You're not just cute! You're fucking gorgeous! The light was doing its work over my chest, accentuating the shadows under my muscles and giving them real, powerful shape. I had suddenly acquired a washboard stomach and the rippling torso of a stud. I pushed my hand down into my pubic hair and pressed the base of my hard cock with my finger. I had already determined to lie there for a good quarter of an hour and luxuriate in a slow, satisfying wank. Since Gary left me, it was something I'd learned to enjoy almost as much as sex with another man.

I closed my eyes and imagined. Usually I conjured up some hunk I've seen on the television or remembered the face of a handsome bloke I've passed in the street. I would let my mind's eye deliver him up, naked and willing, into my bed. This time, however, I couldn't bring anybody into focus. Every dream lover I could come up with was being torn away from me just as I got his face in front of my closed eyelids.

Then it occurred to me that maybe it was too light. I don't have curtains at my window and, though I've never experienced the sunlight interfering with my wanking habits before, even with my eyes closed I was finding it a little brighter than I was used to. Whatever the reason, after a while I stopped trying. I was pleasantly sleepy and I wasn't so horny that I had to come right away. I lay there in the increasingly hot sunshine, playing with myself without any great effort.

I know we're nearing the point in my story where every sane person is going to smile politely and leave the room, but what I have to say is true. Being an entirely rational individual, I told myself I must have imagined it, but nevertheless it didn't seem unreal at the time, or on subsequent occasions.

The warmth around me became tangible. My hands may have left my genitals of their own accord – I wasn't aware of having consciously removed them. I found myself lying flat on my back with my arms spread above my head and my legs wide apart. The warmth across my body was beginning to seem like the heat of another man lying on top of me. I couldn't see him and couldn't actually feel him but I knew he was there. I may have even moaned a few words of encouragement: something original like 'Yes, yes – take me!'

My penis was responding all right. And the thing was, when I looked down, it was flat to my belly, as though it were being squashed by the pressure of another man lying on top of me. I knew there wasn't really anyone there at all but I felt weight; I felt heat – and particularly, I felt that sweaty, lovely, intense warmth around my cock and balls that comes only from having another man pressing his own tackle against them. I even fancied I felt real breath against my cheek. I wasn't about to let my common sense in to spoil the effect – if this was what going bonkers was like, I was all for it.

I opened my legs wider. I wanted to see if I could dictate what was going to happen to me or if my visitor was the dominant type who would insist on calling the shots. I swear I heard him laugh.

The presence swept down my body: leaving my face – I felt the cool air of the room return to it – and, stopping to kiss each of my nipples, it went across my chest, down my stomach and so towards my cock. He kissed over my genitals – briefly and gently, just to let them know they hadn't been forgotten – and then did exactly as I had hoped he would: he nuzzled in between my buttocks and pushed what felt for all the world like a moist tongue right into my shithole.

If it was a tongue, it was a more flexible one than I had ever had up there before. He was able to get right inside me – jabbing at my prostate gland and turning me to jelly. I hope it doesn't seem like I'm greedy, but I couldn't help but be impatient for what his cock was going to do to me.

As soon as the thought entered my head, I was given his erection full into my mouth. He achieved the 69 without any sort of difficulty. I was just grateful for the throbbing hot, salty thing that plugged my face. I sucked on it as if it was a nipple, confident (I don't know why or how) I wouldn't choke or feel any discomfort. All the while the stimulation of my insides continued and, added to everything else, my cock was encircled by strong hands. They pumped it slowly, stopping every so often to stroke the thin, stretched skin along its sides or carefully tease the primed nerves around my piss-slit.

I started to experiment. I had already worked out that this creature – if that's what he was – was reading my mind. I wondered if just by changing my thoughts I could dictate what he would do to me. I concentrated like mad on having dick inside my arse. I imagined being fucked by a lovely man who was, at the same time, kissing me passionately, our arms around each other – the full romantic thing.

And it worked.

The slippery tonguing in my rear end and the hard ramming into my mouth interchanged without any sort of break. My gut was now full of stallion-like cock. It was a hard, thrusting lump inside me which felt like part of my body but which I knew belonged to another. My insides gripped around it as with each push it went deeper and deeper into me. Meanwhile, the more loving, careful attention of his tongue met with my own. My arms encircled – what? I didn't yet know and I couldn't yet see.

Without knowing how I knew, there were things I understood about him. I understood, for instance, that this sex was for me and whatever I wanted I could have. In return, there was something I would one day have to do for him. I didn't know what it was and, in truth, I didn't care, the only precedent I was aware of being Dr Faustus. who I always thought had quite a good deal. Anyway, whoever my visitor was, I was pretty sure he wasn't the Devil.

Meanwhile, the heat was growing. It was already more intense than I had ever known it, even when I recalled my recent holiday and the blazing Egyptian sun over the Temple of Luxor. The memory of that place was strong in my subconscious and gradually I began to know and understand more.

I wanted to see him. This could have been a most unwise decision: I've had my fair share of fucks in the pitch black of the back rooms and I've thought I'd found true love, only to emerge into the seedy light of night to find my Romeo looks like Caliban in a leather vest. I dismissed my fears: this just had to be different. Besides which, it had crossed my mind that maybe his looks were up to me.

I was right: they were. That was when I saddled him with blond hair and blue eyes – and all the rest. I don't think he was all that bothered. After all, he'd been seen for centuries as having a decent body but with feathers and a beak up top. At least with the looks I've given him, he needn't avoid the gay bars in Old Compton Street.

His body was, in any case, visible only in my mind. The experience of fucking with him was all to do with feeling, not with vision. My spunk was simmering in my sac and I realised it was going to boil over any second. I wondered what the protocol was when one was being screwed by a higher being. Did one help him to come first? Did he want to come at all? My doubts were quietly and firmly taken out of my mind as soon as they arrived there. This was the ultimate relaxation – better even than being massaged by the impossibly gorgeous Sean at my local sauna.

Without anything to worry about and aware that a firm visual image would be elusive, I lay back and concentrated instead on the feeling. The building orgasm had seized every part of my nervous system and put it on red alert. I felt as though I was going to burst.

And burst I did. My come shot out of my dick in one long, uninterrupted spurt. It had never happened to me like that before, but then I'd never before bedded a deity. Every hair on my body stood to attention as though I'd been swept over with static electricity. The tongue in my mouth seemed to envelop my whole face in its loving caress and my erogenous zones – all of them – buzzed with ultimate pleasure. It must have lasted for over thirty seconds or more. It felt like minutes. Then it was gone and I found myself (I think) waking up at the start of a glorious sunny day. It could have been a wet dream but I hoped and trusted it was not. The only thing I knew for certain was that I had come as I'd never come before. The bedclothes were saturated.

I couldn't get the incident out of my head, no matter how hard I tried. I followed my instincts and spent some time in the library looking at books about ancient Egypt. It wasn't a productive thing to do as none of them told me what I really wanted to know. In the end I went to see the old priest who runs the Egyptian society in Fulham. I pretended I was doing a thesis. He told me a whole lot of stuff I already knew about the preservation of the dead and sacred boats floating off to the afterworld, but when I mentioned sex he clammed right up.

You may be thinking, as I was, Why me? Why didn't some more worthy male have the chance of getting his end away with the Lord of the Skies? In answer I'd hazard a guess that maybe some more worthy male isn't a thieving little bastard and therefore didn't nick a certain little bauble as a souvenir of his Egyptian holiday.

It's called an ankh and it looks a bit like a cross with a sort of loop at the top of it. It's made of stone and I 'found' it at the base of a pillar in a part of the temple where some archaeologists had been beavering away. At the time, I wondered briefly about the propriety of taking it but persuaded myself it was just a bit of stone and nobody would really miss it. My friend, David, said that I should be careful. He reckoned there's a mummy's curse that goes with that sort of activity. I'm sorry to say I scoffed at the idea, but what's happened to me since is just as unbelievable as a curse, so maybe I won't be so sceptical in future. This sort of curse just happens to be more pleasant than dying of typhoid or a snake's bite or whatever.

Yes, I'm a lucky sod. I've stolen a magic, sacred talisman and, instead of vengeance raining down on me from above, I get fucked rotten by the horniest, sexiest, loveliest god who ever made his face to shine down upon me. Nothing bad can happen to me − I know it.

Strange then, that I get this vague feeling of apprehension. It's probably nothing, but I wish it would go away.

★

It's the height of summer and I have decided to take a holiday in Egypt. With all that's happened to me, I just can't get the place out of my mind. It's been beckoning me back ever since I left.

My ethereal love affair has become so much a part of my life that it's almost routine. It needs a bit of pepping up. He has not asked for anything other than to please me, but sometimes I have had that niggling 'oh, not you again' feeling that eventually put paid to me and Gary. It seems necessary for me to meet my Ra on his home ground. Egypt may weave its magic around my jaded soul and help me to appreciate what I have. Whatever the case, I don't really think I have a choice – I have to be here.

I haven't enough money for the Winter Palace, so I'm staying at the Pharaon, which is some way down a dusty road out of the centre of Luxor. I've brought the ankh with me and it's tucked safe and snug under my pillow. I arrived some two hours ago, by night. He hasn't yet appeared to me. A handsome lad who brought me clean towels has offered to wank me for ten Egyptian pounds but I said no, though I was tempted.

The night is hot and airless. It seems to be lasting for ever. I swear that a full hour has gone by since the last time I checked and the clock doesn't seem to have done much more than look cheap and nasty – which it can't help because I paid only a few quid for it. Maybe it's broken as well as hideous.

I can feel my cock becoming engorged. To be honest, I'd rather it wasn't. I like sex and, in the normal course of events, I'm game for it at any time, but it really is impossibly hot, and besides I want to save myself for the ultimate experience, which I know will be mine first thing tomorrow.

The hard-on won't go and I can't sleep.

My hand encircles my shaft and takes a few tentative pulls on it. My cock leaps to full life like a dog who's just heard 'walkies'. I debate, briefly. I have the choice of wanking now and maybe getting some sleep – in which case I may not be able to come tomorrow morning – or I can have a sleepless night and hope I will be up to it when those welcoming beams filter through the window.

I haven't had this problem since the first time he came to me. I haven't felt the slightest desire to attend to myself. I take a few more tantalising pulls at my dick and feel like a two-timer. Then I feel angry that he has this control over me. I have a right to pleasure myself if I want to. Even people who are in conventional relationships toss themselves off when their partner isn't around to do it for them.

The clock still doesn't appear to have moved.

It isn't the most satisfactory wank I've ever had. I have to really tense my whole body in order to coax the come out of my balls. When it arrives, it's just a splodge and the effort has made my head hurt and my limbs ache.

I still can't sleep and, according to the clock – which is still ticking – no time has passed.

I think I'm dreaming – like in other dreams, I know anything can happen and probably will. Unlike in other dreams, I feel absolutely conscious and I remember that earlier I couldn't sleep.

I am drawn towards the window. Across the blackness of the Nile lies the western desert, which the ancients thought was where the spirits lived. All I can make out are mountainous lumps of darkness against the marginally lighter sky. The moon can't be seen and this strikes me as odd because there isn't any cloud; one doesn't expect there to be over the Nile.

I am naked. My body is sweaty and heavy. I expect some sort of breeze from the river, but I don't get any. There's something in my hand. I look down and realise I am clutching the ankh. I have a sudden, inexplicable rush of panic and I drop the thing on the floor. It shatters.

When I turn back into the room I am surprised to find a stranger lying in my bed. You may think that by now nothing should surprise me, but the sight of this youth gives me a hell of a turn. At first I suppose it to be one of the hotel staff, out to make a quick buck. (The locals are amazingly resourceful and quite unabashed at the prospect of male-to-male coupling.) I approach slowly and silently because the lad has his eyes closed and I would rather he stay that way until I find out who he is and just what he thinks he's doing in my bed in the middle of the night. He's lying flat on his back with the sheet artistically screwed around his loins as though he was about to be committed to canvas. He has smooth, even features and long, dark hair. The bones under his face are shaped and fine. His arched brows and long, girlish lashes, his full, large mouth and his pert little button of a nose are all quite enchanting. He's not an Arab or an African: his skin is not dark enough. In fact, it seems to glow.

He stirs as I draw near and gives a contented, heavy sigh. His arm cradles around his head and I get to see the tuft of precocious black hair in his armpit. I have lost my fear and replaced it with an overwhelming lust. I reach out and touch the gently undulating stomach, drifting my hand upwards to his tightly packed pectorals and the wonderfully smooth, dark mounds of his nipples. I lean over and take one of them carefully into my mouth. He opens his eyes dreamily.

'Your time is soon come,' he says. 'You are tomorrow's day.'

I don't know what this means. In this half-asleep state it's not that easy to ask sensible questions and I'm quite ready to take it as a compliment.

He reaches for my head and runs his hands through my hair. I still have his nipple in my mouth but he carefully extracts it and turns over. The sheet falls away from his arse and shows me two perfect cheeks with dark, inviting hair profuse between them. He reaches behind himself and pulls them apart to show me his arsehole. He hands me a condom. I don't need further encouragement.

Entering him takes no effort whatsoever. I sink into his backside in one, easy movement. Once there, I feel his young body gripping around my erection as though it were devouring it. My balls are hot against his bottom but, strangely, his body is lovely and cool. I even fancy my cock feels cool inside him. I want to fuck him hard and fast but I am compelled, I don't know how, to take it slowly. He responds by bucking luxuriously against my thrusts. I put my arms around his hard chest and pull him towards me. I can feel myself coming and it seems to have taken a night of bliss to get there.

It churns out of me in bucketfuls. Holding me close to him and with my softening penis still encased in his arse, he rolls both of us on to our sides and presents me with his own small, perfect cock, nestling there in a bush of black pubic hair. I grip it and he strains around to kiss me. Our tongues mingle as I rub the small of his back against my stomach and feel his rounded, stubby, hot little penis with my fingers.

I know he's come because his breathing gets ragged and I feel the sticky fluid spill on to my hand. His tongue stays where it is, in my mouth, for minutes after. He has his hand on the back of my head and he's holding my face close to his own. My dick is still inside him. I'm going to have to withdraw carefully now, gripping the condom tight on my shaft.

The dawn is beginning to show. Here, there isn't much of a preamble about it: one minute it's night and the next it's day. I am suddenly panicked. He smiles at me.

'You have not been unfaithful to him,' he says. 'The glory of the sun is reflected by me, who am the moon. Heat must have coolness and the strength of light depends upon the gentle dark. I am part of him and he is part of me. I am Thoth, who was born of the seed of Horus through the body of Seth. I am the measurer of time and scribe to the immortal ones. As for you: now is when you must pay your debt and, in so doing, attain your greatest reward. You must cast off your human shape and embrace the light. You are Today.'

The dawn is coming to me in a great rush, like a wind of fire sweeping out of the sky at full pelt, a meteorite, dead on target. That target is me.

My cock jumps obscenely to attention. I feel again that static tingle that makes my skin seem like one whole mass of wonderful sensation. My backside is suddenly and wonderfully invaded by warm flesh. My nipples are stiff and erect. My stomach turns over and over. The heat has ceased to be unpleasant and is now exhilarating. The night sky changes into a blinding, white light which has no edges. I am no longer standing on solid ground but I have no fear of falling.

The only pain I feel is in my hand. I look down and see the imprint of the ankh seared into my palm. For some reason I find myself smiling.

Divine Lover

David MacMillan

The sun was white hot, bleaching the blue from the sky. Broken stone from the temple glimmered in the heat and starkness of afternoon.

I was in Greece all right.

Before me lay one more scattering of the dried bones that were classical Greece. Another wraith of what once was and never would be again.

I was in Arcadia, in the southwestern corner of the land that gave birth to Western civilisation. Far from the crowds of fat, red-faced tourists and their unruly children, far from the hawkers who catered to them and pretended to know their country's past. Ancient Greece was still here in Arcadia, as serenely natural as it would have been when Socrates thought and Homer composed. I needed only imagination to feel it as they had.

I climbed the wide steps of the ruined building and crossed what had been a columned portico to enter the temple proper. The walls and ceiling were gone, of course; I stood in but a reminder of Greece's dead past. A reminder bleached white as bone.

I smiled and the movement split the sheen of perspiration covering my face. I pulled out a handkerchief and wiped away the sweat. The brochure from the Greek Tourist Bureau I had picked up in London labelled this the last known temple built to Hades, the god of the underworld. It stood on the bottom slopes of the mountain named in honour of a nymph whom that god ravaged. Minthe had become the mint plant and the world had come to love the herb she became, as much as Hades had once desired her body. Mount Minthe and a living herb versus the ruined temple to Hades. I wished the nymph had got the better of the arrangement, but wasn't sure.

I was mildly surprised at the debris that littered the floor. I had idly thought scavengers over the millennia would have stolen everything but the dust that covered the stones beneath my feet. Curious, I moved towards what had been the rear of the temple, another scavenger seeking inspiration from a long-dead civilisation and its gods.

I came to Greece looking for a story, taking the journey I had promised myself each of the thirty-three years since I graduated university in Edinburgh, searching for the same inspiration this land once gave its most brilliant sons. Writer's block had held me firmly in its grip for far too long. I needed another bestseller to regain confidence in myself and had come to the land whose legends gave birth to my first and only major success.

My name's Iain Campbell.

That's right. The chap who sold twenty million copies of *Beasts of Chaos* in thirty languages. The same Iain Campbell whose novel frightened more people than even that grocer's daughter from Grantham who became Prime Minister. The Iain Campbell the BBC labelled the Scottish voice of terror. I had not written anything since *Beasts*.

My muse had deserted me after that success. Five long, fruitless years of pretending to be a writer when I wasn't, of living on past glory, as Greece had done since freeing itself of Turkish rule more than a century ago.

I stopped before a small pile of rubbish and kneeled to explore it. And I smiled. I sensed, almost felt, I could find an escape from the writer's block that held me so completely. My fingers explored the small pile of chipped, broken, stone fragments before me.

Almost immediately, they closed on a strangely shaped stone. I lifted it to my face and blew the dust and grit away.

The stone was marble, perhaps an inch long, and fluted. Perhaps half an inch in diameter, the fragment came to a puckered point at one end. The other end was jagged from where it must have broken off whatever it was attached to. The thing looked oddly familiar.

I chuckled then. The bloody thing looked more than a bit like the foreskin-covered tip of a penile helmet. I snorted as the realisation came over me. 'It's been much too long since you had a good shag, Iain, m'lad,' I told myself aloud, and had a good laugh at myself.

I wrapped my fingers around the strangely shaped piece of marble and stood up. My gaze moved around the floor of the temple again, attempting to imagine what had been here. Near where I stood, the god's statue would have towered above those who came to petition him. Before that, his altar would have stood. The stone warmed in my hand, absorbing my body heat as I began to move about.

Near the edge furthest from the mountain, I found what could have been the slab from a small altar, perhaps three feet long and of darker stone. It lay shattered on the floor and should have felt out of place where it lay. I had the strongest sense, however, that it was where it was supposed to be.

A strange thought struck me and I placed the stone in my hand on to the largest piece of the slab of rock. The idea of offering up a piece of a god's body to that god grew in that part of my mind that had not created a story for five years. I was thinking more of the Egyptian Osiris than of a Greek god and wondered what horror such an act would create in the novel I knew was beginning to form in my mind.

The temple floor shuddered slightly beneath me as I released the stone. The white-hot sun above me seemed to blink for a moment. I looked around me, imagining an earthquake, but everything was still and as it had been the moment before.

I chuckled at my overactive imagination now that it was returned to earth, and moved to the steps. I had some planning to do. My muse had returned and I had a novel to write. I wanted to get on with it.

I woke to fingertips gently skimming the hair of my long, thin legs and making it stand up in their wake. Long and smooth, the fingers moved until they were above my knee. They were getting close to my thick bush and the penis that nestled there while I had slept.

I was definitely and quickly climbing towards arousal. Skin pulled back as my bell end grew wider and hardened. My shaft wasn't yet steely hard but it was already supporting my helmet.

I was in a bed in a small room above the one taverna in this part of Arcadia. I didn't have a lover, and I hadn't brought anyone to my room with me.

I was supposed to be alone.

Fingertips nudged my thighs apart so that the palm of the hand behind them could cradle my bollocks. I was totally hard, prepuce pulled tight behind the helmet's collar.

I forced myself to open my eyes just enough to see around me, and remembered Stephen King's story about a writer kidnapped by a deranged fan. I sought to focus my eyes. Had anyone recognised me? Bloody hell! Was Greek one of those thirty languages I had been translated into? Did I have a mad Greek in my room with me?

I could make out a figure squatting beside the bed where my waist was. Eyes twinkling with captured light from the window watched me speculatively. I sensed more than saw his smile.

'You are awake,' a deep but melodious voice announced.

'Who are you?' I demanded, pulling myself up on the pillows so I faced him.

He chuckled softly. No, the room around me chuckled softly. Strangely, I grew even more erect. 'That is not really the question you want to ask right now, Iain.'

I stared at the silhouette that was the man whose hand rested on my knee. He knew my name. He also had a voice that belonged in the older brothers' version of the Vienna Boys' Choir. And, though slight, there was a definite accent there, not exactly like those I had heard in Athens or here. But recognisably lower Balkans. I began to leak.

'How did you get in?' I demanded quietly, my voice sounding loud in the silence of the room.

That soft chuckle again. As if the small room was breathing humour. How in bloody hell would I capture the combination of desire and fear I was feeling? How would I put them on paper? It would be like combining the very best cinematic elements of *The Exorcist* and *Poltergeist* to capture it fairly. And capture it I must. I would outdo myself with the book already well forming in my mind.

'I came to you, Iain, from – somewhere else.'

'What do you want?' I growled, remembering I was in a locked room above a Greek village taverna with some stranger touching me up.

'You finally asked the right question.'

I sensed his smile broaden across his face even as my room became uncomfortably silent. 'What do you want?' I asked again.

'You.'

I choked. 'I don't do gratuitous sex,' I grumbled as I reached down and brushed his hand from my thigh.

The touch of skin on skin, of a wrist with a hand growing out of it, reassured me. Hair on the arm. The guy *could* have been a ghost, an angel, or something. But supernatural beings weren't corporeal. Church, mosque and synagogue made them out to be spirits, not bodies.

So, I had some Bedlam escapee who managed to get up a flight of steps inside an unsecured taverna in a village where crime was unheard of. Now, all I had to do was get him out of my room without getting myself killed.

But it had been so long since I'd had a man – since I had returned from my first book-signing tour to find the man I loved moved out and me alone.

'Who are you?' I demanded.

That damned chuckle again. It was spooky as bloody hell. My continuing erection and the amount of pre-come dripping down on to my bush was even more spooky. I ought to be scared shitless and I wasn't. I was hornier than I had ever been.

'I am called by many names,' the man at my waist answered.

'So, what do I call you?' I asked, fighting against my whole body's desire to get into sex now. Every hair on my legs and chest was standing straight up. My thatch would be, too, if it wasn't so wet with pre-come. My arsehole itched and I hadn't done bottom in thirty years. Fucking hell! I didn't even know what this guy looked like.

I sensed him shrug. 'I am from this land.' He laughed then. 'You would label everything.' He sighed good-naturedly. 'Call me Greek if you must have a name for me.'

'OK, Greek. Next order of business is to see what you look like.' I reached to the lamp. And my hand stopped. My fingertips couldn't have been more than an inch from the lamp switch. But they weren't moving any more. It was as if there was an invisible wall around the lamp. 'What the fuck?' I growled.

'We do not need light to know each other, Iain.'

'Like fuck we don't! You could be a five-hundred-pound gorilla with human vocal cords for all I know. I take a real close look at anybody I do anything with. Understand?'

Silence followed my outburst. Yet light began slowly to coalesce beside my bed, in small increments. It took me more than a few seconds to realise what was happening around me. Light came from the window and through the closed blinds, from the dark Greek night beyond, from nowhere and everywhere. And stopped there about the Greek. Like the room chuckling a moment before, this was the kind of shit that just doesn't happen. I shivered in anticipation and hoped I was having a dream. My imagination was indeed finally working. Overtime.

The Scottish voice of terror indeed! The new book was going to scare anything that could read. The human voice of terror was more like it. No one could match what my mind was coming up with.

Soon, it was as if the Greek held a torch to his face. I hadn't seen any more of him than that but I was already in love and wallowing in lust.

Ebony locks caught the light and concentrated it. Curls formed a frame around the most beautiful face I had ever seen. I would wager even Alexander the Great wasn't as beautiful – regardless of what those old sycophants claimed. Why did he want me? He could have any man he wanted. I grew harder. And leaked steadily.

The Greek was beautiful – totally masculine: high forehead, dark brows and long lashes; high cheekbones, perky flared nose, wide lips and absolutely perfect alabaster skin. He even had a damned cleft in his chin like those celluloid gods of yesteryear. He looked to be in his late teens but I sensed he had seen aeons.

He watched me studying him, a little smile turning his full, sensual lips up at the corners. I saw his eyes then, the light accentuating them. They were black and as deep as space, as distant as the farthest galaxy, as knowing as the most experienced courtesan of any Renaissance court. I could fall into them and fall for ever.

'I am not a five-hundred-pound gorilla, Iain,' he said finally, and I had the sense that the light was going to return to wherever it came from.

'No! I want to see all of you,' I groaned. I didn't care how the son of a bitch got into my room. I'd worry about that after we had done the dirty deed. After he had fucked my bum raw. After I had held him and touched him and tasted him everywhere. It may be my citizen's duty to report a burglar or whatever to the local constabulary but, right now, I had more important things facing me. All of which I was looking forward to – with my tongue lolling.

'All of me?' His lips spread into a smile. The room chuckled again. I didn't cringe but my balls tightened. 'You would not want to feel me instead?'

'I want to feel you but let me see you, Greek. All of you. Please.' I realised I was begging and didn't care. This guy was beautiful enough to be an angel, at least one of those Italian models the old masters used. I'd be a fool not to want to look.

Light continued to come to a point beside me, beside my bed. It coalesced around the Greek. He stood up, still smiling as he looked down at me. Wide shoulders appeared beneath a long, graceful neck. Wide chest. No hair. And I was sure he didn't have any in his armpits, either. Same alabaster skin as his face. His areolae were wide and chocolate-looking. Small, dark chocolate nubs pointed out at me.

My mouth watered. My bollocks threatened to erupt. I grabbed them and pulled. The feeling passed. It felt as if I was in a Renaissance church with hidden, recessed lights focused on the statue of the dead rabbi, casting shadows everywhere.

My gaze found a deformity in the sculpted perfection unveiling before me: a strange pucker above his left nub, a wound of some sort. Healed now but a disfigurement nonetheless.

My mind passed that puckered imperfection, revelling in the beauty unfolded before me. There were no shadows on the Greek's body as it became exposed before me. I could see every line of his neck up under his earlobes. I had the sense I could walk around him and see each part of him as clearly as I saw his face and chest. But only those parts where the light had already reached. There was still impenetrable shadow below what had been exposed.

His waist was narrow, tight even. On a teenager, he would have a swimmer's build, smooth and tight. His hips were pronounced, accenting his pelvic bones over his tight gut. But he wasn't skinny. He was simply perfect.

I saw the first curls of his pubes and surrendered to every lustful thought I had ever had in the forty years since I entered puberty. They were as dark as the hair on his head. They were thick, a furry ebony mat. My balls tightened again but I didn't even think of them. I stared. I just wanted to see what the next two inches of illumination brought.

I sensed substance centred between his legs even as the Greek sat on the bed to face me and spread his legs to give me an unimpeded view in the growing illumination. The light caressed him, staying one with him as he moved on to the bed.

I reached out to touch that pucker above his left breast, the only disfigurement to his body. Stiff, hardened flesh greeted my finger. I glanced questioningly into the man's ebonite eyes.

He smiled. Neither friendly nor unfriendly, just from a far distance. 'I have always competed against one of my brothers.' A smile touched his lips. 'He has what I would have and guards it jealously. That time, he was rougher than usual in resisting me.'

'He could have killed you,' I mumbled as my fingertip explored the depression between the puckered walls of hardened skin.

He chuckled and sat up straight, dismissing further discussion of his family.

My gaze dropped to his groin then and I gasped. There was real size there, reaching for me, nothing fake or man-made about it. No silicone implants for this Greek hunk: his twelve inches were all his. They were regal, even divine.

I studied his manhood as light dispelled the last of the darkness between his spread legs. A pole planted firmly and accurately and perfectly in the centre of his pubic triangle, skin pulled back to bunch behind its collar. Sticking straight out with no droop and no curve, it was a perfect pole, long and thick.

His hand returned to my leg and settled halfway up my thigh, his long, slim fingers touching the hairs on the bottom of my tight scrotum.

I want you, Iain, the room breathed about me, and the Greek's eyes watched mine, beseeching me.

My mind became a turmoil of conflict as I gazed at his colossal cock and weighed pleasure against pain. Then, in betrayal, my legs spread in silent invitation as my balls churned.

'Do you want me, Iain?' the Greek asked softly, his fingers beginning to encircle my dick.

'Fuck me!' I moaned and hated myself. I wanted it. Bad. An itch had started deep in my arse I couldn't reach. I knew the Greek could. And would. His stout dagger would scratch that damned itch real good, just as soon as I got him between my legs.

His fist pulled my skin down on to my shaft and his lips touched my helmet with a butterfly kiss. Every muscle in my body leaped into a living rigor mortis. The fingers from the Greek's other hand passed my navel and spread across my chest to jump-start my heart again.

His lips opened and my prick filled his mouth, his throat muscles clutching at the helmet all the way to bloody well near the root as he buried his face in my pubes.

I moaned. My muscles locked up as I shoved myself even deeper into his throat. I beat the bed with my fists. I erupted like a first-time wanker. It was my biggest orgasm in more than forty years of knowing what my manhood was about.

My heart pounded. My ears buzzed and the Greek sucked me dry, my dick and my bollocks. I didn't have anything left when he was through. My whole body began to shake until he finally let me go. Then I just collapsed. I didn't care. I sank into myself.

He slipped further between my legs – his shoulders and arms, his ribs, his stomach muscles. His lips trailed up my body and pulled it into a new reality. He was on his knees and lifting my long legs up over his smooth chest on to his perfect shoulders. His tongue reached the little hollow between my neck and chest. I was hard again.

My hands reached behind him, fingernails digging into his sides as they slid over his perfect skin towards the mounds of his backside. His lips nibbled at my chin and moved along the jaw to my ear. I felt his perfect helmet line up against my wrinkled pucker, slightly pushing it aside as it took up its position at my entrance.

'I want you, Iain,' the Greek mumbled against my ear.

I stared down my body at him, poised at my entrance, stared at the perfect body illuminated by a light that knew no shadows. The walls about me oozed assurance. The air sang the chorus. I looked at him, his face inches from mine. At his reassuring smile.

I opened up – for the first time in the thirty years since I decided I was a topman. I opened like a blossom becoming a flower. For the biggest slab of meat I had ever had in me. Dry. For this bloody Greek.

He entered me. His wide head slipped into my bowel and my body knew not to resist. The Greek gently sank down to meet my spread buttocks, his dick sliding into me. No pain screamed through nerve endings to remind me of why I gave up bottoming. Forgotten sensations coursed through me, better than I ever imagined, and became reality. My head pounded with exultation at having his dick buried inside me.

His eyes were shut as his lips moved unerringly towards mine. I smelled mint as they touched. His pubes scratched the bottom of my scrotum. My mouth opened and his tongue entered it as he ground his hips against my bum. My balls tightened around my hard shaft.

His body moved against mine as we kissed. Mine moved against his. I wanted him in me. More than anything in my fifty-four years I needed his dick. It seemed to concentrate its attention on my love gland, though I knew he was far bigger than that.

I kissed him back, my tongue duelling his as we shagged across the bed above the taverna in Arcadia. His dick continuously massaged my love gland with a constant prod. His heavy balls caressed my backside each time he bored into me. My dick leaked thick pre-come. My fingers dug into his backside and I was raised to the heights of lust.

I ground up against him as he thrust into me. Our lips remained locked together. His fingers explored my chest and the sparse forest that spread across it. They roamed down to grip my hips to give him better leverage.

I shot a load that my balls couldn't have had in them, spunk spreading across my stomach, as the Greek continued to shag me slowly. He possessed me thoroughly. And I gave myself to him completely.

I slowly came to realise that a stutter had begun to develop in the perfect world of lust through which we rocked. His thrusts became quicker – faster and shorter. His groin pounded hard against my arse cheeks. I gasped in ecstasy as I again exploded.

The Greek broke from our kiss, rising up on his knees above me. He carried my arse with him and only my shoulders and head were on the mattress. He pushed everything he had into me, stopped, and smiled down at me. He wasn't even breathing hard. 'Not this time, Iain,' he said as he laid me back on to the bed and withdrew from me. I sat up and pulled myself to him.

I cuddled against him, my legs still against his chest, my backside against his groin. I liked the feel of his erection in my cleft. I liked his fingers playing in my chest hair. I accepted his possession of me, that I had given it freely, and wanted it never to end. His smooth cheek nuzzled my shoulder. 'What may I give you, Iain?' he whispered, his lips playing at my ear.

I chuckled and wiggled my buttocks against him. 'You've given me enough.'

His fingers moved down on to my stomach muscles. 'I would give you more.'

'I have everything I ever needed now,' I mumbled and grinned, drifting along on a sea of complete satiation.

'May I come to you tomorrow?'

'You're leaving?' I asked and forced myself back to the shore of that satiation. My hand went to his backside, instinctively trying to hold him to me.

'I must. But I shall return tomorrow evening.'

I smiled. 'You'd better,' I told him and was asleep.

I was instantly awake the moment my eyes opened the next morning. I sat up and tore open my suitcase. The box of condoms sat there unopened, silently accusing me. I checked the floor and the rubbish bin. Not a used slicker in sight. I had let a fucking burglar between my legs. There was no telling where he had put his damned dick before it went into my bowel. I knew I was going to be frightened for the next two months before a test would tell me if I had made a fatal mistake.

The skin of my stomach and chest glistened with a sheen of perspiration in the early morning of a Greek summer. I frowned. Where was the come I had shot the night before and not cleaned up? Come from two orgasms.

I hopped off the bed with more energy than I had felt in years and threw the duvet back. I ran my hands across every inch of the bottom sheet looking for the dried come that should have been there. If the guy shot a load up my bum, he'd still be leaking while he held me when I was falling asleep. Jizz would have oozed out of my hole during the night. And, even if he had pulled out without ejaculating, the Greek had still sucked me dry. I had erupted again when he fucked me. There had to be plenty of dried jism splattered across the sheets.

There was nothing anywhere, not even a stray hair on the pillows. Just my sweat.

Perhaps it was just a dream.

I allowed myself to hope that as I made my way down the hallway to the bathroom. After all, my options were that last night was a dream or I was ready for a long rest at Bedlam.

Or, perhaps, my imagination had created a scene for the new novel beginning to develop in my mind. It was a possibility now that my writer's block was gone.

Perhaps. But I didn't remember anything as intense as last night had been playing out in my head as I had written my bestseller.

I pondered my options as I squirted toothpaste on the toothbrush. Something grew on me as I went through my automatic preparations – something terribly wrong that I wasn't catching. 'Iain, you're psyching yourself up with this bloody mess,' I told myself and pulled myself back from the precipice to which my imagination had led me. I stepped up to the lavatory and lifted the brush to my teeth.

I had almost decided the young, blond guy gazing at me with a toothbrush against his teeth was a damned good-looking lad when I realised where I was and who I was looking at.

I was staring into a mirror, after all. That was supposed to be me there. But it was me when I was in my early twenties. Thirty years ago.

I was blond and there wasn't a grey hair in sight. The sagging cheeks and crow's feet of middle age were gone. The delicate bone structure that had so characterised my middle age was again hidden beneath fleshed-out skin. Blue eyes gazed back at me and showed their surprise. My skin had become tight and elastic once again.

I stepped back to view more of myself. My chest was again covered by a light sparse forest from my collarbone to the bottom of my ribcage. There was no gut to suck in. There were no protruding hip bones, either. I stared at the slim, well-built, good-looking young man in the mirror in total disbelief. The near-ravished appearance I had given off the past decade was gone, covered by tight skin over hard but understated muscle.

I dropped the toothbrush in the basin and marched quick-time back to my room and the bed that awaited me there.

Even through the thick walls of this taverna, the morning sun of a Greek summer made the room hot; but I lay in my bed with the duvet drawn up to my chin and shivered.

'Iain,' I told myself forcefully, 'this simply *will* not do, old lad.' I looked about the room slowly as rivulets of sweat ran down my cheeks into my sideburns and on to my neck. 'You're a fucking writer – think it out, mate. Damn it all! Plot it out. Nothing happens without a bloody reason.'

That pulled me from the embrace of the shock that held me – treating my experience of the night before as a knot in a story I had to unravel by plotting it out. Perspiration still covered me as I again pushed myself from the bed, but I was no longer chilled.

I made my way back along the hallway to have a bath and shave quickly. Downstairs in the taverna, I ate a late lunch without tasting my food. Outside in the heat of the day, I made my way down to the beach and contemplated the recent plot change in my life that did not make sense.

I noticed the appraising glance of more than one of the youths I passed along the way. I even nodded to one or two of the cutest of them. They were still lads, however, in their twenties, and the Greek was . . . What in bloody hell was he?

Last night had been a dream, an insane delusion – or it had been real. Those were my choices. The reality of what I had found in the mirror this morning seemed to negate the possibility of either a dream or delusion. That left me with the greatest sex I could remember and the loss of thirty years as reality. An impossible reality, but reality nonetheless.

If reality, then who was the Greek who had loved me so well? Who had given me my youth again?

A god? A voice from deep within the recesses of my mind suggested quietly.

Not bloody likely!

As Sherlock Holmes had once suggested to Dr Watson, however, when one has eliminated the impossible, whatever remains – however improbable – must be the truth. I was not about to suggest that making love and sculpting thirty years off my body was a crime but Sir Arthur's logic was nonetheless irrefutable to me.

I leaned against a boulder facing out on the Mediterranean as I finally reached this conclusion. The sun was near to setting and purple streamers began to spread across the darkening sky.

A god?

One of those many Greeks adored and elevated to divinity so

long ago? Could such be possible? Could that whole pantheon be real? Even one of them?

And, if so, why me?

Later, as night spread across southern Greece, I sat in the growing darkness of my room. I was naked in anticipation of my lover's promised return. I didn't know what to think. But part of me was willing to believe. At least, it was willing to hope.

On a most esoteric level, I was in a quandary. A fifty-four-year-old man simply did not wake up one morning on holiday looking *twenty*-four. He definitely didn't look as if he had had a whole-body tuck. If he didn't but I did, the only difference between me and my hypothetical gent was the Greek's arrival in my life. Which would make last night's lover supernatural but real.

If the Greek of last night *was* real, however, I was confronted with his being not exactly human. No one had unlatched the door and entered my room last night, especially not the Greek. And no human could ever be so damned beautiful (well, OK, that one Australian lad on the cover of the March 1996 *Outrage* – but one human being out of seven billion?).

If the Greek wasn't exactly human, then what was he?

I already had the answer to that. He *was* a god. But I was not especially happy with that answer. It wasn't exactly reasonable in a day and age where reason had replaced superstition in enlight-ened societies.

I didn't like it, but I was damned close to admitting that the Greek fell into the supernatural category. I didn't know how I felt about that.

I had to accept that there were heroes, demigods and gods; there were gods who possessed more power than other gods. One small pebble of improbability became an avalanche of ignorant superstition. Yet it was the only explanation that fitted from all directions. If it was true, however, I was going to have to uproot nearly everything that governed my life and start anew. I definitely was not fond of that probability.

My room became dark as night unrelentingly possessed Arcadia. My dick was hard and drooled in anticipation of the Greek's promised return. Somewhere near on the nine-inch mark the inside of my gut itched fiercely. And my pucker was exercising its new and improved stretch-and-grip routine in preparation for another workout.

Light began imperceptibly to coalesce in the centre of the darkened room. It took me long moments to realise it was there, expanding and growing stronger. My head snapped to face it as I forgot my hard dick, as I forgot all the questions that had plagued me throughout the day.

He was back.

I hadn't been dreaming. I wasn't a delusional maniac. The Greek was real. Even if he was some sort of god.

The light continued to expand and grow in the centre of the room before me. The night pressed against it, resisting its growth but also moulding it into the shape of a passage. A corridor that extended into even deeper night.

'Iain, may I enter?'

The words came at me from all sides of the room around me, from the air that touched me, from deep within the corridor that stretched from the light into nothingness.

There was no one in the bedroom with me. Just me and the room. I stared into the night at the depth of the corridor. My dick drooled a serving of pre-come in greeting. My sphincter joyously spread wide enough to take the whole mattress.

'Please!' I mewled, ready for a bacchanal that would make me forget all my thoughts and doubts and fears from the day now behind me.

I heard footsteps ring on stone. The sound of them was as distant as the stars, yet as close as the other side of the room. They came towards me. I shivered in anticipation. Another helping of pre-come trickled from my prick and slid down my shaft into my pubes to ooze on to my bollocks and between my thighs, wetting me.

My lover had returned to me. A god who wanted me. My divine lover.

A gate creaked open near to me – one the light did not illuminate for me. The walls chuckled as my lover took in my anticipation and understood it.

The Greek stood at the foot of my bed. Nude, beautiful, hard, perfect. He pulled the light from the hallway to him, eclipsing everything else in the room but himself. He studied me for a moment before he nodded. 'Yes, Iain, you do look better younger. It pleases me that I thought of it for you.'

He climbed on to the bed and crawled towards me.

'How . . .?' I began and forgot my confusion of the day just past. I lay back and my legs spread in welcome as I watched him near me. A day's worth of questions lay forgotten in the depths of my mind. I just wanted him in me. My arse ring winked at him, my dick oozed again.

He skirted my legs even as his fingers found my knee and moved up towards my bollocks. He lay beside me. 'I thought of you,' he said, his face inches from mine.

God, demigod, or hero, whatever the Greek was I wanted him. I reached for his face with both hands and pulled his lips to mine even as I rolled us over. He fell back and smiled up at me as I straddled his thighs with my knees and bent to taste his lips. His fingers spread across my back as our tongues met and mine immediately acknowledged his supremacy. His hands slipped to my buttocks and gripped them, pulling me against him. Between us, his prick duelled mine and there wasn't even a contest.

My hands explored from his ebony curls and long, slim neck to his wide shoulders. My fingers found again the pucker of skin above his left nipple and played with it. It was the only imperfection on my Greek's body.

My hands moved from his smooth chest to his perfect abdomen – to his perfect manhood. I was past lust and was into adoration. My bollocks rode my dick as I ground my backside against him, capturing his manhood within my cleft. I wanted him in me. I wanted to ride him as if I were some Valkyrie riding out of Valhalla. For ever.

But his slab of meat wasn't getting any closer to my arsehole where I wanted it. It took a while but I finally realised the Greek wasn't ready to shag me. He wanted something else for now. The scent of freshly crushed mint filled the room.

I sat up and grinned down at his hard dick pushing its way out from beneath my bollocks. I took in the perfect body lying beneath me and looked into the most beautiful face I had ever seen and was almost overwhelmed by the rush of lust and desire. For sex. For him. For his perfection.

'Will you go with me, Iain? That I might show you something of me?'

My face grew blank as I tried to leap from lust to intelligent conversation. 'Where?'

He smiled up at me. 'To my bed. To my home – my palace. In Tartarus.'

'Where?' I frowned.

Tartarus? I had heard the word. Knew it. From somewhere. One of the mythological lands ruled by one of the principal gods of classical Greece. I racked my brain to dredge it up from among those many Greek legends I had incorporated into my last novel. It eluded me and I was surprised at how sluggish my thoughts were.

I was caught for a moment between instinct and intelligence – both out of hand's reach. I was suspended between both. His fingers touched my brow and I forfeited my search for references to Tartarus. To this god who had chosen me. I had my divine lover and he was all I would ever need. I relaxed and settled down against him, his arms moving to my back to hold me to him. I was home as long as I had him with me.

He rose from the bed and I with him. Levitating. My arms went about his chest and gripped him tightly.

We moved parallel to the bed until the floor was beneath us. We tilted then and my lover was perpendicular to the planked floor beneath us. He walked to the centre of the darkened room, his arms around me as mine were around him, his prick in the cleft of my buttocks.

Air shimmered about us in southwestern Greece as we returned to the portal through which he had entered, pulling light into itself. The soft movement of air over our naked bodies quickly became screaming gusts as we hurtled through what I had thought of as a corridor. My room above the taverna disappeared and we sped faster than I had imagined possible between walls of shimmering grey nothingness.

My knees gripped the Greek as they would a runaway stallion.

I pressed against him and clutched my hands together in the centre of his back to hold on to him. As I put my head down beneath his chin, my stomach did flip-flops and my hard dick shot a splash of pre-come on to his perfect belly. The only thing that could make my mysterious ride any better would be his dick buried deep inside me, where I wanted it.

We erupted from the corridor into a large stone room. My Greek held me to him as we came to an abrupt halt in the centre of the room. He wasn't even breathing hard. Over his shoulder, I watched in horror as the corridor we had come through blinked out of existence.

'Where are we?' I groaned, unsure whether I wanted an answer.

He chuckled and kissed the top of my head. 'My palace in Tartarus, Iain.'

'Tartarus?' I released my legs' hold on the small of his back and slid them over his hips. My hands moved to hold his arms. His prick still jutted between my legs and mine pressed against his stomach. I looked into the Greek's face and saw a distant resoluteness I had not seen there before.

I looked again at the room in which we stood, studying it in an effort to gain my bearings. A grey light was upon us, surrounding us in the centre of what I saw now was a great circular hall – an ornate hall vaguely like one in the greatest of our castles, but strangely different at the same time. Above us I could not see the ceiling: there was only darkness above the light illuminating us. Around us, at the extreme reach of the light, I could make out the stone railings along the walkway of the second storey. Beneath us lay a mosaic that stretched the length and breadth of the floor. I saw no source for the light.

'The –' He paused, seeming to search for the correct word. 'The novel that gave you your fame, Iain Campbell – what is its title?'

'*Beasts of Chaos*,' I mumbled suspiciously.

He smiled at me watching his face. 'An interesting tale – and far too accurate for the world in which you live, Iain. Where did you find your information?'

'The ancient Greek poets mostly, and in the depths of classic Greek mythology.'

His eyelids closed to slits but I knew he still looked at me. 'A strange word, "mythology" is. It feels stranger still when one is considered a myth.' He shook his head slowly. Almost sadly, I thought. 'Beneath you is the picture of Chaos, Iain.'

I looked over my shoulder at the mosaic spread across the floor. Though it was lighted, I could not make out more than a jumble of colours.

'It's impossible for a mortal mind to comprehend it standing this close,' he told me. 'When you can do so of your own will, you may view it from the ceiling, Iain. You can see how close you came to capturing what my father contained and my brothers and I destroyed.'

'You and your brothers destroyed . . .?' I mumbled, my mind grappling with the impossibility of what was happening to me, of who this man – being – could be. The only brothers I remember from any mythology eliminating Chaos were Zeus, Poseidon and Hades. He nodded and I knew he had read my thoughts. I took a deep breath and, reassured, knew this god before me was not Poseidon – at least, not unless I had suddenly learned to breathe water. That left Zeus and Hades from whom to choose.

My gaze found the puckered scar over his left nipple then. Over his heart. My eyes widened in a combination of disbelief and fear as realisation spread across me. 'You're Hades!' I gasped finally.

He nodded and I felt my heart slide towards my gut. My erection was lost as it succumbed to my growing acceptance of where I stood and who my lover was. I wasn't sure my heart still beat.

'Am I dead, then?' I managed somehow to ask.

He studied me, his face unsmiling and his eyes blank to me. 'I am not Death! I shelter the shades of mortals, but I do not reap them. You returned to youth, Iain. If you give yourself again to me as you did last night, you gain immortality when I give you my seed to nourish your body. It is yours if you decide to accept it – and me.'

'If I don't accept?' I asked, watching his face as I pushed against his waist. I slid out along his engorged manhood, its helmet an inch closer to my entrance.

He shrugged. 'I return you to Gaia and you live out whatever life remains to you.'

'Then I die and return here,' I grumbled and pushed off him completely. This was not a discussion to have with a dick poised at one's back door.

'To Tartarus – but not to this palace, exactly. To the underworld I rule. You would be but one more shade populating the land between the five rivers. Judged by the three Kings and guarded by Cerebus so that you do not attempt to escape.'

'And if I accept?' I took a step back from him so that I could see him better.

'You live with me for eternity,' he answered simply. Far too simply. What did a god's fucktoy do with himself when not being buggered?

Hades chuckled as he read my thoughts. His long, perfect finger reached out and touched my cheek before beginning to trace my jaw. 'Our sort has never been especially monogamous, Iain. Most often, we live for the moment, accepting whatever pleasure we find. If you live with me, you may go anywhere and do anything you choose to do – as long as you come back to me after you've done it.'

I studied the god Hades watching me as he awaited my answer. The offer of immortality sounded too good to be true. I remembered then that the Olympians were considered more than a bit fickle by the mortals who once worshipped them. 'I can go anywhere and do anything I wish?' I asked and hoped to pin him by his words.

He looked me in the eyes and said, 'I swear it on the Styx itself, Iain. That's the strongest oath I can give you. On my word, you shall live for ever, you may go wherever you will, and do whatever you choose. I cannot hinder you. If your action doesn't include me willingly, you may still do it and no harm shall befall you. And I shall welcome you back upon your return.'

I studied him a moment more and asked, 'Where's the catch, Lord Hades?'

His lips twitched. 'Only that which you would pursue alone is yours alone to undertake.'

'And you swear this on the river Styx?' I asked quickly. He nodded. I remembered that Persephone was bound to six months of every year to the underworld because she had eaten six pomegranate seeds. 'I'm still alive,' I mumbled as suspicion again flooded over me. 'I've got to eat and drink. You aren't going to bind me to this place through what I eat, are you?'

Hades laughed, his eyes twinkling as he met my gaze. 'I make that too part of my oath to you, Iain.'

'I'll be like you and the other Olympians?' I asked, still hesitant to believe what Hades offered me.

He dark eyes became distant. 'More like my brother's old flame.' He nodded. 'Yes, like Ganymede. You are as free as you make yourself be, Iain. It is mine to make you immortal and young for ever. The rest is yours to create.'

I smiled finally. My fingers moved between us and found him as erect as he had been in the hallway. They wrapped around his manhood. I peered about the great hall. 'Where is your bed, then, My Lord?' I asked.

Gooseflesh crawled down my back and into the cleft of my backside. His fingers touched my hips and moved to possess my buttocks as we climbed the stairs to the second storey of his palace. His fingers trailed up my back and we both knew I was his – no matter how we had come to be together.

Warmth enveloped me and I gazed into those ebony eyes watching me so closely. As we reached the landing, I moved closer and brushed his cheek with my lips. My erection returned at the nearness of our coupling. My fears had been banished with Hades' assurances. He lifted me and my knees went around his waist, my heels crossing over his buttocks. His prick again possessed my cleft. 'I'm yours, My Lord,' I whispered at his ear. And meant it with every fibre of my being.

He laid me on the bed that occupied the centre of the room we entered. I watched as Hades climbed on to the bed at my feet and pulled his knees under him. 'Let me ride you – please.'

He gazed at me for a moment and I wondered what his

thoughts were. Then he lay back and his thick twelve-inch pole stood proudly from his smoothly muscled abdomen as if the Union Jack flew from it. Its cowl was pulled back and settled beneath the collar of his helmet.

My dick oozed pre-come as I climbed over his stomach and rose to my knees so that I could put his dick where it belonged. And I moaned my pleasure as I impaled myself on that wide-bodied slab of meat.

My guts rippled and gripped at the sides of his pole as I pushed myself up along him. I dribbled pre-come on his perfect chest even as my balls crawled up against my dick.

'Come with me, Lord,' I groaned when I knew I couldn't hold it any longer. Though it seemed impossible, my dick swelled even more. My helmet was filled to its limit with blood. I ground against his thatch with all of him in me.

I lost it. I blew. A rope hit him on the forehead, another slid down his shoulder and sizzled against the sheet. 'Give it to me!' I howled and my voice echoed through the palace of Hades as my arse muscles clinched at his dick.

I felt it then, as my load of jizz became a meek dribble. The head of his dick spread my bowel wider than it had ever been before. I gasped as he gushed deep into me, hot sperm spreading up my gut into the rest of me. Throughout all of me, claiming me. For him. For eternity.

Naked, I moved slowly along the great hall, my hand trailing along the stone wall. A nude Hades sat on the landing above me and watched me. He chuckled and I turned to look back at him.

'You're my first male, Iain – since man first walked across the face of Gaia.'

'Are you ashamed of yourself then, Lord?'

'No! Definitely not that. I'm quite surprised I didn't try it before. That there weren't others before you. Through the aeons, Zeus certainly had quite a few.' He sniggered. 'I emulated him quite nicely when you turned my head.'

'How's that?'

'He was so infatuated with Ganymede that he made him immortal. I'm so smitten by you that I've done the same.'

121

I had continued moving as we chatted. My fingers had continued to trace the wall. I was near on to an eighth of the way around the great hall from where I had started. I began to realise that I had felt no seams in the stone. I turned and studied the wall before me closely.

'Where are the openings?' I demanded as fear washed up over me.

'Openings?'

'The many gates this palace is supposed to have.' I turned to stare up the stairs at him, sensing my entrapment closing about me. 'The corridors like that one we came through.'

'I think you may have read too many Greek poets, Iain.' He rose and began to descend the stairs.

'Where are they?' I howled, turning back to the blank stone wall of the great hall.

'You make them yourself, Iain. With your mind.' I heard his steps on the stone stairs growing closer but I did not turn. I couldn't. I was frozen as I stared at the wall before me.

'The corridors like the one we travelled are paths through the planes of existence. You can enter them only through your mind.'

'I don't know how to do that!' I wailed.

'Then you shall stay here until you learn how. You shall remain at my beckoning call. Or go with me where I choose to go.'

I turned back to face him as he crossed the mosaic in the centre of the floor. 'You lied! You're already breaking your oath –'

'No!' he growled and halted his approach. His eyes grew darker as he sneered at me. 'I committed to honour your freedom when you exercised it. *You* must exercise it, not I.'

Clothing began to wrap itself about his body. 'I'm going to visit Zeus,' he told me, his voice barely under control. 'The servants will feed you while I'm gone.' He smiled and I knew it was unfriendly. 'They are all shades, horror writer. You won't be able to satisfy yourself with them.'

I watched as he took a step away from me and disappeared. My jaw dropped in shock as I realised I was alone in the worst of all possible worlds.

I screamed.

Into the Fog

Jordan Baker

The *Ice Maiden* was in international waters 310 miles northeast of Thule, Greenland, when we hit the wall of fog. We were looking for dinosaur flatulence. A group of American investors seriously believed that millennia-old remnants of dinosaur farts were percolating below the sea, waiting to fuel the world once mankind ran out of petrol.

Right.

Still, as long as their pockets were deep enough, the Yanks could be as insane as they pleased. It offered an opportunity to go a-yondering, as my dad used to say. We sailed from Labrador early in the autumn with plans of mapping as many methane deposits as possible before the sea turned to ice.

The fog was more of a nuisance than a threat. Instruments sensitive enough to detect million-year-old dinosaur farts shouldn't have any trouble guiding us through fog. Still, no sailor likes to sail blind.

'What do the weather satellites show?' I asked.

The first mate refused to look me in the eye. Instead, he shuffled his feet and said, 'It appears to be a perfect rectangle, exactly two hundred miles long. It hasn't moved since before the first weather satellite went up. It's just sitting there like a big cereal box.'

'Navigational advisories?'

'No problem there. But nothing sails up here – even the Danes stay further south.'

I sensed then that he was holding something back. 'What is it?' I growled.

'Our radar shows there's something out there. An island, has to be.' He frowned. 'But the infrared satellites don't see it. We're the first to find it.'

'Let's see it,' I said, barely able to keep control of my excitement.

I could understand why satellite photos of the area missed it. Radar images showed craggy mountains rising from a level sea. The centre could be more frozen peaks or the lost city of Shangri-La for all we knew.

I didn't care.

Even if it were nothing but frozen waste, it was mine. I discovered it. I would name it. I would explore it. I would name it. Brantz Island. Or maybe just Jeff's Isle.

The crew weren't enthusiastic. The monetary value of our discoveries determined their bonuses. A gleeful captain was nice, but not particularly profitable.

My first mate made that argument quite eloquently. I accepted his judgement and asked him to take command of the ship. Rodgers and the *Ice Maiden* would continue the voyage while I explored the island. Everyone would be happy.

Even that proposal drew criticism. I thought Rodgers suspected me of loafing. After all, I would be on a camping holiday while the rest of the crew went about business.

'That's not it,' he insisted. 'I'm worried about you dying out there. Anything could happen. We might not even find the island again.'

I laughed. They had longitude and latitude, global positioning systems and the most sophisticated sonar and radar available to oceanic wildcatters. Finding the island again would be child's play.

As for my survival, that may not be as simple, but it wouldn't be dangerous. I had supplies, training, experience and common sense. That was all anyone needed to survive in the wild. The island was inhospitable, but it was no more deadly than any other wilderness. I'd outfit my base camp with a month's worth of supplies and a short-wave radio. We would maintain daily contact.

I would be fine.

'Look, Jeff,' the mate argued, 'a captain doesn't just abandon his ship to go off exploring on his own. We need you on board.'

That, too, was nonsense. Rodgers could handle the ship. He was actually the better captain. Lack of funds and ambition were the only things stopping him from owning a ship of his own. He preferred keeping me around to worry about payroll and taxes. When it came to sailing, salvage and exploration, even I admitted he was the better seaman. And I told him so.

'I'll remind you of that when I need more money,' he retorted. 'But I still think this is a mistake.'

I prevailed eventually. Given the choice of leaving me to my own devices for a couple of weeks or tying the entire expedition up on a fool's errand, Rodgers relented.

I watched as my ship sailed away. I made base camp, set up the radio, and heated a tin of rations. Chilli con carne with beans. I'd got a good deal on American military MREs and stuffed the emergency pantry with them before leaving port. They were perfect for a camping trip.

I dreamed of a man, a tortured poetic soul with a glint of mischief in his emerald eyes. His hair was a dark, flaming sable red. His face was lean and pointed like a fox. He was small and slender and beautiful and a hole ached where his heart should have been.

He was the most beautifully tragic figure I'd ever seen. The dream seemed so clear, so prophetic, that in that moment I knew it meant something vital. I knew it would change my life. Then I lost the thread. Like so much else in my life, it degenerated into a wash of sex and sensation.

I felt his lips on my cock, his foreskin sliding back beneath my hands. We grappled in the darkness. I had an impression of flames at the edge of the night, stone walls arching into dome, jumbled images of stones and fire and blackness.

Through it all, the one constant was the feel of skin on skin.

His cock was seven inches long and uncut. It burned in my hand. It burned in my mouth as I took him inside me. I expected his pre-come to scald my tongue. Instead, it was cool, almost sweet. I became greedy, sucking his entire length into my mouth, vacuum-locking it.

I gave him everything I had, tugging hard at his cock with my mouth, pressing it tight against the roof with my tongue. I hummed contentedly as I worked his cock. The stranger's moans rewarded my efforts. His hips punched against my face. His cock head slipped into the back of my throat.

I cupped the silken sac of his balls in my hand and pulled them away from his body. He gasped as I tugged them tighter. His cock began to twitch in my mouth and his bollocks tightened in my hands.

My own cock pumped in sympathy as he came. I swallowed jet after jet of the stranger's come. My own come was burning against my stomach. Spurt after spurt came until I thought I'd pass out.

That was what woke me from the wet dream – the feel of my own load burning against my skin.

I fell back asleep laughing. In the darkness, the redhead's eyes laughed with me.

The next morning, I strapped a backpack over my parka and explored the base of the cliffs. A wind had grown up during the night. I hoped there would be no need to scale the mountains. I'd have to fight to avoid flapping like a flag against the side of the rocks.

I found a break in the rock almost immediately. In retrospect, maybe it wasn't fortune. Maybe it was fate. Maybe I was led. The crevice wasn't even on my planned exploration route. Something just tugged me towards it. When I started out from camp, I felt an overwhelming urge to change direction.

The hunch paid off. The mountains parted for me and I followed the winding crevice through them. After what seemed like days of struggling over loose shale and gravel, I broke through into open space again.

I stared at the ruins of a city before me. To be more accurate, I was staring at what remained of the ruins. This had been no city of stone, built to withstand the ages. It had been made of logs and iron. The logs had rotted away centuries ago and the iron was turning to flakes of rust. A few stones here and there marked where hearths had been and helped mark the boundaries of long-vanished walls.

The well-preserved condition of the site surprised me. It should have been buried under snow and ice. That was when I turned my face upwards and found the sky was missing. A massive dome of grey stone covered the entire valley. The crevice I'd followed had become a tunnel at some point and I hadn't noticed.

Even knowing I was in a vast cave didn't make the reality easier to understand. The stone was the same leaden grey shade as the sky. At first glance, I'd thought the dome was low cloud cover.

Then, there were the trees. That was what threw me. I'd never seen trees growing inside a cavern. I'd never seen trees like these. Their bark was a lustrous shade of silver and the leaves were a soft golden green. As a breeze tickled them, they shimmered in the soft light of the cave.

That was the point when I should have asked myself where the light was coming from. The valley was bright as summer while, outside, there was only leaden skies and fog. I should have noticed that. Not that it would have changed my destiny one whit. If anything, it would have hastened my fate. I would have torn through the ruins that much faster in an effort to find the source of the light.

Maybe that was what the creators hoped would happen and I was just too dumb to co-operate. Instead, I fiddled about for the next four hours examining every relic I encountered. Tools and weapons littered the ground. The design was blatantly Viking. So was the layout of the ruins.

I assumed that some band of warriors had been shipwrecked here and had taken refuge in the cavernous valley. The ground was too rocky for agriculture and none of the tools I found appeared to be farming implements. The inhabitants had either starved or found game.

It was possible they could have fished the waters surrounding the island. From the variety of spear points scattered about, it was more likely that they hunted. Judging from the size of the eighteen-centimetre points, whatever they hunted was large.

I banished visions of polar bears, yetis and Grendel's mother from my mind and continued exploring. Eventually, I noticed a sparkling glow high up on the south wall of the valley. It was more than four hours later that I found the second tunnel. The light tipped me off.

At first, I suspected mineral deposits glinting in the sun. I realised slowly that there was no sun. The source of light for the entire world seemed to be pouring out of that hole in the wall.

Reaching the opening was ridiculously easy. My grappling hook caught the mouth of the cave on the first toss. Hand and foot holds pocked the rock wall. It was as if something wanted me to find my way there.

A few moments later, I realised what that something was.

The man I'd dreamed about was in the cavern. I found him strapped to a stone altar, his heart pierced by a stalactite.

'It didn't exist when they strapped me down,' he said conversationally. 'I watched it grow from a bump on the ceiling.'

When I failed to respond, he sighed and continued.

'I spent an entire millennium watching it slowly grow towards my chest and thinking that it was going to hurt. I was wrong. Stone grows so slowly that I got used to the pressure over time. It's not much worse than a bad headache. Still, it is quite inconvenient. Would you mind freeing me?'

'How?' I asked.

I looked down at my climber's axe but the stranger shook his head.

'It'll take months to chip through the stalactite with that,' he said. 'I've got the time, but your ship will be returning soon.'

'How do you know about my ship?' I asked.

'I sensed it,' he shrugged. 'Your ship is the first to have passed within range of my senses. I've been sending you dreams for a fortnight to draw you here. This island was a bore even when it was inhabited.'

'Last night was the first time I dreamed of you,' I said.

'It was the first time you *remember* dreaming of me. You

moderns have lost the gift of remembering your dreams. You don't believe in anything you can't take a bite out of and it's made you weak. A Viking could have shattered this stone with his bare hands and his belief in the gods.'

'I can get better tools when my ship arrives,' I said apologetically.

'It's bad enough that one mortal has seen me like this,' he sighed. 'I'd rather not expand the audience. Just use the axe blade and hack through my rib cage on this side. I may swear a bit, but I'll survive it.'

A sense of unreality swallowed me. I didn't so much hack his body free as watch myself hack his body free. By the end, his blood covered me and he was screaming so loudly that the mountains trembled. I remembered something about the red-haired trickster of the Norse pantheon being a god of earthquakes and forest fires.

The fine mist of blood splashing me with each stroke gave a red tinge to the air and I grew hot from exertion. His screams and the rumble of mountains shaking on their foundations gave a hellish feel to the cavern. I think, perhaps, I was insane at the time.

Maybe it never happened. Maybe it was a hallucination brought on by exposure. Maybe the ghosts of the former inhabitants of the island possessed me.

How else could I explain hacking a human body in half with an axe, only to watch the halves knit themselves back together and the man thank me for my assistance?

How else can I explain the man introducing himself as the god Loki?

When I asked him why he was chained to an altar with a stalactite through his heart, Loki shrugged and mumbled, 'Never trust an ettin. They have no sense of humour.'

He smiled as if that explained everything. He was so charming, so beautiful, that I accepted the explanation. I wondered for a moment why he hadn't been able to charm the ettins as well. Perhaps the two-headed giants were immune to his charm. More likely, with two heads, one was able to watch for deceit while the second was charmed.

'I thought Loki was half ettin,' I stammered.

Again, he flashed that marvellous smile. 'All the more reason for them to hate me.'

And for me to distrust you, I thought. It seemed I couldn't even trust my own senses if this were happening.

It would have been so easy to dismiss it all as temporary insanity. I *wanted* to dismiss it all as temporary insanity.

'I should fuck you,' I said. 'I should whip out my cock and ask you to suck it.'

'What?' Loki said. He appeared genuinely amused.

'This is all just a dream. I fell down the cliff or slipped in the rocks and cracked my skull,' I explained. 'This isn't really happening. I'm dreaming this and you're beautiful and I should just fuck you because it's all only a dream and it might as well be a good one.'

His laughter shook the mountains as easily as his rage. I wondered what his orgasm would do. Visions of tidal waves capsizing small fishing vessels filled my mind.

'If that is the reward you wish for releasing me, I would be happy to fuck you,' Loki said. 'I'm flattered you'd think of that before wealth and power.'

Now I knew it was a dream.

'It's been millennia since I shape-shifted,' he said. 'Give me a moment and I'll give myself a female form.'

'Pardon me?' I said as my wet dream began going horribly wrong.

'You're a male,' he pointed out. 'I'll need a female form so that we may have intercourse.'

'Why?'

Loki paused to consider the implications.

'You want us to have sex – while we both remain in male bodies?'

'It's the way I normally have sex,' I said, feeling sheepish. I can handle hostility when people learn I'm gay but incredulity is different. Loki seemed to be having trouble understanding the concept of homosexuality.

'Truly?'

He seemed shocked at the idea.

'Look, it's no big deal if you don't want to. I didn't mean to offend your sense of decency. If you don't like men, that's your business.'

'No, it's not that,' he said. 'I've had sex with males before. It's just that normally I make myself into a female first. In one case, a stallion impregnated me and I gave birth to Odin's great steed. I'm hardly a prude. It just never occurred to me to have sex with a male while in my natural form. You find that enjoyable?'

'Look, I don't have to justify my orientation to you –'

Before I could finish, he kissed me. It was a deep, wet kiss. His tongue probed my mouth. I was stunned. I was dizzy. I forgot what we were arguing about.

My hands automatically circled his waist and drew Loki closer to me. I wanted to pull him through me. I wanted to pull him inside me. I wanted us to merge, to be one person.

His hands were busy as well. My parka was gone. I didn't remove it. It simply vanished. His hands were moving under my shirt. His palms were cool and smooth as they slid over the flat of my belly and along my ribs. He caressed my shoulder blades and the tops of my shoulders and his hands slid down my chest.

I felt as if his fingers electrocuted me as they brushed my nipples. I moaned aloud and he smiled. Loki was always smiling. He dipped his head to my chest and began kissing my nipples. His lips formed a ring around one and then the other. Then the tip of his tongue fluttered over them.

I was in heaven.

Furs appeared on the floor of the cavern. We sank into the deep, soft sable furs together, luxuriating in their warmth and the warmth of our bodies. Nothing generates as much heat as skin on skin. Loki blazed with some form of internal fire. Passion, maybe.

He kissed his way along my belly and down to my thighs. I thought I'd go insane – more insane – when his tongue began tracing the line where my thighs join my crotch. He lifted my bollocks with his tongue, kissing beneath them.

I shivered. I expected a blow job, but instead he lifted my legs, rolling my knees back to my chest and exposing the puckered opening of my arsehole. I felt his breath on it and then his tongue.

Loki lapped at it, his tongue stroking across the opening, teasing it. Each stroke felt as if it might be *the* stroke – the one where he penetrated me with his tongue. It never was. Each time, he either brushed across my opening or stopped and wiggled the tip of his tongue against the hole.

'Fuck me,' I hissed. 'I want to feel you inside me now.'

I felt his voice in my head. He was laughing as he said, 'As you wish.' Then his tongue speared my arsehole and I screamed. His tongue filled me, opened me. It opened me too much to be a tongue. I felt as if I had a long, wet prehensile cock inside me, sliding in and out, circling, bobbing and weaving.

I couldn't stop coming. I couldn't believe anything could feel that good. Loki surprised me again. He was laughing as he rose above me. His cock slipped into my arse, effortlessly thanks to the probing of his tongue.

He drove himself deep inside me, grinding his pelvis against my arse cheeks. Even when he stopped thrusting, his cock seemed to continue deeper inside me on its own.

I lost all sense of reality, all sense of time, space and identity. I forgot who and what I was. I became a hole, a wet, sucking hole that wanted Loki's huge, beautiful Viking god cock to fill me. Loki sensed that and began slamming his body into mine, driving me deeper into the fur. I bit down on my own forearm to cope with the intensity of the feelings he gave me.

I came like a volcano or an earthquake. My mind and body and soul became so filled with sensation they couldn't contain it. I shook and screamed and exploded. I felt as if my whole being was dispersing into atoms, filling the universe. My consciousness was reduced to flames and shadows and impenetrable darkness.

I awoke in my cabin on the *Ice Maiden*. Someone had undressed and bathed me and put me to bed. I was still trying to get a handle on things when Rodgers entered.

'Good to see you awake, Captain,' he said. 'We thought you were a goner.'

'What happened?'

'Well, when you didn't answer any of our radio hails the second day, we decided to return for you. Good thing, too. With the fall you'd taken and the cold, you'd have frozen to death. I warned you no good could come of exploring that rock.'

'I guess you were right,' I said ruefully. 'How long was I unconscious?'

'Two whole days, sir. I hope your little pleasure trip was worth it.'

I thought of the dreams of Loki and smiled. In a way, it had been. The dreams had been so real I even felt sore down there.

'I must have landed on my arse when I fell.' I laughed.

'You landed on something hard all right,' a mellow voice called from the door.

Startled, I looked over to see an enormous red-haired sailor standing there. He was dressed in a crew uniform. Noticing my look, he smiled.

'Hope you don't mind, Captain,' he said. 'Most of my clothes were lost when my boat went down. I had to tear up the shirt I was wearing to bandage you. I borrowed these from your mate. Good thing we're the same size.'

Rodgers saw the look of horror on my face and moved to push the redhead from the cabin.

'This is no time to be bothering the captain,' he said. 'Let him get his strength back up first.'

'No,' I said. 'You saved my life?'

'I kept you warm until your ship arrived,' he said. 'I'd say that makes us even since you saved me from being stuck on that piece of rock for eternity.'

'We'll give you a ride back to port,' I said. 'It's the least we can do.'

'No hurry,' the sailor said. 'Actually, I was hoping you might have a job for me while I get my bearings back.'

Rodgers coughed discreetly and nodded when I caught his eye. The sailor picked up the gesture and smiled.

'Looks like I have your mate's approval,' he said. 'If you're feeling up to it, I can tell you my qualifications now.'

Rodgers excused himself and went back to his duties. My mind was a jumble of images as I tried to sort out what had happened. The most likely explanation was that I'd found a shipwreck survivor on the island and incorporated him into my fevered hallucinations after taking a fall. Instead of a large, gruff sailor, my subconscious had made him a small, slender god.

I wasn't insane. The world wasn't upside down. Reality was falling back into place again. Sighing, I asked the red-haired sailor what experience he had with ships.

'I built a nice one from the fingernails of dead men once,' he said. 'And I've gone a-Viking many a time with Thor.'

'What?' I said, looking up just in time to see the redhead shrinking into his clothes.

'Ah, that feels better,' Loki said as he arranged himself in a chair. 'Your mate is a bit larger than I am so I have to shape-shift a little to look good in his clothes.'

The truth was slowly dawning on me as Loki laughed. 'We're going to have to work on your stamina,' he said. 'What kind of relationship can we have if you pass out for two days every time we fuck?'

Song of the Sea

Bill Crimmin

Just beyond Wick, I crested yet another hill and saw the shallow valley spreading out before me in the distance. In my mind's eye, I could see the stone houses that led down to the sea and remembered disjointed snatches of my boyhood spent in Girnigoe.

I'd driven up from Berwick that morning, the small car permanently climbing ever deeper into the Highlands and its engine wheezing with the effort of it. With every mile, however, the misty landscape had taken on an increasingly ethereal beauty. A heavy evening mist spread over the village's valley and the sea beyond, a warming lilac blanket that came to this part of Scotland only in high summer.

Through the open windows of the car, even at that distance, I could hear wild waves crashing against the cliffs, the impact making a huge cracking sound – as loud as thunder. I drove on in silence, drinking in the wildness of the landscape and listening to the crash of the waves beating on the purple rocks. It was the sound of home.

I'd come to Girnigoe to wind up Aunt Meg's affairs – as executor and sole beneficiary of her will. It wasn't a task I looked forward to, but it was not one I intended to shirk, either. It was quite strange, actually, her death. Her neighbours had found only her shoes down by the shore, but the body had never turned up.

As I parked before Aunt Meg's cottage – my cottage now – the soothing sound of the sea called to me. I smiled and nodded to myself, remembering the solitary boy I had been – a boy whose every spare moment seemed to be spent strolling along the shore. I left the car and started along the cliff walk towards the break in the rocks I knew so well, the steep, short path that led down to a rock shelf jutting into the sea of the sheltered inlet.

Walking towards the water, I heard a sound, a pure, melodic note cutting through the crash and bubble of the sea. It was singing, but I could make out no words. It was familiar, but I couldn't recall where I had heard it before. It was beautiful, and it was seductive. The voice captivated me; the rise and fall of the notes seemed so eloquent, so powerful, so moving. Yet, there was no tune to it that I could have sung and no rhythm I could follow. I realised I was holding my breath, my entire body taut and alert, completely taken over by the mysterious singing. It made me want to weep.

Thinking I'd glimpsed something moving in the sea off to my right, I turned and looked out towards the waves. At first, I saw nothing, but then I became aware of movement, about twenty feet from the shore. A silvery flash above the water, then a splash. Something gleaming and fluid was moving out there, sometimes above the water, sometimes just below the surface. I pulled binoculars from their case at my side and trained them on the spot where I had seen the movement, adjusting the focus. Three, perhaps four, seals were playing out there, diving and leaping through the turbulent water. Their sleek bodies gleamed in the dim light, their wet kitten-like faces smiling in delight. Their deep, round, dark eyes looked straight into my soul.

Could the seals be making the sound I'd heard? I didn't think so. I'd never heard of seals singing and I'd spent enough time living in the Highlands. Then, just at the edge of my field of vision, I saw a man. Sitting on the rocks, just in the water, was a naked man, singing. He looked up at that moment, saw me, dived into the sea in a fluid movement, and swam off in the direction of the seals.

Having put the binoculars back in their case, I rubbed my eyes and realised how tired I was. I'd spent more than half the day driving and had little sleep the night before. I dismissed the naked man as a figment of my imagination and my tiredness. I returned to the cottage and let myself in with the key I had carried with me ever since I had left Aunt Meg to enter university.

I was grateful that the lawyer had arranged to have the heating switched on and the bed in my old room made up. In the evening shadows, I walked wearily up the steep, narrow stairs, stripped off, and climbed between the welcoming sheets. I was asleep in moments.

I woke up slowly and the room was pitch black. There was a familiar and comforting scent in the room, but it was sufficiently out of place to pull me from my sleep. There was a sharp, salty, ozone tang to it and I recognised it, even though I was still half asleep. 'It's the sea,' I told myself and nearly believed it.

I shut my eyes and began to drift back into sleep. But something kept tugging at me and I slowly became aware that there was another element to the odour, a musky, animal quality to it. That too was familiar – almost like sweat. I roused enough to lift the duvet and sniff, wondering if I had avoided taking a bath for too long.

It wasn't my smell. It wasn't my sweat. I woke up then. I was not frightened, rather I felt a growing sense of not being alone, followed only by curiosity. For a moment, I had thought it was Aunt Meg, sitting at the foot of my bed, waiting patiently for me to wake up so that she could give me a morning hug. I reached to the bedside cabinet and turned on the electric light. I pushed myself up to sit against the pillows.

It wasn't Aunt Meg – it was a man, a young man. I knew in that instant who was in my room with me.

He was the man I had seen singing on the shore. He was still naked and beautiful. Even sitting at the end of my bed, he looked tall. He was lean and muscular, but not overdeveloped like some of the London muscle Marys I'd met. He was lithe, compact and sleek-looking. His chest and legs were virtually hairless and his skin was a deep golden colour, like toffee. His skin was still damp, his shoulder-length black hair slick to his head, his entire body gleaming with water; yet he didn't seem cold. He was looking directly at me, his eyes, huge and round and almost black, mesmerised me. They peered straight into my soul. He just looked at me, half smiling, expectantly almost.

My prick took on a life of its own as I sat under his gaze. I took in his black hair, his wide, hairless chest the colour of toffee. His dick was already tumescent – its glans nearly escaped its cowl. His pubic hair was sparse, wetly slicked against his tight belly. 'Who are you?' I managed through the force of the arousal claiming me.

'You may call me Andrew,' he said, his voice musical and sexy, leading me deeper into overwhelming need. 'Mannan mac Lir sent me to you.'

I watched as his dick grew fatter and firmer, inching down his leg. I licked my lips, wanting it – all thought of the strangeness of his presence forgotten. I knew Mannan mac Lir was the Celtic God of the sea – a lad couldn't have grown up in the Highlands and not have heard of him. But all those gods were just myths – weren't they? And what was this Andrew?

'Your Aunt Meg is very special to him, to all of us,' Andrew continued, his face a friendly smile. 'He asked me to come to you, to take care of you.' As he spoke, I watched spellbound his bell end become completely exposed, his foreskin stretching back along his shaft. My mind blanked out my questions; my body ached for his touch.

'How?' I croaked, barely able to find my voice.

He chuckled and inched his buttocks over the duvet, moving closer to me. 'However you need me, Stuart,' he answered. 'Whatever it takes to give you the happiness you deserve.'

I'd never known such absence from fear. Here was a total stranger, naked and in my bedroom – uninvited. I was on the brink of shagging him, and I felt not the slightest apprehension. I felt no fear, no doubt and no hesitation. I wanted him and I wanted him now.

I reached out my hand and touched his nearest thigh. It was warm, slippery and smooth – almost oily. I leaned forward and, with one finger, gently stroked his erect cock. It seemed to swell under my touch and he shivered slightly. Holding my arms wide, I looked directly into his mysterious dark eyes and whispered, 'I want you.'

Lifting the duvet, he slid into the bed beside me and pressed his body against mine. His skin was warm and his chest slid against mine. We kissed, his soft, full lips meeting mine, his tongue finding its way between my teeth and possessing my mouth. He tasted of oysters.

He slithered on top of me and I was surprised by how heavy he was; he'd seemed so lithe. My hands roamed over his sleek back, slid over the bones of his long spine and came to rest on his round, smooth buttocks. His rigid cock was pressing against my thigh and my own hard prick was digging into his flat belly as I pulled him towards me.

He kissed my neck, his lips moving to my collarbone and then my pecs – all the time sliding downwards. He took one hard nipple between his lips and teased it with his tongue and lips until it was hard and swollen. Moving to the other, he nibbled on it until that was hard too. He nuzzled in my chest hair and, moving ever lower, licked my belly button, tracing the line of hair from my navel to my pubes with his probing tongue. He settled himself between my parted thighs. He took my engorged member in one hand and slid my foreskin gently back and forth over the helmet.

My slit leaked pre-come. He smiled, and licked my helmet clean. I shivered under his touch as he took all of my cock in his mouth. Swallowing me to the root, he tongued the sensitive underside of my glans. Cupping my balls in one hand, he began to suck me hard. Long, sensual strokes up and down my rod with his warm, wet mouth. In, until I could feel his hot breath on my belly, and out until only his lips were still in contact with my cock. Deep, powerful strokes I could feel in my guts.

His eyes were closed as he worked on my prick and he had an expression of pure bliss on his face. His mouth worked its magic on me. A tingling heat filled my balls and my belly and spread deliciously through my veins. I felt it move to my chest and almost stopped breathing when this divine glow of pleasure entered my head and flashed through my brain like a wave. I gasped and moaned with pleasure as his lips took me ever closer to ecstasy.

I wanted him to fuck me; I had to have his fat, toffee-coloured cock inside me. I had never wanted anything so much. I touched him gently on his head and he looked up at me. 'Please fuck me,' I said simply.

He smiled and raised himself up on his knees. I lifted my legs then, spreading them, presenting my eager hole to him. A moment of doubt darkened my spiralling need when I realised we had no lube (I hadn't exactly planned on getting fucked when I'd packed my bags in London). His finger gently touched my opening and slipped easily into me and my concerns disappeared. His slippery finger slid inside easily, closely followed by another, and I sighed as he stroked my cock with one hand and probed my arse with the other. His fingers left my twitching hole to be replaced seconds later by his tongue. He rimmed me slowly – licking, sucking and probing my relaxing ring.

I felt him climb to his knees again, his stiff rod now up against my hole. I felt him push the thickness of his manhood past the muscles of my sphincter and claim me as his own. I felt only pleasure and excitement as he pushed deeper into me. I couldn't wait for him to fuck me. As if in answer, he began to ream my arse. Long, slow strokes tantalised my prostate and made me feel as though my own cock would burst. He was up on his haunches as I lay beneath him on my back, my legs raised. Between us my rigid dick leaped and twitched on my belly. My bowels were churning fire now; my fist closed round my own cock, and I knew I was close to orgasm.

'I'm going to come.' I hissed as the first wave gripped my balls and spurts of come began to pour on to my belly. My arse muscles pulsed and contracted, gripping his thrusting cock even tighter. My climax crashed and peaked like the tide hitting the rocks; it seemed to go on for ever and I was weak and sweating.

Andrew began to pound my bum in earnest then. Hard, fast strokes rammed into me with increasing speed. His movements took on a rhythm of their own. His prick throbbed inside me; his breathing was shallow and fast.

Coming down from the crescendo that had been my orgasm, I

watched him as he fucked me, his face nuzzling mine. He was lost in the sensations of the moment, eyes darting and fluttering beneath closed lids. Over his shoulder, I saw that his buttocks were a blur as they shoved his rod into me again and again. His whole body began to tremble as he pumped my arse with quicker, shorter strokes.

He threw his head back, his face a mask of pleasure. Then I heard it. At first I thought it was just moaning – a sibilant rush of breath escaping between taut lips as he came – but it was more than that. It was crying – no, not crying, singing almost, a sort of keening. A pure, piercing note which filled the small room and my mind. A shiver of recognition ran through me – it was a sound I knew. I'd heard it only hours before on the beach, and it was a sound I'd never forget. He was singing.

His rigid cock pumped spurt after spurt of hot seed inside me. He sang as he rode me, his enchanting song becoming more and more joyous, more and more abandoned as his climax reached its crescendo. He stayed inside me after he came, his head resting on my chest. His voice, quieter now, wove a tapestry of sound around us as I held him tightly against me.

We continued to lie there like that even after his breathing had returned to normal. He moved to pull from me but I grasped his arse cheeks and held him in me. His hands came up to hold my face as he lifted himself on his elbows to look down at me. I knew that I had never had another man do for me what this one had. I knew, too, that I would never willingly give him up.

I noticed his fingers then as they traced my brow – the webbing joining one to another. Slowly, I released my grip of his buttocks and raised them that I might see the webbing that joined my fingers as well. I looked into his eyes then, suspicions growing in my mind that I did not like.

'Do you know what I am, Stuart?' he asked softly, watching me closely. 'What we both are?'

'Your fingers are like mine,' I said and dropped my hands to either side of the bed. I no longer wanted to touch him. I didn't want to meet his gaze. He was going to tell me something I didn't want to hear.

'Yes,' he replied. 'You are one of us. You are a silkie.'

'Silkie?' I mumbled, trying to remember the childhood tales Aunt Meg had told me. 'The seal people?'

He smiled and nodded. 'We're more than just humans who dress in sealskins, Stuart. Or creatures to scare little children into obedience. We are the children of Mannan mac Lir – and your Aunt Meg.'

'No . . . No!' I shook my head. 'That's just old Celtic legend, nothing more. There are no sea gods.'

'How do you explain the webbing between your fingers and toes then?'

'A genetic mutation, like haemophilia from inbreeding –'

He smiled and clucked his tongue. 'Ah, yes – the beauty of science is that it can explain that which it doesn't know. Stuart, I am here to help you come home.'

I should have been shocked by this news, but I wasn't. Not most of me. I felt a sense of truth to his words. I had always known that I was different but had never understood how. Still, I wasn't buying it completely. Not sight unseen. Andrew I could accept as real, but snorkelling through a wintry North Sea was another kettle of fish entirely.

'If I am a silkie too, why don't I sing?'

'Silkies sing through joy,' he explained. 'You've never experienced the freedom of the sea, the rushing water massaging your sides, the fellowship of Mannan mac Lir and all his creations. A silkie cannot be happy on the land: you will always feel unfulfilled, incomplete – until you join us.'

'I can't join you. I have my work, my life, my friends,' I quickly responded.

'Do you?' replied Andrew. 'Do you really have those things?'

I pushed myself further up on my pillows, pulling off him. I didn't like the emptiness I felt when he was no longer inside me. 'I think you'd better go,' I said as I moved a leg under him and made ready to stand.

'I'll come tomorrow night, Stuart.' He sat up and smiled back at me. 'I suggest you think about exactly what you have before I see you again. Your aunt left you something that you will need, but you have to find it.'

★

I had slept soundly once Andrew left me – deeply and dreamlessly – and woke with the dawn. A cloudless day greeted me when I stepped from the cottage, and the crash of waves against the rocks called to me. Hesitantly, I answered that call, following the path along the cliff down to the sea.

My mind sought to sort it out. Andrew had said I was a silkie, the same as he was. That was the hardest part of the night's events to accept. Silkies were mythical creatures, like mermaids and Sirens from the old Greek religion. I held one hand and then the other up before my face. The skin that spread between my fingers, connecting them to each other, told me I was not like other people I had known the past thirty years. The only people I knew who had such webbing were Aunt Meg and I – and Andrew. Last night I had come close to accepting that I was one of these creatures. Sitting on the rocks beneath a cloudless sky and facing the sea, I found it difficult to pull back from what I had bordered on accepting in the darkness of the night.

What was a silkie supposed to be anyway? Human-formed, definitely. I smiled as I thought of Andrew's form and began to grow erect as I remembered his well-formed prick inside me. They donned sealskins to swim in the sea, but went nude on land. If a human found his or her skin, the silkie became his slave. I snorted as I remembered myself as a ten-year-old child lifting rocks along the shore, looking for a silkie's skin and longing for the companion who would be mine for ever.

I looked out over the sea and wondered what it would be like to be free – totally free, like the birds in the sky or the fish in the sea. I knew I would like that – as long as I had Andrew beside me. I grew more erect as my thoughts again turned to him, being with him. Not once had I felt so complete as I had last night with him inside me.

If the legends were true, however, I had to have a sealskin to be a silkie. Either I had one or I was for ever land-bound. My heart stopped. A memory began to form in my mind. Aunt Meg standing on a chair, taking down a shoebox from the top of her bedroom cupboard. I was only about ten.

The first thing that had struck me when she eased the flat lid off the box was the odour. I had smelled the sea; I had smelled the cool, ozone scent that was fresh and clean the nearer one got to the seashore. Then I had seen it. A neatly folded piece of sleek fur. Silver-grey and gleaming in the morning light, it was unmistakably an animal's pelt. Reverently, she had lifted it out of the box and shaken it loose. It was a sealskin. She had told me it was a great treasure, something very special. I was never to play with it, or tell anyone that I had seen it. Now I finally knew what it was. It was the skin of a silkie.

I knew then that it was what Andrew meant when he had told me Aunt Meg had left me something I would need. She had kept it safe for me as I grew into manhood and tried to fit into man's world.

I pulled off my sweater, pushed off the rock, and hesitantly made my way back to the cottage. I told myself that, if the skin was there, last night and Andrew were as real as the sun warming my shoulders. If the skin was still in her cupboard, I was a silkie and belonged in the sea.

I couldn't take it in as I followed the path back to the cottage. If my aunt was a silkie who'd chosen a human life out of love for my uncle, why did she stay after he died? She could have taken down the sealskin, put it on and dived into the sea off Noss Head, leaping and diving in the waves with the other silkies. Why had she stayed?

Image after image materialised in my mind. Aunt Meg, sitting on the end of my bed, her round, dark, kitten-like eyes gleaming with love. Aunt Meg sitting beside my father, clapping until her palms hurt, her soft face glowing with pride, as I collected my degree from university. Aunt Meg's voice bubbling with excitement when I telephoned her from whatever part of the world my assignments took me. I knew she had stayed because of me. She had made that sacrifice for me.

Having reached the cottage, I climbed the stairs with ever-increasing hesitation. What if there wasn't a skin? Andrew would be just another dream and I would be alone again. And if the skin was there? I didn't know which thought frightened me more.

I reached her room and opened the cupboard I remembered. My fingertips barely reached the top shelf, even when I stood on my toes. I frowned and stepped back, trying to see into the darkness that enveloped the top shelf.

'Bloody hell!' I growled. I pulled the chair from her dressing table and placed it before the opened cupboard. Holding the cupboard door to steady myself, I stepped on to the chair – and was staring into the dimness at the top of the cupboard.

I pulled every dust-covered box I saw off the shelf and opened it. Skirts, sweaters, stockings – all things women from the 1940s and 1950s might think to save. But no sealskin.

In spite of myself, I sniffed, wiping a tear from my eye in frustration as I accepted that one more dream was gone. I told myself that I should have known better. Dreams were only for children.

I was making to step down when I decided that I owed it to myself to search the shelf thoroughly. After all, I was already standing on the chair and had made a fool of myself. Besides, there was only myself to witness this one more act of foolishness before I was completely grown up.

My fingers found only the rough board of the shelf as I dug into the dark interior of the cupboard. I felt the grit of dust clinging to my sweaty hands and arms. And I knew finally that there was nothing there.

Tears welled in my eyes as I shut them. 'Damn!' I groaned as I placed my forehead against the face of the cupboard. 'Damn! Damn! Damn!' I cried in the silent cottage, surrendering to the frustration that had been my whole life.

My fingers touched an unusual abutment deep in the blackness that was the back of the shelf. My conscious mind didn't register awareness of the fact for several moments. Instinctively, though, I traced the outline of the thing I had found and felt it move across the shelf.

I blinked, curiosity breaking in on frustration. Hope rekindled in me, and I pulled the thing into the light. I stared at the outline of a shoebox and dared to wonder if it was the one I thought that I remembered. Fearfully, I took it into my hand and raised the lid.

The smell of the sea, fresh and clean, washed over me even

before I had the lid off and could see the sealskin that lay in the box.

I thought about my life that afternoon, how there had always seemed something missing. Some elusive, seductive possibility always there just out of reach. Now I knew what it was. I was a silkie and I belonged to Mannan mac Lir and the sea. And I knew that I had no choice.

Trembling with apprehension, I reached out my hand to Andrew. It took only seconds to slip into my sealskin but, by the time I had put it on, my silkie companion had slid into the sea and was swimming out on the tide. His sleek, fluid body glinted in the sunlight that was beginning to creep above the horizon. I hesitated a moment, uncertain and afraid.

He began to sing. Clear, flutelike notes filled the pure air, fluttered and soared. The sound filtered inside my skull, seemed to take over my consciousness and reach my soul. I slid into the sea, moving through the cold water in a supple, fluid ripple of my silky flanks. I felt the vast universe wrapped around me, as familiar and comforting as Aunt Meg's shawl once had been.

I heard the voices of the other creatures sharing the water with me, felt their minds, knew somehow that we were all part of a shared consciousness. I swam alongside Andrew and he began to dart and dance around me, his streamlined form moving through the dark water expertly. He was still singing. As we bobbed and leaped in the waves my own voice joined his in a plaintive duet of joy and freedom. I was home.

Taming Loki

Jon Thomas

There are days when being a god really sucks. This past weekend has been a bunch of them – all rolled up together.

I'm not knocking the powers, the lack of most ordinary worries, that sort of thing. But immortality can have serious drawbacks, and I've just run up against one of the most serious of all.

I've fallen in love with a mortal.

This is not just a torrid, passionate affair that lasts a season or a few years and then fades away – this one seems to be the real, 'till death us do part' thing.

Trouble is, one of us – me – isn't going to die. I go by Luke O. Danesbrough these days, but, if you want the original, it's Loki Odinnsbrør. The Trickster, the Wily One. And I've fallen for a mortal. I'm sure the Æsir are busting their guts laughing, not that I particularly care.

The worst thing is that I never saw it coming.

I run the web operations for an occult supply house in Chicago. Actually, I own Asgard, the company – though I conceal that fact behind proxies and dummy partners. I leave the daily running of the business to those who enjoy it, and I concentrate on what I like. The arrangement has been mutually beneficial: my partners receive a sizeable profit, and I pay myself a handsome enough salary to explain my style of living, though I could live in any style I liked without ever having to spend a penny.

I met Keith as a consequence of my job. He had dropped me a note when he couldn't get our online catalogue to work. I fixed the problem, and he wrote back to thank me. Mundane, dull and commonplace.

We wrote back and forth across the miles after that – moving from getting acquainted to beginning to dig into more serious matters. There were some personal details exchanged; but the majority of our discussions involved the sort of sharing one expects to go on between friends of long standing, not two people known to each other solely through email.

In January, Keith wrote that he was planning to be in Chicago in a few weeks' time for some job interviews. He suggested a possible meeting while he was in town, if that was convenient. I felt what was for me an uncommon excitement when I dispatched an affirmative reply – and flagged it for urgent handling.

Keith flew in on Friday afternoon. We were planning on having the weekend for getting acquainted in person before he started his round of interviews on Monday. I even toyed with asking him to drop in for an interview at Asgard, but decided to wait until I'd had the chance to size him up myself.

He had wanted to get a hotel, but I quickly put an end to that idea. Not only did I have ample space in my flat, but the only other places convenient for him to stay rated a minimum of two stars and had prices to match.

The best-laid schemes of mice and men – and sometimes even those of gods – are apt to go awry, as mine did. The day Keith arrived brought a double dose of winter to Chicago. There was drizzle and fog, backing up all incoming and outgoing flights. By the time his plane finally set down, the leaden sky was beginning to unload a great deal of snow.

Keith and I had been corresponding for nearly six months, but everything I'd learned about him in that time was overwhelmed by what passed between us when our eyes met in the crowd at the airport gate. It became obvious that there was much more to this young man than met the eye, and that I wanted him as more than just another friend or even an employee – though if that were the only way to keep him around, I'd offer him a job in a heartbeat.

We were similar in build – wiry and compact – and in colouration. Both of us had fair skin and red hair, though mine was a dark auburn while his was a light copper that turned into molten gold in the right light. His eyes were the deep clear blue of a mountain sky in springtime.

We kept our conversation to necessities at the airport and on the overly long cab ride back to my flat on Chicago's Gold Coast. We made up for it at dinner, which we ate in front of a floor-to-ceiling window overlooking the twinkling lights of Chicago – when they could be seen through the thickly flying snow.

When dinner was over, we adjourned with our brandies in front of the fire. I turned down the lights and left the blinds open on the windows overlooking the city. We settled into the soft cushions a companionable distance apart and listened to the warm crackling of the fire.

At length, I broke the comfortable silence that had enveloped us. 'May I ask you a personal question, Keith?'

'Of course,' he said, sitting forward.

'That order of yours that went haywire last fall – you were working on a love spell, weren't you?'

He blushed and said, 'Guilty, I'm afraid. How did you guess?'

I chuckled. 'I asked myself what red candles, lavender and attar of roses had to do with the autumnal equinox and drew a blank. Then I hit on the connection they had with each other and the pieces fell into place. I've got to say, though, I'm surprised someone like you needed the extra help. I'd have thought you'd be fighting them off with a stick.'

He hesitated before answering. 'I've always had plenty of offers, but lately all anyone seems to want is sex. Nobody ever bothers to look any deeper than the surface me. Sex is wonderful, but I want more out of life.' He took a deep breath.

'Also,' he went on, 'I think I told you that my last serious relationship ended two and a half years ago. What I didn't mention was how it ended. One night Al couldn't sleep, so he went into the spare room to let me have a little rest. When I

149

went in the next morning to see what he wanted for breakfast, he was gone.'

'Gone? As in disappeared?'

'No, gone as in dead. A brain aneurysm according to the coroner, though he'd never shown any signs of a problem when he was alive.'

'How old was he?'

'Not even thirty-five.' He looked down at the snifter in his hands and I felt his grief.

'Keith, I'm sorry –'

'I'm OK now. It's good to talk about it, though. Anyway, Al was dead and I'd just started graduate school. Until I could work through all of that, I wasn't really interested in relationships. Most days, it was all I could do just to put one foot in front of the other.'

He looked over at me and smiled sheepishly. 'Towards last October, not long before the festival of Samhain, I felt like the Wheel was beginning to turn in that direction for me again. I was feeling ready to date again, but I figured I was so long out of practice that I'd better not leave anything to chance. So –'

'You checked your supplies and found you needed a few things,' I interrupted.

'Exactly. And the rest is history. No definitive results from the working as yet, though I have hopes in a few directions.'

I leaned towards him and murmured in his ear, 'And might I be one of them?'

Surprised, he caught his breath. 'You guessed?'

'Not until just now, no.'

'It does seem a little odd at first blush – falling in love with someone you've never even seen except in a photograph – but it felt right to me, every time we'd talk on the phone or shared something special online.' He studied me for a moment. 'Can I ask how you feel about the idea?'

I realised suddenly that my feelings for him ran just as deep. That was when I felt as if I was sitting atop the San Andreas Fault during the Big One everyone says is coming one of these days.

The more prudent side of me sounded the alarm klaxons. What kind of future was there in a relationship with a mortal? Could there even be a relationship, especially if I let him in on my not-so-little secret? All that – and more – flashed through my mind as I groped for an answer that wouldn't trample on his self-confidence. I was astonished then to hear myself say, 'I'm for it.'

A tentative smile broke over his features, and the worry line faded from his forehead at my reply. 'You seemed to hesitate a little there, Luke,' he said. 'You aren't sure?'

'Well,' I replied, still feeling the aftershocks of my realisation, 'no more uncertain than anyone is at a time like this. I do have a few concerns, yes, but not major ones. I'm older than you are.' By quite a lot, I added to myself. 'And very much out of practice in relationships like this.'

Keith moved in beside me. 'I like older men that I can train as I please,' he said, wrapping an arm around my neck and pulling me to him for a long kiss that cut off any further protests.

There had always been a spark of understanding, almost prescience, about Keith. Even in the early days of our correspondence, I was often surprised by the depths of his insight. When our lips met, it was as if some of the rightness he'd been feeling about us was transmitted to me. I began to worry less about the future and more about the present situation.

'I want to be with you tonight, Luke,' he whispered to me when at last he broke the kiss.

Keith made as if to remove his pullover with his free hand, but I stopped him with a look. 'No,' I said, 'let me get that for you.'

I kept the pace slow, almost playful, as I pulled the tails of his shirt out of his jeans and worked it up over his chest. With his head still entangled in the folds of clothing, I ran a finger lightly upward along his torso, following the very faint line of fair red-golden hair that began at his navel and bisected his abdomen before fanning out into the valley between his pecs.

Keith soon took matters into his own hands and eased the turtleneck over his head. He looped the discarded garment around my neck and used it to pull me down for another kiss. After several moments I felt his fingers fumbling at my shirt, and broke off the kiss to give him better access. He smiled when he saw the russet thatch covering my chest, and paused repeatedly to run his fingers through it while undoing the rest of my buttons.

151

My shirt joined his on the floor. The touch of his bare chest against my own awoke memories that had almost been forgotten – times when other bodies had pressed against mine, of the warmth of shared companionship and pleasure. With the memories came a renewed ardour, and I reached to undo the button of Keith's jeans.

I pulled the zipper down.

The fly opened to reveal a pair of grey cotton low-rise bikini briefs, with a very prominent spot of darker grey to show that he was leaking. His scent and his cologne made an intoxicating mixture that had my head in a whirl. I pulled him upright with me and let his jeans fall to the floor.

Keith's lips sought mine once more as his hands undid my belt and the fastenings of my trousers. When they were past my knees, we sank back on to the cushions, still locked in an embrace. His hardness ground against mine.

Firelight bathed us in a warm, orange-red glow that accentuated the golden highlights of Keith's hair and gave his alabaster skin the hue of finely burnished copper. 'You're very beautiful,' I told him.

'You're not so bad yourself,' he said in a light tone. His smile told me he was pleased by the compliment.

My lips and tongue caressed the light dusting of hair on his chest. I pleasured his nipples, delighting as they hardened and stood out. Keith's rapid breathing told me I'd found a particularly sensitive spot. My fingers touched his belly and moved lower until they brushed against the thin fabric of his briefs, and over the hard flesh inside. I reached beneath the waistband and gripped his manhood. It was substantial.

I concentrated on stroking him, smearing the pre-come over and around the head with my fingers and thumb. Keith sighed and surrendered himself to my attentions. I eased his briefs off and his cock jutted proudly from a nest of ruddy golden curls. A nice piece of meat, and one I wanted to become more intimately acquainted with. I nuzzled its length with my cheek.

I felt Keith's hands on my shorts and, before long, my own member was swinging freely in the flickering light of the fire. A warm wetness quickly enveloped it, and I looked down to see

Keith's lips fully two-thirds of the way along my shaft. As I watched, he engulfed the remaining two inches with the ease of a born cocksucker, sending a wave of pleasure washing over me.

That was nothing compared with the sensations produced on the upstroke, when he gripped the base of my cock with his hand and pulled my foreskin forward over the helmet. No sooner had the last of it slipped free of his lips than Keith was burrowing his tongue beneath the folds of my overhang.

I shuddered and he pulled off me to look up at me. 'Did I hurt you?'

'It felt so damn good that I almost lost it!'

'Can't have that now, can we?' he chuckled and returned to his labours.

I rode the waves of pleasure he generated in me. Almost mindlessly. But, deep within my being, forgotten memories began to work their way into my consciousness. Desires that had built for centuries became fierce. I wanted to feel his thick pole driving into me, filling me up as I had not been filled since the time I conceived and bore my blood-brother Odin's great horse Sleipnir.

'Fuck me,' I told him.

'Are you sure?' he asked, letting my cock slip from his lips.

'Hell, yes! I want to feel you all the way inside of me.'

'Hold that thought then,' he said, pushing himself to his feet and starting for the guestroom. 'I'll be right back.'

I guessed he was going for condoms, the one reality of gay sex in the age of AIDS. I thought about telling him not to bother. I knew I couldn't catch anything from him. But Keith didn't know what I knew.

He returned with a box of condoms and a bottle of lubricant. 'I was hoping I might need these,' he said, 'though I was expecting it would be you wearing one of them and not me.'

'We might be able to arrange for that,' I told him and, taking his hand, pulled him on top of me. His body touched mine at every point, his manhood a spear pressed against mine. Eager to help the process along, I pushed him up to a sitting position astride my thighs and leaned forward to suck on him.

It was quite a mouthful. It was difficult to keep my teeth from dragging across its tender skin. Though many of my brother gods would laugh derisively to hear it said, I have a rather small mouth.

'You'd better stop that soon,' Keith said after some time, 'if you want me to fuck you tonight.'

'Decisions, decisions,' I teased as he withdrew from my mouth and began rolling on the condom. 'But we do have all weekend.'

If I had any remaining doubts about getting involved with Keith, they melted away when he entered me. My rosebud opened to his invading probe as a well-oiled scabbard received the blade. There was no pain as he took me, only a deep pleasure that increased with every stroke of his thick cock into and out of my channel.

'Gods, but you're tight, Luke!' he grunted.

'It's been a while,' I grunted as he pushed into me.

His helmet worked a primal magic on my prostate – a pearl of pleasure dripped from the slit of my cock to pool in my navel and spread slickly over my lower belly with his every thrust. I hooked my heels over his shoulders and said, 'Ram it on home, Keith – I need everything you've got.'

Without a word, he picked up the speed and strength of his thrusts. His breathing began to come in ragged pants. The sheen of sweat on Keith's body caught and reflected the fire's light. On his own initiative, he pushed my hindquarters toward the back of the couch, bending me almost double beneath him. My stiff cock waved in my face as he pounded deep into me.

'Just like that!' I encouraged him. 'Fuck me!'

'Better get ready, Luke,' he gasped. 'It won't be long now – I'm almost there.' He mashed his pubes against my cheeks in one final, tremendous thrust. Deep inside me, I could feel his engorged cock growing thicker still, pumping his seed into the condom. A slight twitch of my foreskin was all it took to bring me off all over my face and neck – and the cushions of the couch behind me.

Keith sank back with me into the cushions. 'Thank you, Luke – that was a good one.'

'It was just what I needed,' I said and pulled him to me. His lips found mine.

★

The winter weather kept us cooped up in my flat the whole weekend. By the time the snow stopped falling, around mid-afternoon on Sunday, we'd had two feet. The winds were piling up drifts deeper still, and wreaking havoc for the clean-up crews. Freshly ploughed streets became impassable again within ten minutes of being cleared.

Not that Keith and I really minded, of course. While I would have liked to show him some of the sights in the city that has been my adopted home for nearly a century and a half, I was just as happy to rediscover with him the pleasures of the bed – or the couch, or the floor, or the shower.

By noon on Saturday all of Keith's Monday appointments had been postponed. 'Will you be able to extend your vacation?' I asked him after the last call had ended.

'What vacation?' he asked. 'My job was an internship set up during my last year in grad school. Technically it ended in December when I declined their offer of a permanent position. They kept me on payroll while I trained my replacement, but that ended a week ago Friday. Now I'm footloose and fancy-free, at least until I find some place that I like.' He grinned. 'I hope it takes a while. I like being able to do whatever I want, whenever I want it.'

'We could maybe take some of the afternoon and go shopping and sightseeing,' I said, 'but right now it's anyone's guess if we'd even find anything open.'

'I vote for staying here where it's warm,' Keith said. 'Got any good movies? We can grab some snacks and just be couch potatoes.'

So we did. The rest of Saturday, all of Sunday, and well into the night, Keith and I snuggled together and watched movies, or listened to music, or just talked if we felt like it. We even made love a couple of times. I couldn't remember a time I felt so carefree and relaxed.

There was one anxious cloud on my emotional horizon. There was still an important piece of information about me that he didn't have. I had no idea how he was going to take my secret, but I had to tell him. It was my responsibility to the man.

I pulled back the bedclothes from Keith's nude body. His

quiescent cock lay to one side on its silky red-gold pillow of hair. I tentatively brushed it with the back of a finger, watching to see if the movement or the touch would waken him. He still slept, but his cock woke quickly and crept towards full arousal.

Leaning over him, I let my tongue take the place of my finger, starting at the base of his column and lapping lightly here and there along the shaft. When I reached the head, I licked more carefully still, not wanting to produce a sensation so strong as to wake him just yet. Slowly, carefully, I worked my way down his hard shaft, still lapping at him with my tongue. Eventually, I had it all inside me, with my nose pressed into the tightening skin of his ball sac. I could just detect a hint of musk there – nothing too strong, but more than enough to set my pulse to pounding.

His cock was at its peak, filling my mouth to overflowing. I held it in me briefly, but then I pulled off to catch my breath. As I did so, a tooth caught on the rim of his glans, and Keith awoke with a start.

He sat bolt upright in the bed.

'Sorry I woke you,' I said. 'I was hoping you'd sleep right up until you came.'

'I wouldn't have minded,' he replied, blinking against the light and rubbing sleep from his eyes. 'I was having a fantastic dream.'

'A wet dream with me in it, I hope.'

'It would've been wet, if it had gone on a bit longer,' he said grinning. 'I felt like I was floating right on the edge of coming, but not quite to the point where I felt like I had to come or I was going to die.'

He smiled wistfully and reached out to touch my lips. 'I wish I could say you were in the dream with me, but I couldn't really see who it was. There was this kind of shimmering veil around him that prevented me from looking at him directly. Definitely a man, though once or twice I'd swear he changed shapes for an instant.'

A sense of anticipation came over me. 'What sort of shapes?' I asked, trying to keep the strain I was feeling from showing in my voice.

'One was definitely a horse,' Keith said. 'Another time, it

looked like a bird – a falcon maybe, or a hawk. But I was never very good at bird spotting . . .'

His voice trailed off, and his eyes grew large as I called upon my powers and began to shape-shift in front of him, taking the forms of horse, falcon and salmon in turn – all of them well-known disguises in my earlier days. There was awe in Keith's eyes as I settled back into human form, and perhaps reverence as well, but thankfully no fear that I could see – or anger.

'I'm sorry, Keith,' I began. 'I wanted to tell you Friday. I was afraid that if I did, though, you'd get spooked and leave. That, and I was having a hell of a time coming up with a way to say it that didn't sound like bad science fiction or fantasy. And if you even think about calling me "lord", or "sir",' I added, mock-threateningly, 'I promise, I'll turn you into a dwarf!'

He looked up and caught the mischievous grin on my face, and that set him off. He was instantly laughing, and it was infectious.

'You know, Luke,' Keith said over his second cup of coffee, 'there's no way I could honestly say I wasn't surprised when you chose to reveal your true self this morning. But now that we're letting all the barriers down, there's an epilogue to the story that seems to have been the first step for both of us on the road that led to this moment. You remember I said I didn't have any definitive results from my love spell last fall?'

I nodded.

'What I did have,' he went on after another swig of coffee, 'were a lot of hints. This morning while you were sucking my dick wasn't the first dream I've had about shape-shifting beings, divine or otherwise. They've been popping up out of my subconscious – or wherever it is that such dreams come from – about once every two weeks. It was happening often enough,' he added, drawing a small book from the pocket of his robe and laying it on the table between us, 'that I picked this up at a bookstore at home.'

I looked at it and saw it was a copy of *The Elder Edda* – the Auden and Taylor translation. The pages were dog-eared and festooned with coloured tabs and odd slips of paper. Obviously,

Keith had gone to some effort to understand the meaning of his dreams.

'Can I ask you a personal question?' he said timidly.

'Of course.'

'Why me? There's nothing in here –' he lifted the book from the table '– that says anything about Loki being interested in guys. And, if you don't mind my asking, what are the other gods likely to think?'

'To answer your last question first, they can go do vaudeville in Valhalla for all I care,' I said.

'I have spoken to the gods, and to the sons of the gods –' Keith began quoting from the *Lokasenna*.

'– what my mind was pleased to say,' I said, finishing the quotation for him. 'Just so. The Æsir tolerate me when they have to, call on me when they get in trouble, and despise me or try to get rid of me the rest of the time. I live my own life, and they'll just have to get used to it – if they don't all die laughing first.

'About this,' I said, gesturing towards the book, 'it seems you've forgotten just how my blood-brother got his horse.'

A puzzled look came over his face, then disappeared as the memory surfaced. 'Anyway,' I went on, 'there were lots of things going on in Asgard that the poets never found out about – and plenty more that they knew about, but which were lost before the stories were written down, or deliberately omitted because they didn't happen to agree with someone's preconceived ideas about how gods ought to behave.

'As for the why of it all, I wish I could say I knew. This whole thing crept up on me so slowly that I was in the middle of it before I ever realised it was there. I'm afraid it won't sound very romantic but, at least initially, a lot of my attraction to you was that you gave me something to do to break up the monotony.'

'What do you mean?' he asked.

'There was something in you that reached out to me and reawakened a lot of cold dead spots inside me that I'd stopped thinking about long ago. I'll always be grateful to you for that, Keith. My only fear is that the fact of my living so much longer than you will come between us and rip us apart.'

'Then don't fret, Luke,' he said quietly and with firm conviction. 'Because you aren't going to live any longer than I do.'

I stared at him in shock. 'Huh? I mean, "Excuse me?"'

'Oh, sure, you've lived more years now than I'll ever manage, and you'll probably last many, many more after I depart this realm for the next. But, really, all either of us has is right now – the present moment.' He smiled. 'But it's way too early in the day for heavy-duty metaphysics – so let's talk about our relationship, and what we're going to do about it. I won't lie to you, Luke – the idea that I've been fucking my brains out all weekend with one of the gods is going to take some getting used to. But I love you for you and what I feel when I'm with you, not because you have phenomenal cosmic powers. I can't promise I'm not going to freak out down the road somewhere, or even that I'll be able to make it a permanent commitment. I can say, though, that I don't want to walk away without ever trying, and I don't think you do, either. Why else would you have chosen to reveal your identity, when you could have fucked me and forgotten me with far less trouble?'

I reached for him and he allowed me to pull him to me. His lips met mine. So to be fair, this was one of those days when being a god didn't suck at all, not unless you count what happened later that afternoon, by which time we were quite happily back in bed.

Ridden by the Ghedes

Johnny T. Malice

Under the vast dome of a moonless indigo sky clotted with a billion stars, Voodoo drums throbbed. The air was still and solid as glass, breathless, blood-warm, blood-close. The year was 1952 and it was the night before All Saints' Day, the day of the feast given for the Ghedes, also known as the Barons. The Ghedes were one of the most important families of *lwa* – spirits – and this festival was one of the most important ceremonies in the Voodoo calendar. Ti-Charles, the handsome young *oungan* for the small fishing village of Croix-Le-Bois, was making his preparations.

The priest was a good-looking young man, lean and ebony-dark with closely shaved hair, large, dark eyes, full sensual lips and broad shoulders. He had a compact hairless chest from which large, dark nipples projected like bullets, and a narrow, waspy waist. His legs were long and well muscled, his buttocks high and firm. There were many preparations to make that evening, many small rituals to perform and prayers to offer up before the greater ritual the following day. But he also had a request to make of the *lwa* before tomorrow, one that had nothing to do with his role as Croix-Le-Bois' *oungan*. A request entirely to do with his increasingly intense attraction to one of the handsome young fishermen of the village, Henri Biassou.

Papa Legba, ouvri baye-a pou mwen
Papa Legba, open the gate for me
So I can go through.
When I return I will honour the lwa . . .

So Ti-Charles chanted, his mind filled with the image of Henri's handsome, large-featured face, his flashing white boyish smile, one front tooth framed with gold, the provocative gap between his two front teeth; his sinuous, mocha-brown body, hard and tanned from each long day out on the limitless blue ocean; the casual, loping grace of his walk as he came up the beach with large marlins slung over his shoulders, or rows of red snappers; the straw hat pushed back on his shaved head; his flat, hairless chest bare, red shirt open to the waist and knotted over his sharply defined abdominals; his sun-bleached denim shorts tight around his hips and bulging crotch and high, muscular buttocks.

Henri was a passionate believer, though not a temple initiate. He attended every service, every festival, and danced wildly to the pulsing heartbeat of the drums, ecstatically possessed by the music, the chanting, the sacred rites, the *lwa* themselves, and yet outside the temple he ignored Ti-Charles – beyond being properly respectful to the priest, and perhaps also a little in awe of him, for the lithe, satin-skinned young *oungan* was also a *bokor*, a sorcerer. Henri would never meet Ti-Charles's eyes.

Still, Ti-Charles made out *veves* for Henri's protection and prosperity, tracing the elaborate symbolic patterns on the raked black earth of the *oufo*'s peristyle with flour and coffee grounds. And he also made offerings in the small, whitewashed hut that contained the shrine to Agwe, *lwa* of the sea, that Henri's boat should travel safely across the vast and swelling waters.

Ti-Charles had gradually resigned himself to the fact that nothing would happen between Henri and himself however much he wanted it to. But then had come the time of the Mardi Gras festival in Lent. The *oufo* had been packed with sweaty, white-robed, red-headscarved dancers throwing themselves around ecstatically to the compelling pounding of the temple's drummers, dancing for hours on end around the *poteau-mitain*, the elaborately carved and painted pole that rose up in the middle of the *oufo*'s peristyle, the sacred pole that joined the sky to the earth, that was the conduit of the *lwa* from the Watery Place to the worshippers. Ti-Charles had led the ceremony and danced and chanted for several hours in the sultry heat, and then he was resting on a carved, raised chair by the door of the shrine to Legba. Henri now led the dancing, tossing his head back, wearing nothing but tight white cotton breeches that hugged his full crotch and lean hips, his ebony skin gleaming with sweat, his short hair a mass of diamonds, every sinew standing out in flawless symmetry. Abruptly his whole body began to convulse and his eyes rolled back in his head: Henri was being mounted, ridden, possessed by one of the *lwa*, his higher soul displaced by one of *Les Mysteres* the Lent festival had tempted forth with its offerings of music, food and sacrifice.

Ti-Charles had, of course, been possessed many times, by *lwa* of both sexes, and had come to understand the deeper androgyny, the profounder openness of *Les Mysteres*. This in turn had helped him to understand his own nature, that of a man who finds the totality of masculine and feminine experience with another man: that he was *massissi*. And so, when he had been fully initiated, he had dedicated his *oufo* to Baron Limba and Baron Lundi, who were, it was said, both male, and lovers.

He had never been able to describe the experience of being possessed, being taken by one of *Les Mysteres*, except to say that the ecstasy of being fucked anally touched on some corner of the transcendental sensation of being utterly opened at the profoundest level by the mounting spirit. It was a fearful yielding that gave the 'horse' a pleasure beyond pleasure, a brief moment of insight into the necessary, unbearable essence of life, a moment of passionate involvement with everything living and beyond living. So naturally in his secular life Ti-Charles looked for a mirror to the ecstasy of possession: a man who would take him as *Les Mysteres* took him, deeply, passionately, unrelentingly.

It was Baron Samedi who had possessed Henri that humid, breathless night in Lent. The muscular, dark-skinned young fisherman – naked except for tight, white, pearl-button-fronted breeches that hugged his bulging crotch and large, muscular butt

– undulated his way over to the rising pole of the *poteau-mitain*, head still thrown back, eyes rolled up in his head, and started to move his crotch against the painted post in eager, thrusting motions. As he did so, he reached down with one lanky, well-muscled arm and ran his hand over the offerings that had been laid out for him. He picked out a bottle of rum and swigged from it, running long dark fingers through trays of rice and chicken stew. Finally he picked up a battered black top hat, put it on his head and fumbled for dark glasses laid there to conceal his white, rolled-up eyes.

Slowly, with swivelling hips, Henri made his way towards where Ti-Charles was sitting, his large erection pushing out visibly against the constraining cotton of his tight, knee-length breeches, his small, dark nipples stiff on the low domes of his sinew-striated pectorals. Ti-Charles's cock stiffened to erection inside his own tight white breeches at the intensely arousing sight, its shaft expanding awkwardly across his lean thigh beneath the close-fitting material. A red scarf was knotted tightly around Ti-Charles's close-cropped head, and his loose white cotton shirt was knotted up in front of him, exposing his supple waist. He himself could see every muscle in Henri's sinewy, hairless body as Henri moved towards him, filled with the chaotic, horny spirit of Baron Samedi, extending a muscular arm, a strong hand, swivelling his hips provocatively as the drums pounded.

And Ti-Charles had reached out and taken Henri's hand and been led into the centre of the peristyle, moving to the relentless, compelling rhythm of the drums as he did so. And he had let Henri grip his narrow, supple waist and turn him around and place his hands on Ti-Charles's hips and grind his rigidity against Ti-Charles's firmly muscular and upturned buttocks, simulating fucking the young *oungan* up the arse, driving Ti-Charles to such an unbearable height of excitement that he found himself willing Henri to pull his trousers down and fuck him for real in front of the whole community.

But Henri hadn't done that: he had pulled back from Ti-Charles and gone and danced with others, men and women of the village, leaving the lean young *oungan* desperately aroused and so frustrated he had become nearly delirious as he was obliged to turn back to performing the rituals that ensured the orderly passage of other *lwa* in and out of the bodies of the faithful. Afterwards Ti-Charles had felt compelled to take a thick, pale wax candle from the shrine to Baron Samedi and pleasure himself by sitting on it, letting the warm, unyielding wax pole penetrate him deeply, moving his arse up and down on it as he moved his fist on his aching erection and moaned Henri's name. But once again, when he had greeted the muscular young fisherman on his way to the village the next afternoon to heal a woman stricken by a fever, he had been all but ignored. It burned Ti-Charles's heart to be so coolly treated and then see Henri laughing and throwing his arm casually around the shoulders of his fellow fishermen.

So finally Ti-Charles had turned to sorcery, to ask Ezulie, the *lwa* of love and matters of the heart, to intervene on his behalf. This was the ritual he was performing the night before All Saints' Day. He had placed offerings of food – rice, goat curry and a large cake – and rum at the altar in her hut and now he was grinding his hips hard against the painted wood of the *poteau-mitain* pole in the centre of the peristyle, crushing his balls against the warm, brightly coloured silk-wood patterned with *veves* and symbols, pushing his stiff cock up and down inside his tight white cotton pants, undulating his trembling belly and flatly muscled chest against its warm, smooth surface, feeling a tense, magnetic energy building in his body as the temple's drummer, Sauveur, pounded the *Petro* drum, the drum of magic, of bewitchment, in a building rhythm. Ti-Charles kissed the pole, licked it with a long, pink tongue, all the time pumping his crotch urgently, trying to bring himself off for Ezulie. At the cardinal points of the peristyle he had also marked out *veves* to Baron Lundi and Baron Limba, that they might mediate with Ezulie, whose passions were powerful. The silk-wood tasted of salt and perfume. Ti-Charles's heart was pounding in his chest.

Give him to me, Ezulie, bride of many grooms. Give me this man and I will serve and honour you.

All Saints' Day arrived and the inhabitants of the village of Croix-Le-Bois busied themselves making the preparations for that evening's services, washing and starching their white robes and red headdresses, and cooking the elaborate meals that would be offered up to *Les Mysteres* at the ceremony at the temple that evening. The day was hot and bright, and the slight breeze wafted clean, salt-tinted air across the whitewashed huts of the villagers. The fishing boats were pulled up on to the dazzling white sand and leaning in the shade of arching palm trees; the fishermen too were making their preparations, offerings to their ancestors, past family members and the *lwa*.

The temple was buzzing with activity. The temple initiates, handsome, firm-bodied young men in red headscarves and tight white cotton breeches reaching only to mid-thigh, placed offerings at the base of the *poteau-mitain* post and swept the dark earth of the peristyle while Ti-Charles went from one hut to the other, performing rituals and placing offerings before the altar to each particular god. Sauveur and the two other muscular, younger drummers practised the music they were to perform in the evening while initiates hung the temple flags and pennants. It was unusual for the initiates of an *oufo* to be exclusively male, but the folk of Croix-Le-Bois understood that Ti-Charles was *massissi*, attracted to the same sex, and had been married both to Baron Limba and to Baron Lundi when he was seventeen. He was now twenty-one, and, since he was a good priest and a healer, they had no objections to his choice of initiates.

After the first set of preparations had been made, Ti-Charles retired to his cabin. There he kneeled before his own personal altar, piled high with ritual objects: mirrors, skulls, knotted ropes, bound dolls and objects hung upside down. Amongst these objects were the cord-bound clay pots that contained the spirits of Ti-Charles's ancestors.

'Guide me, Father,' Ti-Charles prayed. 'Guide me, Grandmother. And so let me guide the faithful to wisdom and happiness as you have guided me.' The image of Henri's dark, handsome and smiling face filled his mind. 'Help me, Legba. Help me, Baron Samedi. Help me, Baron Lundi. Help me, Baron Limba. Let me give my love to this man. Help me win his love. You too are *massissi*. Understand me and help me and I will honour you.'

★

Dusk fell, heavy and purple-skied, as the villagers, bearing offerings and lighting their way along the narrow, winding track with oil lamps, made their way towards the sound of drumming that had been coming for some time from the direction of the *oufo*. Its walls rose luminously white from the dark greenery that surrounded it and its gates stood open in welcome. As they filed in and deposited their offerings at the base of the *poteau-mitain*, feeding the *lwa* and giving them the strength to intervene in human affairs, the drumming ceased and the initiates paraded the *oufo*'s flags. After this had been done, Ti-Charles led the invocations of the different *lwa*, incorporating into his chants long Catholic prayers and the liturgies of the saints to the loud, repetitive, ever-varying and compelling drumming of Sauveur and his friends. The muscular young male initiates led the dancing, followed by the villagers. Ti-Charles's eyes often lighted on Henri as he danced vigorously and near naked among his fellow villagers to the music, losing himself to the sounds and the ritual.

After the invocations had been made and the offerings given, Ti-Charles drew the *veves* on the freshly raked black soil of the peristyle of the *lwa* that were to be summoned. The tempo of the drumming increased, and the singing of the initiates built in intensity, as did the frenzy of the dancing, building, building as the air got warmer, closer, blood pounding in veins, ears, the air, the trees, the stones, all life suddenly acutely sentient, everything compellingly interlocked, connected, energy flooding down from the sky into the *poteau-mitain*.

And suddenly the spirit was moving into Henri; he tossed his head back, eyes rolling, pelvis thrusting, soul displaced, every sinew in his dark, lean, muscular body straining as his whole body arched up and he fell backwards. But the initiates were there to catch him before he could fall to the ground and injure himself, bearing him upright and away from the centre of the peristyle, kicking and convulsing, cock thrusting to visible instant erectness in his shorts. One after another various villagers and initiates became possessed by different *lwa*, some invited, some not, taking on their different characteristics, and Henri became lost to Ti-Charles's sight. In the meantime he had many rituals to lead, many things to attend to.

166

Then Henri was dancing forwards, wearing an undertaker's battered black top hat and dark glasses, a purple neckerchief around his sinew-corded neck, his torso dark and hard and defined, glossy with sweat, small nipples erect, waist liquid. He came forwards and took Ti-Charles's hand as he had before and led him into the dance, and Ti-Charles shook his *asson* above the two of them like a benison as the two men ground their crotches together, each straddling the other's thigh, rigid cocks erect and straining against the tight white cotton of their breeches. Ti-Charles gazed into Henri's mirror-shaded face and saw his own large eyes, his own full lips slightly parted with desire.

'Who are you?' Ti-Charles whispered under the pounding of the drums, his voice throaty with fear and desire.

'Baron Samedi,' Henri said in a hoarse, nasal voice. And he threw back his head and laughed a full, rasping laugh, reaching out with strong fingers for Ti-Charles's flatly muscled chest and gripping one of Ti-Charles's protuberant, bullet-shaped nipples brazenly. 'The Ghedes sent me, so I come. And I want you.'

'Are you mocking me?' Ti-Charles asked breathlessly, arsehole clenching and unclenching, his shaft aching, glans throbbing, knowing all too well the *lwa*'s reputation for practical jokes and provocative behaviour.

'No, man. I do not mock you. I give you what you want.' And Henri slid a hand down the back of Ti-Charles's tight white shorts in front of the whole celebrating village, pressing a long, strong finger against Ti-Charles's receptive sphincter. 'I want to mount you human-wise through the one you desire, the one you love. Ezulie sent me. Lundi sent me. Limba sent me. And tonight, man, tonight I must ride.'

The heat of Henri's body, the scent of cocoa butter on his skin mingling with the cooler night smells, the background scents of the offerings of the food, of oil lamps and candles, all intertwined sensually in Ti-Charles's nose. He was powerless to resist the needs of the *lwa*, his own needs also.

'Ride me, Baron,' he whispered breathlessly in Henri's ear.

'Come to my altar,' Baron Samedi answered. Then he swung the heavily erect and unresisting young *oungan* up into his arms and carried him through the parting crowd of initiates and

167

villagers. Ti-Charles no longer cared: let them all see he was *massissi* without dispute. The drumming rose to a new height of intensity and the most senior of the *hounsis* led a fresh chant as Baron Samedi pushed the elaborately patterned black curtain at the entrance to his shrine aside with one elbow and carried Ti-Charles in.

Inside the air was heavy, thick and still, scented with candle wax and heated by the many candles that lit the small, white-washed hut. There was a strange intensity of energy in there, like pre-storm air before a violent downpour, even though the sky outside was clear. Baron Samedi laid Ti-Charles down gently in front of his altar, before plates of rice and goat curry, bottles of spirits, *wanga*, mirrors, candles, the skeletons of snakes and human skulls. He kissed Ti-Charles on the mouth, the taint of cigar smoke on his breath, pushing his strong, muscular tongue between Ti-Charles's full lips, the top hat still pushed down on his shaven, sweaty head, the sunglasses still covering his eyes. Ti-Charles wrapped his arms around the mounted Henri's strong, broad, well-muscled back, sliding his pink palms over smooth, hot, mocha-dark skin, sucking on Baron Samedi's probing tongue, gasping muffledly as the possessed Henri slid his hand down over Ti-Charles's lean, trembling stomach and began to massage his erection firmly through his skin-tight cotton breeches. Ti-Charles opened his thighs to give Baron Samedi's roving hand greater access to his balls and round between his legs to his buttocks and arsehole.

Tentatively – shy both of the young fisherman and of the *lwa* possessing him – Ti-Charles slipped one hand round from Baron Samedi's broad back to his muscular chest, fumbling for a small, stiff nipple. Finding it, he elicited a groan of pleasure from the top-hatted young man bending over him, and he moved his hand down over Henri's ridged stomach and explored his full and rigid crotch.

Suddenly desperate to suck the possessed fisherman's cock, Ti-Charles broke the kiss and turned his head so it was pushed into Henri's bulging crotch. Baron Samedi arched back and pushed his rigid basket into Ti-Charles's face. Ti-Charles nuzzled the stiffness behind the well-washed fabric, then pulled eagerly at the buttons of the fly, getting it open, then tugging the tight breeches down over the mounted Henri's large, muscular butt and down over his smooth, well-shaped thighs to his knees. Baron Samedi's large, stiff, veiny cock sprang up, the dark, satiny foreskin sliding back to reveal its glistening, lighter-brown head. In its piss slit a drop of pre-come glittered like a diamond.

Ti-Charles extended his trembling tongue and licked the salty drop from the opening in Baron Samedi's bulging glans. It tasted more intense than any man juice he had ever tasted before, and he felt a strange, ecstatic energy pass through him as he closed his mouth over Baron Samedi's crown and slid his lips down over his stiff, veiny shaft, swallowing Henri's cock head down his throat as he gagged all ten hot, hard inches down and pressed his full lips into the tight, sparse coils of pubic hair at its base. The ridden fisherman gripped his head with strong fingers and began to fuck Ti-Charles's face rhythmically. Ti-Charles's heart began to pound excitedly as Baron Samedi took control of him, another form of possession.

And yet even as Ti-Charles gratefully swallowed Baron Samedi's large, stiff and pulsing cock down his throat over and over again – the face-fucking rhythm mirroring the muffled rhythms of the drummers outside the shrine, even as he gasped and gurgled in pleasure as Baron Samedi massaged and kneaded his bulging crotch while fucking his throat – Ti-Charles wondered if this was the *lwa*'s joke: to give him Henri and not, to mischievously fuck him with the knowledge of the whole village through the one man the *mystere* would know Ti-Charles could not refuse. And yet surely the other Barons would not permit it?

Ezulie, I will give you much honour, he thought, opening his throat so Baron Samedi could slide his cock further down towards the young *oungan*'s stomach with each firm thrust. I will build a shrine for you next to the shrines of Baron Lundi and Baron Limba in my *oufo*.

Henri slid round on top of Ti-Charles and pushed his strong, smooth, muscular thighs in between Ti-Charles's open ones. Ti-Charles stared into his own face reflected in Baron Samedi's sunglasses, pretty, boyish features bloated by excitement. Henri's skin was hot against his, and Ti-Charles knew he had no power to refuse the possessed fisherman anything. Henri slid his hands firmly down Ti-Charles's body and pulled his shorts down and off in one confident movement. Ti-Charles's large erection sprang up and slapped against his flat, trembling belly, making him gasp, and the warm air felt cool around his heavy, hanging ball sac between his legs.

'Fuck me, Baron Samedi,' he begged breathlessly. 'Fill me with life in defiance of death. Give me your cock, your seed. Fuck my arse. Come up me.'

Sweat running glistening down the sides of his shaved head, top hat still firmly in place, the otherwise naked Baron Samedi reached around to the piled offerings at the foot of the altar. Next to a bottle of rum was a small pot of chicken fat, offered up by one of the shrine's supplicants. Baron Samedi pushed long fingers into it, coating them with thick, waxy grease. Ti-Charles opened his long, muscular, cocoa-brown legs receptively, then threw them wide, rolling back on the altar's base so that his legs and buttocks were up in the air and spread, and his receptive arsehole was made as available as possible to the horny Baron's fingers and his large, stiff dick, longing for deep, profound penetration into his body, into his anal cavity.

'Oh, yes, oh, yes,' Ti-Charles moaned, closing his eyes in pleasure, letting his head fall back over the edge of the altar base as Baron Samedi boldly pushed two fingers into the young *oungan*'s brazenly offered arsehole straight to the knuckle, making Ti-Charles grunt, and his own stiff dick buck. Baron Samedi worked a third finger in alongside his first and second fingers, and Ti-Charles was surprised to find he could take it easily, as if his body was yielding to the possessed Henri on some deeper level than just being fucked by a hot and heavily aroused young fisherman. 'Ride me,' he begged Henri/Baron Samedi. 'Mount me and ride me.'

With a wide grin and a coarse laugh, Baron Samedi nodded and slid his long fingers out of Ti-Charles's now open bottom, dipping them into the small pot and greasing up his large, rigid erection with confident strokes. The watching Ti-Charles hooked his leanly muscled arms up and under his thighs, raising his lower back, pulling his arsehole up as high and spreading it as wide open for the Baron as physically possible.

Baron Samedi kneeled on one knee and guided his large cock head towards Ti-Charles's waiting, well-greased anal star. Ti-Charles groaned as he felt its smooth, hot, egglike curve push against his now accommodating sphincter, then gasped sharply as Baron Samedi slid his crown in past Ti-Charles's now stretched anal ring and pushed his throbbingly rigid ten-inch shaft all the way up Ti-Charles's arsehole. Ti-Charles's stiff dick kicked and pre-come beaded at its head, but he didn't try to grip it to give himself any manual relief as Baron Samedi began to fuck him with long, deep, passionate strokes, instead giving himself up to the total anality of the experience, to the ecstasy of being fucked, penetrated, filled so completely on every level, by the large and throbbing cock of the riding *lwa*.

Ezulie, give me this man.

Baron Samedi's smooth cock head rammed repeatedly against the sphincter deep inside Ti-Charles at the top of his rectum, each firm thrust pushing increasingly milky drops of pre-come out of the young *oungan*'s now gaping piss slit. Ti-Charles lowered his arms so he could brace himself up on his elbows and push his large, muscular buttocks back on to Baron Samedi's thrusting dick in rhythmic response, forcing it as far up himself as possible. Outside the drums pounded and Ti-Charles felt the tug on his spirit as he was opened up on every level at once. Ti-Charles felt as if he was melting, as if the lining of his arse had become the skin wrapping the *lwa*'s large and rigid pole ramming in and out of his backside, possessed by spirit and man together.

And came Baron Samedi's voice hoarse and loud and ribald: 'Keep your arse up in the air so I can fuck it deep, man. Kick stars with your heels and open your back door wide. Spread like Limba when Lundi takes him from behind. Open to your rider, man. Let me mount you and ride you deep.'

And Baron Samedi rammed Ti-Charles up the arse with all the muscular strength he had until Ti-Charles was gasping high and fast and hard, time dissolving, eternal, Ti-Charles's cock heavy and vibrating, his balls tight, Baron Samedi hooking the turned-on young *oungan*'s smooth, long legs up to his shoulders, then twisting Ti-Charles around so he was fucking him on his side, then from behind, stretching Ti-Charles inside, adding to the young priest's ecstasy as Baron Samedi shoved his large hard-on into Ti-Charles's rectum from every possible angle, even swivelling its rigidity inside the young *oungan* to really open his anal passage up to the pleasure of being fucked.

Without withdrawing his wood-hard ten inches from Ti-Charles for a moment, Baron Samedi rolled Ti-Charles back round on to his back, hooked the young man's knees over his shoulders and began to fuck him with hard, deep strokes that rammed up against Ti-Charles's prostate with practised assurance. The *lwa* was an expert butt-fucker, and Ti-Charles's achingly stiff dick bucked uncontrollably with each thrust as he threw his lean arms up over his face, his chest heaving, every muscle in his body trembling, all control thrown away.

'Oh yeah, fuck me, man, fuck me,' Ti-Charles gasped, pushing his buttocks back on to Baron Samedi's crotch with small thrusts, his heart hammering, his lungs compressed. 'I'm open to you, completely open.'

Baron Samedi's top hat tumbled from his dark, shiny head as he fucked Ti-Charles as hard as he could, his lean hips slapping sharply against the globes of Ti-Charles's buttocks. He laughed hoarsely, tossing his head back as he pushed all the way into Ti-Charles, then swivelled his erection inside the young man, making him grunt and gasp and beg for release even as he prayed for this arse-fucking never to finish.

And then strangely the Baron's whole voice and even his breathing changed in some strange and subtle way, and he looked down on Ti-Charles and his face was different somehow – younger, more innocent. His cock seemed suddenly larger, stiffer, hotter inside the young *oungan*'s rectum. His large erection still buried to the root in Ti-Charles's arse, the young fisherman now rotated his pelvis more gently, and he reached up with one hand and took the sunglasses from his face. Ti-Charles stared up into Henri's dark, wide eyes, totally present eyes, pupils dilated with – what? Fear? Desire? Surprise?

Then Henri bent forward and kissed Ti-Charles on the mouth and his breath tasted sweet, and Ti-Charles wrapped his arms around Henri's broad back as the horny young fisherman began to move his hips rapidly back and forth against the heavily aroused passive *oungan*'s upturned and freely offered buttocks.

'You want me?' Ti-Charles asked breathlessly as the leanly muscled young fisherman broke their kiss so he could brace himself up with his strong arms and fuck the *oungan* more deeply and more fluidly, staring up into his handsome, shining brown face.

'I always wanted you, man,' Henri replied as he slid his throbbing pole in and out of Ti-Charles's slack, open arsehole. 'But I was afraid. I was just a fisherman. Why should you want me? I would never have dared to do this. And then suddenly I am here –'

'I wanted you from the first moment you came to the temple,' Ti-Charles replied breathlessly, trying to keep his eyes on Henri's, but finally having to let his head fall back and yield to the ecstasy the young fisherman's large, stiff dick was producing in his rectum. Henri rammed deep into Ti-Charles, thrusting up hard, giving his lover his whole length with each assertion, then pumped rapidly, thrusting himself to a climax inside Ti-Charles's arsehole, each push making Ti-Charles's own throbbing hard-on heavier, ramming the spunk out of his balls and along its shaft, Henri literally fucking the come out of Ti-Charles's aching dick as, with hoarse, loud gasps that were almost bellows, he exploded inside the young *oungan*'s anal passage, flooding it with hot white jism. The pressure of his climax made Ti-Charles explode with a cry too, come spattering thick and white up the length of his arching torso, drops landing on his chest, in his clavicle, one even hitting his chin.

They stayed like that, Henri inside Ti-Charles's body, for some time, lying at the base of the altar of the Ghedes curled up around each other, listening to the service continuing outside.

'The *Mysteres* are satisfied, yes, man?' Henri said eventually, his voice soft and grainy in Ti-Charles's ear.

'The *Mysteres* are never satisfied,' Ti-Charles replied. 'But tonight we have honoured them.'

'If it is what the *lwa* will, I will honour them in this way every night,' Henri whispered, leaning round from behind Ti-Charles and smiling. Ti-Charles turned his head and the two young men kissed softly on the lips.

'It is what the *lwa* will,' he said, smiling too.

The New Recruit

John Patrick

I often dreamed of flying. Of being unconnected. Of being unattached. High in a sky that is in Technicolor and Cinemascope.

And finally I got to fly. It was a great adventure, as it turned out – mainly because I never left the ground. Not in a literal sense.

It all began when a massive snowstorm in the northeast grounded everything north of Atlanta. I was at the Tampa airport with my duffel bag and a parka that I hadn't worn in two years, not since I was living in Buffalo with Mom and Dad. I wasn't going anywhere.

Outside the terminal, it was a balmy seventy-five degrees. When I told my folks what the weather was like and how I couldn't believe it was so bad where they were, there was dead silence. My dad hated the idea that I never had to shovel snow; that was what kept him going all winter, telling me to shovel out the driveway while he watched football on TV and got drunk.

My lover was stranded as well. We had planned to meet in the Big Apple after I had seen my folks. He was already in the city for a conference, and he was waiting for me to join him for a 'second honeymoon' to celebrate our first anniversary. Now that wasn't to be and, as far as I was concerned, it was just as well. Better, really.

Anyhow, there I was at the airport with everything cancelled.

I hoisted my duffel bag to my shoulder and returned to all that Florida sunshine. There was a long line at the cab stand and I cursed myself for not driving and paying the long-term parking rate in the lot.

My lover, however, had convinced me that it would be cheaper to take cabs, considering we would be coming back together. Yeah, right! Frowning, I easily laid the lack of available cabs at his feet. It was all Bob's fault. It seemed that *everything* was Bob's fault these days, and there was a lot of shit happening in my life recently.

I stood there trying to make up my mind that I simply was going to have to leave Bob. We had grown too far apart recently and I didn't see myself wasting my time trying to patch something that no longer worked.

I saw him – or I became aware of him. He was standing two people ahead of me, and his beauty was so total that it took my breath away. He was a god come to life.

He felt me staring at him because he turned and smiled at me. I smiled back, and he let the two people ahead of me and behind him take the cab that was next up. 'We seem to be headed in the same direction. Do you want to share a cab?' he asked.

'Sure,' I said, without thinking about it. He turned and watched the next cab inch towards our line. I started to reflect on what he'd said.

How could he know what direction I was headed? There was the obvious destination, of course – the noticeable bulge at his crotch which I couldn't help staring at as he stood next to me. That, coupled with the buttocks I had so admired while he was standing ahead of me. Confronted by such abundance, I always turned dumb and my thoughts turned off. I couldn't think of a thing to say as we came closer to the front of the line.

'Looks like I got out of Atlanta just in time,' he said. 'Mine must have been the last flight out. And I've been looking forward to getting in some fun and sun for a long while.' He winked. 'Lots of fun especially.'

'Where are you staying?' I managed to ask.

'With you,' he said matter-of-factly.

Before I had a chance to respond to this outlandish news, we were in the cab.

This perfect stranger, this god, gave the driver *my* address.

'But how –'

'It's on your tag,' he said, pointing to my duffel bag.

So it was, but how could he have read it at that distance? This, I decided, was as close to being with Superman as I was ever likely to get and settled back into the seat to enjoy the ride.

It was ten minutes to my apartment from the airport. In that time, he introduced himself as Terry and got from me more details about my life than I have shared with anyone – let alone a total stranger.

It seemed, from the questions Terry asked, that he already knew the answers. I didn't know whether he was clairvoyant or what, but, at that point, it hardly mattered. This gorgeous number was coming home with me for the weekend! I'd worry about questions later.

I showed him to the bedroom and told him where he could hang his clothes in the closet. I didn't care that I was pointing out the hangers where Bob's shirts usually hung. 'First the sun,' he said and dazzled me again with his smile.

'OK,' I said, heading for the bathroom for my swimming trunks.

When I opened the door after changing, Terry was just slipping into his trunks. I saw he was strawberry blond all over, and the promise of the bulge was a reality. His cock was unusually thick and mouth-watering as he pulled the fabric over it. 'All set,' he said.

'Me, too,' I said, staring as he turned around. It was as if he was showing off, making sure to remind me the rear view was every bit as good as the front.

As he strode purposefully out through the sliding glass door to the courtyard, I muttered, 'First the sun,' as if I was reminding myself to behave. There would be time for fun. Lots of time.

★

'I've come to recruit you,' he informed me when I finally managed to get him back into the bedroom. We'd had the sun: I wanted the fun.

'Recruit me?' I asked, removing my wet swimsuit.

'Yes, for some very important work.'

'Oh?' My cock was already hard. His, I noticed, was getting there as he slipped his trunks over his thighs. They fell to the floor and he walked over to where I was standing.

'Do you know,' he whispered, his tongue flicking at my ear, 'why I was chosen to persuade you?'

'Chosen by whom?'

'It doesn't matter.'

Like hell it didn't. But I had other things on my mind now, so I answered his question. 'Because you're the best?' I asked, stroking his cock for the first time. Now it was fully hard.

He gazed at me, fluttering his impossibly long lashes. 'No. We must concentrate on the pleasure of others. I was chosen not because I am the best. Because I'm the worst. The clumsiest, the laziest, the most distracted. The least adept at sex.'

I tried to pull him to me. He grinned and wiggled away from my hold on him. 'I have to explain this first.' He smiled and went on to say he had wandered the world as an orphan, alone in life as he had been alone at birth, and he had imagined that solitude was his destiny. But he had been offered another destiny, one that was his for the believing.

'Who offered you this?' I asked. Terry didn't answer, and continued with his story. When offered this new destiny, he had only to say yes. And he did. He was offering me that as well. I started to speak but he pressed his fingers against my lips, closed his eyes tight.

'This is what we do. This can be your destiny too, if you'll take it. To share. It's how we find peace.' He opened his eyes; they glowed brilliant and fierce, like green fire. 'So, you've got to say you'll join us.'

The air was hot on my skin, but I could feel a chill all the way down to the marrow of my bones. 'I don't know what to say,' I stammered.

'Just say yes,' he said, as he dropped to his knees and began sucking me.

'Oh, yes,' I sighed at the feel of his lips tight on the root of my cock.

My mind raced even as my body was succumbing to his magic. It was all so bizarre, so unreal. I realised I didn't really want this to be real. I just wanted him to be a guy with a libido as big as mine. A weekend of mutual gratification and he would be gone. Barring that, I wanted him to be a dream I'd conjured up – a jerk-off fantasy that would last the weekend.

A tingle like static electricity built up in my fingers. I looked down at Terry pleasuring me, but it seemed that I was looking *through* him, directly *into* him – into the essence of him. I took his head in my hands, trying to control his hunger for my cock. I told myself that this was flesh and blood that lay under my hands, but rainbowing swirls of light were all I could see. Maybe I was going nuts. Maybe the dud ecstasy I dropped last summer was finally taking effect. I gasped as I began to understand. We're all made of light, I thought. Sounds and light, waves and particles, vibrating.

Moments later I saw that, under my hands, the rainbowing pattern of the lights was unblemished. The lights had faded, had become flesh and bone and skin. I was holding Terry's head in my hands once more. The tingle left my fingers, and I dropped my hands. I had come, but he had not swallowed it. He had caught my entire load in his hand. He smiled.

'Thank you,' I said.

'You have a wonderful penis,' he said, squeezing the last drops of come from it.

He rose and went to the bathroom. I collapsed on the bed. My cock wouldn't stay still. I stroked it back to hardness. When he came back into the bedroom, his cock bobbed deliciously before him. I sat up so that I could kiss it, suck it, play with it.

He joined me on the bed and we began to make love. It had been so long since I had enjoyed the pleasures of long – and tender – lovemaking. This god, this dream, this Terry was not Bob. There was no rush to completion as there was with Bob. Instead, Terry was wooing me by repeated kisses and caresses.

And I knew that, when he did enter me, it would be gentle. Ours would be a slow ride to the peak of sensation.

Eventually he could stand it no longer. He sat up, gleaming with all the vitality of youth and health. I rolled over on my back, took hold of his jerking stiffness and pulled him towards me, my legs parting wide to offer myself to him. But he stopped. He got up, went to his trousers and pulled out a condom.

'I won't get pregnant, I promise,' I joked.

'I know,' he said soberly, putting the condom on and coming back to the bed.

I grabbed his cock and guided him quickly to me. He pierced me with a long thrust, his lips finding mine as more and more of him entered me.

His hands began kneading my arse while he slid backwards and forwards. Each forward thrust found my joy spot, nudging and massaging my prostate. I moaned with delight and jerked under him, my head upturned on the pillows. My legs were as wide open as they would go, and my belly heaved against Terry's as he plunged into me.

His fingers were digging hard into the flesh of my shoulders and my head lifted up from the pillows to bring my open lips over his and force my flickering tongue into his mouth. In my feverish excitement, I began jerking my cock. Terry was plummeting me to my very depths; and a moment later, in a crescendo of small whimpering cries, my back arched off the bed, lifting his weight on me as I came.

I collapsed under him, my head rolling from side to side on the pillows, while Terry fucked on, his cock massaging my prostate with its every thrust. I rode yet another wave of pleasure. I squirmed beneath him and moaned. His mouth covered mine and sucked at it. I began to swing my hips upwards to meet his strokes, crying out from the excruciating pleasure his cock was giving me.

Terry's breathing finally became laboured; his orgasm was near. The tempo of his possession of me changed. He rammed fast and deep into my aching, slippery hole, his belly smacking against mine brutally until he was filling the condom.

Shaking, he took me into his arms and we lay quietly together as his sheathed cock slowly slipped from my opening.

I peeled off the rubber and dropped it on the floor next to the bed. I wanted to suck him some more, but he insisted on washing first. I followed him, and stood behind him at the sink, watching him. My cock would not stay down. I stepped up behind him and my cock pushed into his buttocks.

He smiled but said nothing. He simply went back to the bedroom and got another condom. He rolled it on to my cock and turned around. He took my dick in his hand and, as he bent over, he brought it to his hole. I couldn't remember the last time I'd fucked anyone standing up. As I entered him it seemed like an entirely new sensation. In the mirror over the bureau, I watched spellbound as Terry took all of me deep inside his bum.

I was excited almost to the point of delirium by the sight of my long pink cock going in and out of Terry's perfect arse. There was no discussion, the way it always was with Bob, of whether or not I was worthy to do the fucking. Terry was not only *allowing* me to penetrate him: he actually *wanted* it!

'Give it to me,' he murmured. 'That's what I came here for today! To show you both ways can be good.' He was wrong, of course – Terry had come here to fuck me, but I wasn't in any mood at that moment to dispute his mistaken belief. I wanted him in bed, with his legs wrapped around me. I pushed him there, and I was on top of him in a flash, guiding myself into him with my hand.

'Oh!' he exclaimed as I thrust home to the hilt. I wasn't sure whether he was expressing surprise, dismay or pleasure. Whatever his emotion, his legs closed over my back like a steel trap. He began moving under me, thrusting his hot loins up against me with fast and nervous little strokes.

I continued to plunge hard in and out of him, but his legs clamped tighter around my waist and his arms went around my back to immobilise me. He held me with his belly tight to mine. Now there was nothing else I could do but lie still while he had his way with me from below. Not that it mattered – the outcome was the same.

My cock throbbed as I stared down in wonder at the face

below me, the eyes locked in a glassy stare, mouth open as he finally released me, jerking himself to bring forth another explosion of come.

I moaned in delight and thrust harder and faster into him, setting his legs shaking to the rhythm of my pleasure. I held his foot to my face, showering wet kisses on the soft sole, then sucking on the toes one by one. My arousal soared to frantic heights, and I plunged into him with greater force. His body shook as I stabbed into him in a frenzy of fucking. My eyes were open but I saw nothing. My body convulsed as I filled the rubber. My mouth pressed in a hot kiss to the instep of his right foot. The sheer momentum of my climax caused his body to buck and writhe on the bed.

When I was tranquil again, I took hold of his ankles and opened his legs to the full extent of my arms, to stare down at my cock, now only half embedded in his arse. Terry raised his head to look along his body to our joined parts, an expression of approval on his handsome face. I straightened my back, sat up on my knees and withdrew my softening prick. I lay down beside him.

'Will you join us?' he asked softly, his gaze never leaving my face.

I stared at him. Who was this man who'd given me so much pleasure on a sunny Florida winter afternoon? Or, if I believed any of his tale from earlier, *what* was he? I sure as hell could get into the pleasure – the giving and taking of pleasure that had been ours. Was that all he wanted? I didn't know if I believed him but I did know I wanted the fullness of pleasure I had known with him.

His features blurred and I saw rainbow colours once again where I knew he was. 'What are you?' I groaned. I needed to know, even as I feared the knowledge.

His chuckle was gentle. 'I'm nothing to fear.'

'Do I . . .?' I didn't know how to say it. I wasn't in the throes of passion and I was still seeing electrical currents and swirls and whatever else I was seeing beside my bed. It wasn't hard to figure that, for me to become that, I was going to have to change pretty drastically. Physically. Like become a god – or a ghost. The next logical step was to figure I had to die.

'Eventually, you'll become like me,' he answered. 'But you can be like us while still in this form.'

I knew I didn't want to go back to the quick gropes, the forced entries – even the self-loathing I had felt ever since I knew I was gay. 'Yes, I'll join you,' I told him. 'But when?'

'Not long,' he said, rolling away from me to the edge of the bed. 'But you must be careful,' he added.

'What do you mean?' I asked.

'Just be careful,' he said. He tilted his head back as he rose to his feet, as if he had heard something. That didn't make any sense, though. We had the whole weekend with Bob conveniently snowbound in New York. Terry dressed quickly and quietly as I watched.

'You're one of us now,' he said as he came to the side of the bed and looked down at me. 'Now you can show him how, too. Show him how good it can be.' As he leaned over me, flickering lights of every colour touched my lips softly.

I stared at him as he became Terry once again. My gaze tracked him as he walked away, across the carpeted floor and through the doors of the balcony. He didn't open the doors; he just stepped through the glass and steel out into the street and continued on across the pavement. A half-dozen yards from the condo, he simply faded away like a video effect and was gone.

I shook my head. 'No,' I moaned softly.

Bob came into the bedroom then. He was carrying his suitcase. He looked more tired and more pissed off than usual.

'How come you're *here*?' I asked, with some surprise.

'The weather eased up unexpectedly. I thought I'd surprise you here, back home.' Then it was his turn to question. 'Why're you naked?' he asked.

I turned to look at him. 'Didn't you see what just happened?'

'Happened where?'

'Here. There.' I pointed to the window.

'What the hell are you talking about?'

'He . . .' My voice trailed off as the realisation hit home. I was on my own with this. What had happened? If I took it all at face value, I realised that I had watched the end of the world the way it had been. It was going to become the world the way I now knew it could be. It was changed for ever. *I* was changed for ever. I carried a responsibility now of which I'd never been aware before.

Ignoring me, Bob began unpacking.

Terry, or whoever he really was, had given me a command, 'Just be careful'; so I let the matter drop. Then my gaze fell to the floor and I saw the glow-in-the-dark condom Terry had worn during our sex. I hesitated for a moment, then reached over and picked it up. My fingers tingled again, and I watched in wonder as the rubber sparkled.

'What've you got there?' Bob asked, looking over at me.

I shook my head. I closed my fingers around the condom, savouring its odd warmth.

'Nothing,' I said.

Bob moved towards me. 'No, it's not nothing. Let me see.'

'No,' I said, as he starting wrestling me.

He overpowered me and pulled the condom from my hand. 'So this is what you do while I'm away?' he demanded angrily, his eyes flashing.

'No, no,' I protested, but he held me down. He had his pants opened and was pulling out his cock in moments.

He stopped then and didn't move. I looked up into his face and saw him studying me, moisture in his eyes.

'I want –' He shuddered. 'All I could think about in New York was you, honey. How everything seemed to be going wrong between us. How I wasn't considering you at all – it's this damned job.' He shook his head and wiped his eyes. 'I love you. I don't want to lose you. Give me just one more chance to make it up to you, honey.'

I stared up at him. He was still in his shirt and tie. His trousers were open and his dick jutted out at me, calling me. All I could think of was how almost good it had been those first months we were together – before Terry came to show me what good was.

Maybe this was what Terry had meant when he said that he had been just like me once. He had gone from hurting to healing, and maybe I could do that too.

Just be careful. It seemed possible. Tentatively, I reached both hands out to Bob. Now it seemed more than possible when I saw the gratitude in Bob's eyes as he climbed on to the bed and leaned through my legs to kiss me. I was flying. Soaring in a Technicolor sky. And I never wanted to come down again.

'Want to fuck me?' he asked quietly when he'd broken our kiss. I kissed him again, a quick peck.

'Have we got any condoms?'

He raised himself up and reached to the night table. 'Your guest seemed to have left these Day-Glo things. Will they do?' I nodded. 'Let me get naked then. I want a good, *slow* fuck, honey.'

The Flame Within

Caleb Knight

The sun god's unrelenting white glare filled the house. The air was as thick as Nile mud. Rami's lungs heaved with the heated air, and the tiled floor of the small chamber burned his legs.

Ipahu, the priest, was dead. Rami's father was dead.

His nakedness was little comfort in the heat. He was only the son of the priest's concubine, but he was still Ipahu's son – and only a week away from completing his courses at Temple School. Prince Khofir, brother of the Pharaoh, possessed him now, as he had everything that had once been the priest's.

The bonds that Khofir's servants had used to bind him felt stronger than bands hewn of bronze. He could still hear Ipahu's demands for an explanation as the soldiers led him away.

Khofir's Nubian eunuch and his guard had sniggered while they stripped and bound Rami. The Prince had seemed gleeful when he informed Rami that all of the priest's possessions now belonged to him – especially Rami himself.

Rami said a prayer for mercy and deliverance, one Ipahu had taught him. As his tongue forced out the last syllables, he heard sandals approach the chamber.

He tried to move into a defensive posture, but the ropes

186

tightened around his wrists and ankles and he toppled sideways on to the floor. He was still struggling to right himself when the entrance curtains opened wide. Khofir strode across the chamber and towered over him.

Khofir's perfume was thick and cloying. Rich gold jewellery shimmered on the man's naked shoulders and arms. Gleaming bands flashed on Khofir's wrists, ornaments more expensive than any Ipahu had ever donned. In spite of himself, Rami felt himself harden. Khofir was strong and masculine. The Prince's gaze roamed over Rami's naked body. His thick lips curled into a frown. 'You've been impatient for my return, I see,' he sneered.

Planting a sandal in Rami's side, he rolled him over. The young man stared over his shoulder in fear and unbidden desire at the Prince of Egypt standing over him. The perfection of Khofir's body was as well known in Thebes as his closeness to his brother the Pharaoh or the blackness of his ka.

Khofir laughed as his fingers caressed the turquoise beads of his whip, tickled the gold strands woven in between those fashioned of leather. 'Of course, you should be eager to see me. A slave should always yearn for his master.' He kneeled and chucked the lad's chin. 'Unfortunately, the delay could not be helped, little one. Pharaoh wished to confer new honours on me for bringing Ipahu to justice.'

Khofir pulled his whip loose from his belt. Rami tensed in fear as he watched, gritting his teeth against the expected jolt of pain. His manhood grew harder. Yet, the metal-studded lash didn't bite into his naked skin. Instead, its tip moved between Rami's open thighs, travelling along his perineum until it found his bollocks. His manhood leaked.

'Those looks you gave me in the marketplace – you wanted me then and sought to hide it. Did you think I didn't notice, you concubine's whelp?' He grinned. 'Now, you will have what you wanted.'

The whip snaked up the valley of the crevice in his buttocks and returned to his entrance. Khofir snapped his wrist so that the whip coiled into his fingers like a trained serpent. Holding it in a tight circle, he thrust it under Rami's chin and jerked his head upwards. Rami tried not to tremble as he blinked into the kohl-outlined eyes.

Khofir motioned for his eunuch. The Nubian hoisted Rami off the floor and dragged him into the hall and down to Ipahu's chamber. There he was tied to a large, four-legged jar stand in the corner.

He felt his legs pulled apart. Prince Khofir nodded as Rami was bent over the top of the stand with his buttocks raised. The Nubian lashed his ankles to the frame, splitting the crease in his backside wide open, then fastened his hands in a similar position. Soon his privates dangled freely into the space where a large jar would normally have sat.

'Open him,' Khofir demanded, and the eunuch moved between Rami's legs. Rami turned his head, watching wide-eyed as the Nubian thrust three fingers into lamp oil, then into his hole. To Rami's shock, he drilled them roughly inside and began to skewer his hole. Raw torment flashed through the length of his body as the Nubian's thrusts grew deeper and harder.

The prodding ceased suddenly, and the eunuch stepped away. Before he retreated to the other side of the chamber, he wiped his fingers hard on Rami's buttocks. Oil streaked the youth's naked flesh, and his face burned with shame.

Khofir laughed and moved close, gesturing for the eunuch. The slave peeled his master's white linen kilt away.

Rami caught his breath as Khofir's manhood was revealed. It was as much a weapon as the rest of his finely honed body. Plump at the base, it grew thicker in the middle before tapering to a narrow crown that had already pushed through its moist hood of flesh. The tip oozed clear liquid.

Khofir pushed the organ towards the new slave's mouth. At the last moment, Rami pulled away but the eunuch slapped his face hard. He shook his head and found himself staring up at the ugly, leering eunuch as Khofir moved out of his vision.

Rami jerked at a fresh sensation at his rear opening. He turned to see Khofir standing between his spread legs. Harsh studs dug into tender flesh, and Rami saw that the handle of the Prince's whip had invaded him. It ploughed into him.

'Leave us now,' the new master commanded, and the eunuch

was gone before the last syllable slid from his lips. Rami could hear the eunuch's high-pitched giggling even after he had vanished. He whimpered as the whip handle wrenched deeper into his bowels.

'Have you ever taken another man inside your body?' Khofir asked, bending over the young man so that his cheek brushed against Rami's ear.

'No, master,' Rami whispered back in shame.

'Then you may consider yourself fortunate,' Khofir told him and pulled the whip handle from his bowel. 'As Pharaoh's brother, I am naturally divine as well. You shall soon know the indescribable pleasure of feeling a god's cock split you open.'

Khofir grasped his new slave's arse globes and forced them apart. He moved between the splayed legs and placed his cock at Rami's entrance. Heaving his hips forward, the Prince buried himself deep inside his new slave.

Pain. It felt as though someone had thrust a lighted torch into Rami's body, then twisted it until his innards caught fire. He gasped, instinctively trying to pull away from the hard, burning pain. Though the jar stand rocked beneath him, his bonds held him tight.

Khofir's groin slapped against Rami's buttocks, his organ sliding in and out of his bowel, raking his entrails. Rami flailed and moaned beneath his master's thrusts.

When it was over, Khofir stepped away and called for his servant. The eunuch returned, along with a nearly naked body slave Rami had not seen before. They washed, redressed and praised their master.

Rami was left bent over the jar stand. He could feel the warm trickle of Khofir's fluids sliding down the insides of his thighs.

Khofir glanced at Rami. 'Feed him,' he told the two slaves, 'and let him relieve himself. Make sure he is clean for tonight.'

The eunuch's stolen caresses as he untied him stirred his flesh against his will. Rami closed his eyes and blushed as the eunuch stroked him, soon reaching an orgasm that embarrassed rather than relieved him. The memory of Khofir's body lingered as he ate the bread and drank the water they brought him.

★

The eunuch disrobed Khofir completely that night, leaving only a gold armband in the shape of a serpent.

'Shall I bind his hands, master?' the eunuch asked, eyeing Rami as he kneeled naked in the corner. 'If he were to steal upon you in the night –'

'No,' said Khofir, his gaze seeming to burn Rami's skin. 'He won't harm me. He knows well enough what will happen to him if he does.'

'The guards will be outside your chamber as always, master.'

'Leave us, then.'

'Yes, my Prince.'

His thick lips twitching in a quickly suppressed grin, the eunuch crossed the chamber, grasped Rami by the scruff of the neck, and pushed him towards their master's bed.

When Khofir was through with him, Rami slumped to the floor and curled his arms around his drawn-up legs. He surrendered to sleep as soon as he was comfortable.

Rami woke sometime later, the tips of his fingers tingling as if someone were sticking thousands of tiny knife points into him. Gritting his teeth, he sat up on his bare buttocks and began to rub the feeling back into his sleep-deadened arm.

Above him, on the polished wooden bed inlaid with ivory and silver, his master slept still, a thin sheet of moisture slicking his smooth body. Khofir's desires were sated for the night – his breathing was heavy, and his manhood lay slack and plump against his thigh, his seed already dried. He slept with an ivory-handled dagger in one hand.

Beside the bed, a small clay lamp was still alight, its flames burning low but steady. Rami guessed that Khofir feared the demons that sometimes came in the night. He had no doubt that many spirits longed for revenge on this man who had become his master.

He raised his gaze to the painted figures on the plastered walls, commissioned at such great expense by Ipahu, lit by the lamplight.

Here, untouched by the intrigues of mortals, the Sacred Ones went about their business: jackal-headed Anubis weighed the hearts of the deceased, Isis and Osiris reigned over their squabbling god children, and conniving Seth sowed his dark weeds of discord.

Dominating the mural, though, was Great Re. Magnificent in his sun boat, he began his progress across the sky, pushing the sacred vessel along with a golden bargepole.

As Rami gazed at the panorama of deities, he felt peace spread through him. He was drawn to Amon Re, god of the morning and lord of the light. He knew that the god had not abandoned this house because of the execution of his devoted priest. He felt the god's presence.

His eyes traced the sleek curves of Amon Re's powerful body – the artist's stylised rendering only accented its aura of power and control. Rami longed to have that kind of power himself – to wield the daylight like a sword, to call the fire from the sky to smite down his tormentors. Or to be protected by it. But he had nothing – no strength, no status, not even a ragged kilt to cover himself or a single withered fruit as an offering if he prayed.

An idea slowly began to take shape among his thoughts. He dared to hope that sincere homage without ornamentation would be acceptable.

He had seen his father set a bowl of fruit and cakes in front of this same mural, then recite a whispered prayer of offering. Rami had asked once why the food never disappeared if the god had taken it as sustenance. Ipahu had explained that the essence of the food was all the god required. Though each piece of fruit looked the same after the god had consumed it, its inner qualities were utterly changed once the Divine One's ka had passed through it.

The youth spread his hands and brushed clean a patch of floor beneath the Great One's image.

His lips barely moved as he recited a prayer his father had taught him. 'Praise to thee, oh Re,' he said, his voice quieter than a whisper. 'Lord primeval, who came into being of thine own masterful will, Lord who gives breath to my nostrils, hear my plea –'

Silence mocked him. Gaunt shadows flickered on the painted wall, but Rami swallowed hard and persisted. He bowed so low that his forehead touched the ground.

'Forgive this poor gift, most Merciful Lord,' he whispered and spread his fingers over his groin. 'But I have nothing more to offer.'

In the flickering light, the god's painted face seemed to change – to shift towards him. The red slash of the Great One's mouth seemed to curve upwards.

Rami sucked in breath and gripped his manhood with both hands. In the flickering light, he watched it fill with blood, forcing the fleshy hood back. He stroked his spear until it reared like a spitting asp in his fists. Finally he felt his stones pull tight on his shaft.

His face flushed with emotion as the first droplets of his life force arced upwards. The lamplight caught the stream as it split the still air, turning it a deep orange red. It seemed to hover there, suspended in time, before it lost its flamelike sheen and dropped to the floor.

Rami squeezed harder. Ripples of pleasure spread through his groin, prompting a renewed gush of fluids. He imagined the god ploughing him but, this time, he knew he would find sexual joy as well. A blush rose to his cheeks when he considered the possibility that Khofir's possession of him had stirred his body more than he wanted to admit.

There was so much semen, as if the god's demand would never end. Exhaustion consumed his body and Rami slumped to the floor. His arms spread wide like the wings of swooping Horus, his legs tucked up under him, and his ravaged backside tilted into the air.

Far away, perhaps from the very depths of his ka, Rami thought he heard the ringing, otherworldly laughter of Great Re.

Before sleep could envelop him, he glanced up at the mural again. Though his eyes were swimming, he saw the image in the mural shift yet again. The Sun God himself seemed to loom much closer. The smile on his paint-rouged mouth stretched larger, wider. Rami even saw the hint of gleaming white teeth flash behind the parted lips.

The lamp beside him went out, and he felt his arse cheeks gently spread open.

Rami gasped when he felt a massive shaft move carefully to place itself against his back entrance. Its enormous breadth was welcomed as it entered him. He instinctively opened for it, allowing it to reach into his depths, and sighed at the pleasure of its possession of him. His man-spear rose along his belly and throbbed in greeting.

Khofir's earlier abuse of his flesh had been nothing compared with this. That had been pain and humiliation. This was pleasure and fulfilment. His buttocks moved back to consume more.

Only Khofir's snores broke the silence that held the chamber as the organ began to thrust in and out of him. Rami pushed back to meet each new thrust, his arse muscles clutching at the man-spear that impaled him.

Pleasure rose out of his bottom and spread through him like a windswept fire. He fought himself to remain silent. Only Khofir's snores held his moans of pleasure inside his throat.

On and on the thrusting went. The force that hammered his bowel knocked the breath from his chest. Every fresh thrust from behind was another wave of pleasure that sent him reeling.

A torrent of his essence poured from Rami. His life force sprayed from him in a long, fiery stream, and the night around him became an even darker blur.

Looking back over his shoulder, he saw nothing but felt the great pillar continue to massage his insides. New waves of pleasure built up within his entrance and flowed over him. His man-spear again rode his belly, hard and strong. He bit his cheeks to keep from moaning his pleasure. His arse muscles clutched at the organ ploughing him.

When the organ inside him finally erupted, it seared through his heart as a bolt of lightning would pierce him. He shuddered and bucked once, involuntarily, as the column roughly withdrew from him. His body made a loud slapping sound as it hit the floor.

His hand flew to the side and jarred the small clay lamp beside Khofir's bed, which unexpectedly flickered back to life. A muted gold haze spread through the chamber, falling over the mural and his master's wooden bed frame.

Khofir still lay perfectly still, his fingers still curled around the ivory-handled dagger. His dark, disc-shaped nipples rose and fell in the slow, steady rhythm of deep sleep.

Ka-lifting awe inflated Rami's heart as he turned once again to face the mural. There, dark-haired and red-eyed, Great Re gazed down upon him. An enormous phallus, streaked and wet, glowed like a hot brand between olive-skinned legs.

He was still staring, open mouthed, when the lamplight faded out a second time.

As he began his second morning in Prince Khofir's service, Rami was convinced he had dreamed the whole thing. The floor around him was cleaner than if it had been freshly scrubbed. Yet, when he touched his privates, still exposed, they smarted as if someone had taken a lash to them. And the opening between his globes felt as though it had been singed by fire.

Khofir, of course, took no notice. Rami kneeled in the corner, as the eunuch washed and dressed his master, then painted his face with kohl and rouge. Khofir sat in the ebony chair, spreading his legs and eyeing Rami. The Prince's manhood soon hardened and throbbed visibly beneath the folds of his kilt. Rami's gaze was drawn to it almost against his will.

Khofir snapped his fingers at his new slave and pointed to the space between his open knees. Rami shuddered and crawled forward.

As the eunuch watched, shifting excitedly from one sandalled foot to the other, Khofir flipped aside the hem of his tunic to reveal himself. As Rami kneeled between his master's legs, Khofir grasped him by the ears and pulled his face to him. The serpent-like organ leaped into his mouth, and Rami choked. He fought off a gag as Khofir drove himself into the depths of his throat. Rami quickly began to suck.

Khofir let out a long sigh of pleasure as Rami's lips and tongue curled around his manhood. At first, his humping was slow and measured, drawing out his pleasures as his slave struggled around the object that impaled his face. As Khofir's stones heated and tightened and his nectar bubbled up through his slit, however, he quickened the pace and force of his strokes. Rami's cheeks drew inwards as the first spurts of seed pelted his tongue.

Khofir put his palm on Rami's forehead and shoved him back roughly. His glistening organ slipped from Rami's mouth, a few ivory-coloured droplets spraying into the air as he withdrew himself.

Laughing, Khofir let his kilt drop down, though his distended organ reached well past the hem. Then he leaned back in the ebony chair. 'Leave us,' he barked at the eunuch, who hurried away.

When they were alone, Khofir looked squarely at Rami. Lifting his organ again, Khofir slapped his softening manhood against Rami's lips. The blow stung and Rami looked to the floor. Khofir's grin never faltered.

'My hope for you, Rami, is that you will come to see the benefits of honouring my wishes without question, even without fear.'

A casual sigh escaped his lips, and he raised one foot until the sole rested against Rami's vulnerable stones. Slowly, he pressed downwards until the young slave winced, then gasped in pain.

'I would prefer to keep you alive,' Khofir said quietly. The pressure of his foot grew harder. 'But I can see that you are wilful, Rami – far too wilful for a slave. It's as though you truly believe your father's heresy, that Great Re himself will aid simple mortals like yourself.'

Something uncoiled deep within Rami's being. Like a fire-storm, it gathered force, scorching his brain, pulsating deep within muscle and bone.

Khofir saw it, too. He sat motionless, his almond eyes widening first with affront, then with surprise, and, finally, with fear. 'Great Re,' he gasped as Rami stood and towered over the ebony chair.

Khofir opened his mouth to call out, but Rami's hands were too quick. They closed around the Prince's throat before he could utter a sound. He began to press down on muscle and bone.

He felt the flesh itself give way. A single, drawn-out choking sound issued from Khofir's throat. His chest twisted and went still and his eyes bulged from a face gone dark with blood.

As abruptly as it had set upon Rami, the fire drained from his heart.

Rami's legs, thin and weak again, seemed to give out from under him, and he sat down and smothered a wail with both hands. 'Great Re,' he whispered, looking to the mural. Why had the once merciful god driven him to this?

Panic seized him when he heard footsteps fall outside the door, heard the high-pitched voice of the eunuch.

Rami's heart nearly stalled in his chest as the carved door swung slowly open.

'Your morning meal, My Lord,' the eunuch said, walking in with a platter.

Closing his eyes, Rami sucked in a breath and prepared himself to die. He heard a deep voice answer from across the chamber.

'You may leave it by the bed,' Khofir replied.

Rami's mouth dropped. Spinning around, he gaped at the figure sitting upright in the ebony chair. If Khofir hadn't died after all, Rami might well meet a fate worse than any the Pharaoh's heartless ministers could devise.

Rami prepared to slip out of the door and sprint past the Nubian. Hearing him move, the eunuch looked at him. The eunuch cocked a silky eyebrow at him, and then at Khofir's chair. 'Master?' he asked.

Khofir held up a hand. 'Leave us, eunuch,' he said.

Rami stood rooted to the spot, his body trembling uncontrollably. Khofir, his hand still extended, moved towards Rami. Stunned into paralysis, the lad searched the Prince's face with astonishment. The deathly blush had vanished from Khofir's cheeks and eyes, and the marks from Rami's angry hands had faded from the smooth curve of his neck. Rami had never seen marks disappear so quickly. Perhaps Khofir, like Pharaoh, really was the living limbs of the Divine Ones.

Either that, or –

Understanding broke over him like the sun. Fingers cupped Rami's chin. Sternly, yet with an underlying gentleness Khofir had never displayed in life, they tilted the naked slave's face to meet his own. Rami saw the flames leaping in dark-red, otherworldly eyes.

'You have always served me well, Rami,' the Great One informed him. 'You and your father both.'

'Yes, Lord,' Rami whispered. His voice caught in his throat. The Divine One had no need of words. He understood everything – past, present and future. A future Rami would now devote completely to him. 'But my master Khofir?'

'From now on,' Khofir's voice answered, though the words were unmistakably the god's, 'you shall have but one master.'

And Amon Re's full lips curled into a smile as he brought them down, hard and hot as the vibrant sun itself, on Rami's.

The People of the Empty Places

J. D. Ryan

'Those who enter the forbidden gorge seldom return, young sir. Those who do –' the Tuareg chieftain paused, his ancient eyes dark above his veil '– are changed.'

I rolled my eyes. It was bad enough I had to spend the summer in the middle of the Sahara desert with Uncle Russ and his boring anthropology project – now the nomad tribesmen were feeding me bullshit about haunted canyons! For crying out loud, I was nineteen, not nine! I shoved my fringe back out of my face with a sigh.

Why did all the guys my age have to be gone to some stupid oasis with the tribe's goats, anyway? If I didn't get away from all this aged wisdom for a few hours, I was going to explode.

I shrugged away the old man's final warning: 'The People of the Empty Places are real! Seek them at your peril.' Sounded to me like he'd been watching too many old horror movies – if they even had television out here in the wilderness!

Barely an hour after sunset, I was skipping towards the forbidden gorge, my heart thumping with excitement. I got clear of the camp before switching on my torch, then I took a deep breath. Even the dusty air tasted better now that I was free.

The eerie wail of a native flute echoed from the canyon ahead, raising the hairs on the back of my neck. OK, so it was a little spooky – but 'People of the Empty Places'? I snorted. Anyway, the Tuareg were so damn scared of the wasteland – why would any of them claim to live there? I shrugged. If whoever was in the canyon had music and dancing, they were one up on the Tuareg.

The rhythm of the drums thumped through me. I slipped into the gorge and followed it upwards, my feet rolling on loose rock and gravel. Something inside me uncoiled at the beat, a slowly rising heat that started in my groin and spread. I rounded a bend and saw a campfire ahead of me. The drums throbbed louder, echoing off the dark canyon walls. This was the kind of music you had to dance to – and the people in front of me were doing just that.

I stepped into the orange glow of the fire. Lithe, brown bodies wove in and out of the light, twisting to the pounding beat. Bare feet slapped the sand, bodies flew into unbelievable spinning leaps.

'Oh, man, I must have died and gone to heaven,' I said aloud. A laugh bubbled up inside me and I was grinning like a fool as I moved towards the fire.

Hands reached out to pull me into the dance, passing me a bottle of something that seared my throat when I drank. Voices rang out in song and laughter. I didn't understand the language, but – what the hell! – we were having a good time.

I eventually tore myself from the circle and stumbled, dizzy from dance and liquor, to the nearest boulder. A slender dancer followed, a bottle in one fist, snickering at my attempts to sit on the boulder without sliding off.

He righted me, running his free hand down the front of my shirt and helping me on to the sand with the boulder behind me for support. He murmured something in a soft, musical voice.

I shook my head and grinned. 'You got some really fine booze, man.'

He reached out, touched my forehead with one finger. A tingle like static electricity stirred my fringe. 'You are a good dancer for a white man,' he said slowly. 'What is your name?'

'I'm Allen. Hey – you speak English!'

'I'm Radwane.' He smiled and shrugged. 'I didn't speak English – I took it from you.'

I glanced at him with one eyebrow raised. Sure he didn't speak it! His was as pure an American accent as mine.

He leaned closer, and I could smell booze and cinnamon on his breath. Thick black hair cascaded over us as he threw one arm about my shoulders and lowered himself to sit next to me. My hand rose of its own accord to that silky mane.

My eyes widened as I caught myself, snatching my fingers away as though they'd been burned. Hell, I must be drunk, thinking like some queer! I grabbed Radwane's bottle and took another long gulp, searing what was left of my tonsils away. I glanced at my new friend as I drank, trying to study him without looking like a pansy.

Strong, white teeth showed in a grin as he stared boldly back. The face framed by that waterfall of black hair was elfin, almost girlish. Wide black eyes, high cheekbones, thick lips that needed kissing . . . I hastily took another swig of the brew, and shook my head to clear it. Back home, the only bodies I lusted after had big tits and no dicks. I glanced at Radwane, confused.

A silver ring in his left nostril caught the firelight as he turned his head to meet my gaze. He probably wore earrings, too, though I couldn't see under all that hair. I wanted to pull back that black curtain to see, wanted to fill my hands with dark hair. I wanted to bury my face in it.

My face flamed at the realisation. I turned my attention to the other dancers, trying to ignore the throbbing between my legs.

'You are pretty,' Radwane said suddenly, reaching out for the bottle. I'd had it to my lips, and choked on my swallow. I whirled towards him, fist raised to defend my manhood. Radwane just grinned and closed his fist over mine on the neck of the bottle.

'Your skin is like the milk from my finest camel,' he murmured, his fingers moving over mine. 'Your hair is like fire.'

My heart thudded in my throat. His fingers were so long – so strong. I felt a rush of heat from my groin. My cock wanted those fingers!

Radwane leaned over and planted his wide lips on mine. His tongue slipped inside before I could react. My whole body stiffened with surprise. He tasted like cinnamon and nutmeg, like some exotic dessert. I closed my eyes and leaned into the kiss. His tongue explored my mouth as we devoured each other, shoving against the roof of my mouth like he wanted to crawl inside me.

His hands unbuttoned my shirt. I flinched. Soft lips caressed my ear as he wrapped his arms around me and pulled me closer.

'Haven't you ever done it with a man before? It's better than with a woman. Let me show you how much better it is.'

Oh, God! I looked at that pretty face next to mine, and something inside me melted. I wanted to learn what this dark stranger was offering to teach me. He started nuzzling my neck, burrowing underneath my hair to nibble behind my ear. I shivered as his tongue probed an area I hadn't even known I wanted touched. We slipped down on to the sand.

'Just – don't try sticking anything up my ass,' I mumbled as I surrendered. I could feel my face flaming as hot as the campfire. I couldn't believe this was happening. A month ago, I'd been trying to get into that cheerleader's pants at the ballgame – now some strange Arab was about to get into mine! I gasped as his hand slipped beneath my belt to cup my ass. His other hand quickly unfastened the belt and wrestled my shorts down around my knees.

The chill of the night air raised the hair on my balls. I struggled for a moment, trying to convince myself that I didn't want this.

Radwane was surprisingly strong for such a little guy, though. His arm clamped me against the sand like a vice. Then his hand slid back up my chest and those strong fingers found my left nipple.

A flare of heat rushed from the nub as he tugged and teased. I groaned and lay back, letting him unbutton my shirt. My cock pumped into life, rising to full-mast in the cool air. Radwane moved his mouth to my other nipple and slurped noisily. His tongue flickered like the flames of the campfire, igniting the heat in my balls.

A shadow fell over us. My eyes widened as I glanced at the dancer standing above us. I shoved against Radwane, trying to warn him. He merely raised his head for a quick look, then returned his attention to my chest.

The newcomer seemed a creature of gold and bronze. His ears sported golden rings in a line clear up to their pointed tips. The lower rings were linked by thin chains to rings in each nostril and each thick, black eyebrow was puckered twice by more gold rings. Brass beads adorned the ends of his hair, and gold and bronze chains encircled his neck. He wore no shirt and I could see that each nipple was pierced with a bronze ring. He grinned down at me.

My lust-fogged brain struggled to communicate with me. *Pointed* ears? 'Who – what are you?' I gasped, struggling to shove Radwane away.

'You know,' came the reply in a forceful baritone. 'It was you who chose to enter our sacred place. You wanted to meet the djinn, and now you have.'

I managed to wriggle out from under Radwane long enough to sit up. 'There's no such thing as djinn!' I protested.

'Then you have nothing to worry about, no?'

Radwane giggled, then dived downwards, his hot mouth nuzzling the root of my cock. I scooted backwards, staring up at the newcomer and trying to escape. He hoisted a bare foot to my shoulder and forced me flat on to the sand again. His foot pinned me down. Radwane acted like the two of us were alone, sucking on my balls like a kid with a piece of candy.

'You knew this was forbidden ground,' the one standing over me stated. 'Are you willing to pay the price of your trespass?'

I tried shaking my head. I didn't wake up. This must be some sort of hallucination – maybe they slipped something into my drink! Radwane's mouth closed over my cock, swallowing me down in one stroke. My body was ignoring my growing alarm and responding to that hot mouth. My hips shoved forward, driving my cock deeper into the waiting throat.

'Wait,' I managed to gasp. Radwane paused, glancing up from between my legs with a mischievous grin. I took a deep breath and looked upwards.

'Dad's rich,' I told them. 'How much do you want?'

The one above me scowled, hands on his hips. 'You agree to pay the price, then?'

I sighed, then shrugged. 'Sure, whatever. Just don't tell my uncle.' My cock wanted that mouth back.

The foot atop my chest slid aside, and I sat up. Radwane made no move towards my cock, so I reached for my shorts, now bunched around my ankles. He grabbed my wrists.

'Never mind that,' his soft voice purred. 'I'm not finished yet.'

'Neither am I,' the baritone said firmly. I gasped as a wave of dizziness swept over me. The air seemed to darken and whirl around me. Electricity crackled, making my hair stand on end. Then the light returned.

The three of us were – elsewhere. Somehow, we'd gotten inside, though the room was like nothing I'd seen outside of some movie sets. Soft yellow light spilled from huge brass lamps to tint the room gold. Ornate tapestries draped every wall, cascading over one another in a riot of clashing colours. The floor was awash in pillows of every imaginable hue.

'I'm in charge here,' the baritone said, 'so you may call me Master.'

'I don't call anybody master!' I growled and shoved my elbows against the floor. I got halfway up before he placed one hand against the centre of my chest and effortlessly pushed me down again. His fingers moved to my nipples, twisting viciously. I yelped.

Radwane ran his hands over my hips, snuggled his face into my pubes.

'Allen, you must not resist,' he told me. 'You agreed to pay for trespassing.'

'Goddamn you!' I shouted, and kicked out as hard as I could. Radwane fell back, clutching his crotch. The other djinn grabbed my wrist, hauling me to my feet and dragging me towards a small door in the opposite wall.

'Time to learn who is master,' he growled, gripping my arm so tightly I felt his nails bite through the skin. I flailed wildly with one arm. The djinn backhanded me across the face, then shoved me through the doorway.

The shock of the blow took my breath. I stood dazed for a moment. This room was much darker, lit only by a single lamp hanging from the ceiling. Other things hung from the ceiling and walls too – things that made my balls cringe upwards. Thick iron chains, many with manacles attached, dangled from heavy hooks. A low padded bench squatted in the far corner, arm and leg restraints attached to its base. A sturdy table along the left wall displayed instruments whose purpose I didn't want to guess at.

The leader hauled me to the table and selected a studded collar, like a dog would wear.

'You will learn to enjoy submitting, Allen,' Radwane murmured, kissing my cheeks. His partner fastened the collar around my neck and snapped a chain on to it. I was so dumbfounded that I didn't resist as each of them took one of my hands and strapped my wrists with leather bands.

I struggled as I felt my arms hauled towards the ceiling, but by then it was too late. They had me standing on tiptoe in no time. I felt like some insane condor perched on a mountain ledge with his wings spread. Only I wasn't going anywhere. Radwane slipped in between me and the wall. His lips moved over my face.

'I thought you were my friend!' I groaned, twisting my head away.

'I am your friend,' he insisted, running his hands down my chest. 'I want to help you learn to obey; I want to show you pleasure.'

'Too much noise,' the leader said and plucked an odd strap from the table. A large bronze figure, with the green patina of age, stood out in the middle of it. I stared at it in horror. It was moulded into the shape of a short, fat penis, complete with wide head. I could guess where he planned on putting that thing and I sure as hell didn't want it there.

The djinn shoved the thing against my lips. I groaned as my jaws were forced open around it. The sharp tang of metal filled my mouth. I tossed my head frantically, trying to spit the horrid thing back out. Radwane fastened the strap behind my head, giving me a soothing pat like I was a dog.

My eyes widened as I watched the djinn with all the metal trimmings reach out a hand. The whip from the bench floated across the room to fall into his hand like it had come home.

He grinned and held the whip up for me to study. It looked as though it was made of dozens of strands of stiff rawhide cord. He tapped the hilt against his palm a few times, then reached out to whisk the thing across my chest.

The rough fibres brushed against my nipples and I sucked in a breath at the sensation. Radwane gasped also, and I glanced to where he was watching with fascination, his eyes following each move of the whip. His cock had swelled beneath his loincloth, and I could see a growing stain on the leather. In my mind he was a traitor. And he was getting off on this.

His strong fingers reached out to strip away what was left of my clothing, ripping my shirt in his haste. He wrapped his hand around the base of my wilted cock. My face flamed, and I kicked out, forgetting I was on tiptoe. Radwane grinned as my full weight slammed down on my imprisoned wrists.

I grunted, but managed not to cry out at the sudden strain. My shoulders were on fire by the time I regained my feet. Radwane's hand never left my cock, and I blushed even deeper as I realised my body was again responding to his treatment. Already my cock was filling with hot blood, thickening beneath those long fingers. My breathing quickened as the whip suddenly slapped across my chest, just hard enough to sting without really hurting. The leader set up a slow rhythm, his lash tingling against my nipples and belly. Radwane's thumb slid over the head of my cock in time with the lash.

I squirmed in anguish, wanting my degradation to end. My cock swelled, leaking – it wanted more.

The djinn leader moved behind me and, before I could understand what that meant, the whip was laid across my back with real force. The thin fibres stung like a hive of bees, and my whole body trembled at the new pain. Shock shot through my body like electricity. I twisted frantically, trying to get away from the next blow.

My feet slid from under me. This time I couldn't hold back the groan. My ravaged back burned as though each stripe had been made with a hot wire. And there wasn't a damn thing I could do to stop them! With a sob, I gave up, hanging limply until Radwane helped me balance on my toes once more. I whimpered as the lash descended again, but I didn't try to escape. I accepted that I'd agreed to their punishment.

Tears ran down my cheeks. My body shook with each blow, then quivered with my sobs. By the time the master was finished, I could barely breathe for crying.

Radwane made some sort of adjustment over my head, and I could stand normally again, though my arms were still held above me. My calves and insteps burned at the sudden return of weight. I wrapped my hands around the chains and sagged in my bonds.

'Are you going to take your punishment now?' the djinn master asked, moving to face me. Face scarlet with shame, I shook my head in acquiescence. He laid aside the whip and stepped close, raising my chin so that we were eye to eye. He began to kiss away my tears. My body trembled with relief. I melted into his caress.

Radwane sponged my abused flesh with soft cloths, moistened in some soothing liquid. He kissed each welt on my throbbing back. I groaned into the gag, new tears streaking my cheeks as the pain subsided. Radwane ran his tongue along my right side and into my sweaty armpit, while the leader moved his mouth down to my belly. They sucked noisily, slurping the salt from my skin. My sobs slowly died away, though my body still trembled with spasms of aftershock.

The two began to work my body in tandem, playing my flesh like some musical instrument. Radwane, at my back, ran his hands along my butt, shoving his fingers into the crack. The leader's fingers tugged at my balls, stretching them away from my body, then squeezing them gently. I flinched as the master joined Radwane, his hands kneading the muscles of my ass. The djinn spread my legs apart.

I jerked when I felt a tongue caressing the wrinkled folds at the entrance to my asshole. One of the djinn slapped my ass cheek hard enough to wring a gasp from me. I struggled, earning a slap on the other cheek. I got the idea. I relaxed my buttocks and allowed the tongue to rim my hole. Strong hands pulled my cheeks farther apart. Hot breath stirred my pucker, making the skin on my balls crawl upwards. My eyes widened as I felt a tongue slide inside, like some slippery animal oozing past my sphincter.

I sucked in a deep breath, and my cock sprang to full length.

The master had found my hard-on switch. I spread wider and he thrust again, twisting and licking until I screamed into the gag. Radwane slid around to face me, returning his hands to my throbbing nipples.

The tongue in my ass kept probing. I was sure there was some place deep inside that needed to be touched – that would explode if the master would but touch it. I spread my legs, straining to take him in further, and, when he suddenly pulled his tongue away, I squirmed in frustration.

'I want you to see what you truly desire,' the master said, stepping into view once more. He dropped the baggy pants, and I felt my balls draw up in surprise. I stared at the instrument of my coming initiation and felt the beginning of fear.

His cock, a lot larger than mine, was fully erect. Blue veins bulged along its length, its huge purple head already wet. The skin of his shaft was studded with little bronze balls, encircling the knob, and embedded in parallel rows along the length of his shaft. His balls sported brass rings, linked with a chain. The thought of taking that monster up my ass made my blood run cold.

'You will want this inside you,' he promised.

'Oh, yes, Allen,' Radwane said, tweaking first one nub and then the other. 'You'll see. You won't need the chains next time.'

At a grunt from the master, Radwane scampered to the table, returning with a bronze flask. The master poured a thin stream of oil into Radwane's cupped palms, then began to oil his own massive tool. I whimpered, unable to look away. I could feel my asshole clamp shut.

Radwane grinned, wrapping his hands around my cock once more. His long fingers set up a firm, steady pressure that quickly had me trembling. My cock rose under his ministrations, and my hips jerked, thrusting my cock between his slippery hands.

The master oiled his hands also, and stepped behind me. I tried not to whimper. I felt his hands slide between my legs, and forced myself to relax. After all, his tongue had felt great; maybe a finger would feel just as good.

I groaned as his finger slipped inside my butt. It wasn't just as good – it was better! I spread my legs as wide as I could, wanting him to go deeper. That spot deep within my ass throbbed, and something inside me shouted, 'Yes!' This was what I wanted after all.

No, I wanted his whole damned hand in there, reaching for that spot. I felt a second finger push at the opening of my canal and shoved backwards to take it in. When the master started moving in time with Radwane's rhythm, thrusting in and out, I tried to help him. I wanted to be able to talk, wanted to tell him to give me more fingers. I nodded frantically when I felt him push the third one in beside the other two.

Without warning, the fingers slid from my ass, and I sobbed.

'Don't worry, I'm not finished, my slave,' he said, reaching around me to pick up the bottle of oil again. He wiped his hands across my chest, pinching a nipple as he did. I couldn't see what he was doing, and started to sweat. My heart pounded, waiting for it. Radwane slowed his massage of my cock, and stared into my face until I blushed.

'I want to see your expression when he enters you,' Radwane whispered. 'Then I will pleasure you again while he takes you.'

I felt hands at my waist, positioning me. I looked into Radwane's eyes with confusion. I ought to be terrified, ought to be screaming. Instead, I was wondering if that huge cock could reach the spot throbbing inside my ass.

'You want it, don't you?' Radwane asked, and I nodded my head. He kissed my cheek, and one hand returned to caress my knob. 'Push down when he enters – then it won't hurt.'

The swollen head of that massive dick pressed against my asshole. I swallowed hard and pushed down. I still felt a flash of pain as the head slipped inside, stretching me further than I'd imagined possible.

Every muscle in my body jerked at the sensation. It felt like I was splitting in half. The master stopped and caressed my chest until my ass muscle had adjusted to his invasion, then he shoved slowly inside. I could feel every one of those bronze balls as they pushed into my virgin hole.

My legs were shoved even further apart, and I nearly lost my balance. It felt like I was taking a steel baseball bat up my ass, like I was trying to shit a telephone pole. I groaned as he kept shoving more into me. Radwane's lips were on my knob, flicking and tickling. I started to relax into his rhythm.

Once I stopped fighting it, the master's cock slid up my asshole like it belonged. I realised with a pang that took my breath that it did belong there. That cock was touching the spot, rubbing what wanted to be rubbed. Radwane sighed as he saw it on my face – I liked having a cock inside me. He started working on my meat with abandon and I started enjoying what the master was doing in my ass.

His bush tickled my cheeks. I could feel that huge dick reaching up my gut – it felt like it reached nearly to my throat. I knew what was coming and nodded. Hell, yes, fuck me good.

His hands holding me steady, the master began pumping my butt, his flesh slapping my ass cheeks with each stroke. Radwane steadied me on the front, pumping my cock with his oiled fingers. The djinn who'd betrayed me to myself reached one hand between my legs. He began running his thumbnail along the flesh between my balls and my filled asshole. I didn't know if I could live through such pleasure but knew I'd die a happy man.

I strained against my bonds, this time trying to fully participate. The master grunted with his efforts, his sweaty groin slamming against me as he thrust his meat deep into my ass. I was grunting into my gag, shoving backwards to meet him, taking him as hard as I could. Radwane milked my cock, waiting to be showered with my come. I screamed around the gag as I felt my climax rising.

The master increased his pace, slamming against my buttocks. My body trembled uncontrollably; I could only hang and let them take me. Lava rose in my balls – molten steel, liquid fire. My cock jerked with the force of the eruption, spraying gallons of jizz over Radwane's hands, thick and hot. My breath stopped; my heart pounded. I groaned and quivered.

Just when I thought the world would end, I felt the molten eruption of my master's release filling me. He pulled me tight to his chest, burying his face in my hair, and shoved hard, his hips jerking with the force of his climax. I trembled with him, leaning into his embrace. God help me, I wanted him. I wanted his rod up my ass every chance I could get.

Radwane supported my limp body as the master released my chains. They helped me to a low bench. As I reached weakly to remove the gag, the djinn master grabbed my wrist. I flinched, expecting more punishment.

'Who am I?' he asked, yanking the thing from my mouth. I rubbed my jaw, wincing at the pain of strained muscle. Then I leaned forward.

'You're the master,' I whispered, burying my face in his pubes. He smelled of musk and sand, like the desert in human form – and of come and sex.

The master grinned. 'Excellent,' he said. 'You're a fast learner. But now I think you might need a lesson in cocksucking.' He pulled Radwane close and unfastened the other's trousers.

I grinned at him as I reached for the other djinn. 'You're the master,' I said again.

Changing Death

Shane D. Yorston

Thanatos landed on the battlefield with blood in his eye as the screams of the dead and dying filled the smoky air. And fell immediately, his feet flying out from under him. He lay where he'd landed, cursing up a blue streak, his voice muffled by the blood-soaked gore and dirt he was face down in.

'Damned berserkers! Never watch the mess they make!' He spat out grit and other unmentionable bits, wiped the gore from his face and started to rise with the deliberate motions of someone unsure of how co-operative their knees were at the moment. He leaned on his staff and ignored the complaints of his joints and spine.

'Arrrgh!' a weak voice muttered beside him.

'Easy for you to say,' Thanatos sighed as the man he'd tripped over died. After countless millennia of seeing humans at the end of their individual ropes, Death had developed a somewhat warped sense of humour. Once upright, he looked over his soiled tunic and robes and threw his hand in the air. 'Look at me! Ares is going to pay for the cleaning, that's all I know.'

'Glllrrrk!'

The old god of death looked down at the warrior he'd tripped over and sighed. 'Still hanging on I see. Ah well, work's never done, is it?' He gingerly kneeled before the warrior and reached towards and through the man, withdrawing the glittering orb of the mortal's soul. He stared at the little thing for a moment, examining the contents of the life he'd just ended and then spat more grit back into the blood-soaked earth. 'Same collection of foolishness as most.'

He let the ball of the soul fall from his wrinkled hand and watched as it sank into the earth, on its way to Tartarus, where it would be judged and filed away to be forgotten.

Thanatos slowly made it to his feet, his shoulders and back giving him more grief than he felt even Death deserved. 'There's got to be more than this!' he exclaimed to the dead in general, though they weren't too supportive, or even vocal, in their response. 'I mean, I knew I didn't exactly draw the long straw on this one. Zeus got the throne, Poseidon got the seas and earthquakes, and Hades got Tartarus. Even the kids drew better than me. Apollo got the sun, Aphrodite love, Athena wisdom. And I got death. Cheery.'

He bent painfully again and started to draw yet another soul from the dying when he heard his name called. 'Thanatos!'

He looked up and saw a woman approaching over the humped remains of the armies raging battle about him. She moved quickly and efficiently, like a prowling beast. He wasn't surprised to see it was Artemis when she stopped in front of him.

'I'm glad I found you, Uncle. I need your help.'

He nodded. 'Only time anyone bothers with me is when they want something. So, who did Aphrodite kill this time?'

'How did you know it was her?' asked Artemis, cocking her head to one side.

Thanatos shrugged. 'That girl's got a big body count for a goddess of love. She'll make Ares jealous before long.'

'She's an ignorant snot is what she is,' replied Artemis. 'She's killed a youth I rather like.'

Thanatos did a discreet double take. 'For a minute there I could have sworn you said youth. As in male.'

Artemis the chaste nodded, looking a little uncomfortable. 'I've never done anything with him. He just – well – worshipped me. He said he'd never have any woman and considered me to be the only one he could ever love.' She hastened to add, 'Not physi-cally, mind you.'

Thanatos nodded. 'Uh huh. And your sister got her knickers in a bunch over him and he kissed her off. So how did she do him?'

Artemis sighed. 'No imagination at all. She made the step-mother fall in love with him. The woman then killed herself and the youth got blamed. His father exiled him and then he was attacked by a sea monster as he left his father's domain.'

Thanatos sighed. 'So Poseidon was in on it as well. Zeus will not be happy. He dotes on Aphrodite, but hates it when she starts getting the others to do her dirty work for her.'

Artemis nodded. 'Anyway, can you help?'

Thanatos looked around the battlefield and its mostly unmoving inhabitants. 'They aren't going anywhere, I guess. Where is he and what exactly do you want me to do?'

'Well, I've already spoken with Aescalapius. He's willing to heal the youth, but I need to make sure his soul doesn't get sent off to Uncle Hades before Aescalapius is done with him.'

Thanatos sighed. 'And I suppose Big Brother doesn't know about any of this? You realise what he'll do when he learns that humans have started raising themselves from the dead?'

Artemis shrugged. 'He'll be mad at first, but he'll get over it. I've already cleared it with the Fates.'

Thanatos winced. 'Going over his head as well. I'd suggest you hie yourself off to some place lightning-proof where he won't find you – as soon as you can.'

'So you will help?'

He nodded. 'This young buck must have meant a lot to you. OK. Where have you got him stashed?'

'Come with me. I took him to Mount Pelion and Aescalapius. We'd better hurry.' She looked over his gory tunic and robes. 'By the way, what happened to you? Lending a hand in the festivities?'

'Long story.' Thanatos raised his staff and struck the earth three times, careful not to puncture any spleens or kidneys that might be lying about.

The air about them rippled and the battlefield melted away, replaced with the pristine beauty of Mount Pelion and its forested foothills. The first thing Thanatos noticed was the body. There wasn't much left of it.

'He's missing parts,' he stated with the technical appraisal of one who had literally seen it all.

'Aesculapius said it wouldn't be a problem.'

'Not for him maybe, but this fellow might miss his legs. Don't suppose you could get them back, though.'

Artemis shook her head. 'His soul is still there though, isn't it?'

Thanatos bent slowly, his back popping noisily. 'Damned bones. Ah, yes. Here it is.' He drew out the ball of light that was this youth's soul and that rose like a flower that hadn't quite got the finer points of phototropism worked out. He studied it a moment and slowly smiled. 'Ganymede would have liked this one.'

Artemis sniffed. 'If you're into that sort of thing, I suppose so.'

Thanatos chuckled as he looked over the remains of the youth he now knew was named Hippolytus. He was well made, or at least what was left of him was. Dark blond hair framed a face that seemed carved from ivory. His eyes were closed in the repose of – well – death, not to put too fine a point on it. The beast that had attacked him had torn the tunic from his body and he lay naked on the ground. He was broad-chested and his stomach was taut. He'd been severed, just below the hips. What remained of his legs looked as if they had been strongly muscled. Not surprising, now that Thanatos thought on it. He seemed to remember the family.

The boy's father was the mortal hero Theseus and his mother was Hippolyta.

Normally Thanatos didn't find himself attracted to his clients; he might have a warped sense of humour, but he wasn't *that* warped. This Hippolytus was something else, however – even with only half the package to view. If Thanatos had been a few aeons younger and Hippolytus wasn't – well – dead . . .

But then if Aescalapius could bring him back . . .

'Well, I suppose we should go get the healer,' Artemis said, breaking Thanatos's train of thought.

'Hmmm?' Death looked up, fastening his rheumy gaze on his niece. 'Oh, yes. Of course.'

He turned to face the mountain and noticed the small dwelling sitting in its shadow. He walked smartly towards the building, the pain in his back and hips forgotten. He rapped on the door with his staff and was told by whoever was inside to hold on a minute.

'He does know we're coming, doesn't he?' he asked the slim, boyish goddess beside him.

Artemis nodded slowly and started studying a sandalled foot.

The door was opened by a middle-aged man with greying hair, dressed in a long white tunic and robe. He held a pestle in one hand and looked put out by the sudden distraction of someone knocking on his door. He stared at the two deities a moment before recognition kicked in.

'Thanatos! Artemis! What brings you here?'

Thanatos looked to his niece sternly. 'He knew we were coming, eh?'

'Well, no. But he can help. I know it.'

'And the Fates?' Thanatos persisted. 'They've cleared this?'

Artemis nodded. 'Yes. For real.'

'Cleared what?' asked Aescalapius. 'What's going on here?'

Artemis spoke up. 'You have to help, healer. A youth who was a favourite of mine was slain by Aphrodite and Poseidon. Unjustly. I need you to restore him.'

Aescalapius motioned them into his house and quickly took a seat. 'Let me get this straight. You want me to heal a dead man. As in no pulse, no breath, and extremely unworried about what the morning after is going to feel like?'

Artemis nodded. 'You're the best there is. You did a marvellous job on Eros that time. You can hardly tell where Aphrodite ate his shoulder. It was so embarrassing. She said she'd never tasted anything better.'

'Eros is a god. I take it this youth is mortal.'

'Hippolytus. Son of Theseus and Hippolyta. That's got to count for something.'

Aescalapius sighed and tapped one foot. 'I'll see what I can do.'

The healer was going to be a while so Thanatos left them to clear off the backlog he had piling up, promising Artemis that he'd not let Hippolytus's soul out of his sight.

He didn't either. He couldn't stop thinking of the youth as he

215

removed soul after soul from the dead. The youth's face and body, or what had been left, kept entering his mind until he realised he was all caught up with giving relief to the dying.

Oh, people were still dying in the world; but, at the moment, no one was officially dead. For the first time he could remember, Thanatos had free time on his hands.

He was standing at the bottom of a cliff; the sea rushed on the rocks and the sun was westering. In all it was a beautiful scene. For aeons now, Thanatos hadn't had much time for anything other than the job. It hadn't always been like this. In his younger days, he'd been able to stay abreast of mortal folly and brevity with ease.

He unconsciously moved to take Hippolytus's soul from the pouch at his hip and stared at the thing. He watched the life the youth had lived, every moment. But it wasn't enough, for some reason. He licked his lips and wondered at what he'd come to. He'd never had thoughts like this about a client.

He closed his eyes and tossed the soul into the air. Instead of falling towards the underworld, the soul stopped about three feet from the ground and started glowing brightly. The light took shape and, before long, Hippolytus – or, rather, the memory of what Hippolytus had been – stood before Thanatos. Since he had to take the form he most recently remembered, he was clothed in a tunic and sandals, his muscled legs whole now and certainly worth looking at.

'Ghosting. Has it come to this?'

Hippolytus looked at death and smiled. Thanatos felt parts of his body he'd thought long – well – dead come back to life. 'You're Death, aren't you?' The youth's voice was strong and steady, no trace of fear or confusion colouring it.

Thanatos nodded. 'Sorry about that, but I don't have much choice about it.'

Hippolytus nodded. 'I guess not. I mean you don't kill people; you just clean up what's left over.'

Now what? Thanatos thought. He's here, but what do I do? It had been a long time since he'd entertained a handsome young man.

'You know, you're not what I thought you'd be like,' Hippolytus said as he walked a short distance down the beach.

'How so?' asked Death.

'Well, you know – a big, dark being, scythe in hand, ready to slice up the world. At least that's what everyone says you're like.'

Thanatos grunted. 'As if my shoulders were up to handling a scythe.'

'Your shoulders look fine to me.' Somehow, Hippolytus had come up on Thanatos without his noticing and now stood very close. 'In fact they look very fine to me.'

With that he bent forward and kissed the god of death on the lips. Thanatos was momentarily shocked. Then instinct kicked in and he returned the kiss. When it broke, the god was somewhat short of breath.

'An old man like me?' he gasped as he stared at the beautiful youth. 'I'm not exactly what I thought you'd go for.'

Hippolytus laughed. 'Old? You don't look all that old to me.'

Thanatos shook his head. That was when he noticed his hands where they rested on Hippolytus's chest. They weren't wrinkled. They weren't spotted. They no longer were swollen with arthritis. They were clean and smooth and . . . young.

He took a step back from the youth. 'What happened? I've never done this before.'

Hippolytus cocked his head and smiled knowingly. 'I have lots of times. I can show you.'

'No, not that! This!' He gestured to his body with a sweep of his hands.

It was all young. 'I'm as old as the universe. I normally look like a raisin.'

Hippolytus laughed. 'I like grapes much better than raisins. Preferably plump ones.'

Thanatos stared at the youth. He knew that, somehow, he was responsible for this. In a forever of service, Death had given the gift of release to humanity. This was the first time anyone had ever given him something in return.

Hippolytus didn't have to do much more convincing after that. Thanatos let go of wondering how his youth had been restored and got down to the basics of what to do with it now that he had it back.

Hippolytus stripped him slowly and Thanatos revelled in his new body. The youth kissed him again and worked his way down, covering his neck and shoulders with kisses as his hands teased Thanatos's nipples. His tongue followed his fingers, which moved lower to tease other parts of Thanatos's body, trailing through the short hairs on his belly as his marvellously adept fingers stroked the insides of his thighs.

The youth smiled up at him as he kneeled before him. 'Plums I like too.'

'Indeed,' sighed Thanatos as the youth engulfed a ball with his lips. He was painfully hard, his cock digging into his navel and his knees growing weak.

Hippolytus cupped the globes of the god's arse, squeezing and kneading as his mouth left one orb for the other. By the time Hippolytus slipped his tongue inside Thanatos's foreskin and spread it across the bulb of his prick, the god of death was ready to explode.

He put a halting hand on the youth's head and sighed deeply. Pulling away, he sat on the sand of the beach and pulled Hippolytus down for more kisses. This time he was the one who teased and licked his way over every inch of that perfect body. Hippolytus, for his part, lay back with his hands behind his head as Thanatos laved his navel and then proceeded to sample a set of plums himself.

Of course, by the time they got worked up enough to want to fuck, they were too covered in sand to do anything about it. Bringing death was one thing, sanding a cock in a hole was another. So, they stuck with tongues, mouths and fingers until Thanatos couldn't hold back any longer. After all, it had been literally millennia since his last bit of tail. His orgasm was, needless to say, life renewing. He was just sorry it was over.

They bathed in the surf, though Hippolytus didn't really need to worry about it. Thanatos dressed and stood watching the youth pull his tunic on. 'You realise that I have to put you back now,' he said quietly.

Hippolytus smiled and nodded. 'I hope Aescalapius is finished.

I realise that you've never done this before for anyone. Thank you.' He moved to kiss Thanatos again.

Thanatos let the kiss linger, a promise for the future, and then 'pushed'. Hippolytus collapsed back into the ball of light that was his soul and Thanatos stood staring at it for a long time.

'Damn Aphrodite! And Eros as well. Wherever you are.'

He returned to Mount Pelion and Aescalapius's dwelling and knocked on the door. Artemis answered and stared at him with a puzzled expression.

'May I help you, boy?'

Thanatos snorted. 'No need to get flippant, missy. How's the healer doing with this youth of ours?'

'Uncle?' she yelped, staring at him in surprise. 'Is that you?'

Thanatos frowned. 'Who else would I be? Last I looked I hadn't switched places with Gaea.'

Artemis stepped back and let him enter the house, her expression still shocked. 'Have you looked at yourself recently?'

'Of course I have. It's not every day I get aeons shaved off. I'm still not sure how it was managed, though. I was never much for all the shape-shifting the others get into. You think that might be it?'

Artemis smiled. 'I don't know, but I like the results, Uncle.'

He chuckled. 'Keep this up and your reputation will be ruined.'

She snorted again and shook her head. 'Men.'

'You didn't answer my question. How's the healer getting along?'

She shrugged. 'I haven't seen him in hours. He won't let me into the workroom at all. Rather pushy for a mortal.'

'There, there, dear. He knows what he's doing.'

She smiled at that. 'You sound funny.'

He sighed. 'I hope I haven't gone too far back. Puberty once was enough.'

At that, Aescalapius entered the room, his shoulders drooped and his face covered with perspiration. 'Done. He's back in one piece.' He looked to Thanatos and frowned. 'I'm sorry, boy, but I don't think I can help you just now. I'll need a bit of rest. Unless it's something serious.'

Thanatos smiled. 'It's me, Aescalapius. Thanatos.'

The healer did a double take and shook his head. 'I'll not ask. If you've got the soul ready for Hippolytus, he's all yours.'

'Right here,' he patted the pouch at his hip and smiled when the hip didn't protest.

Hippolytus was laid out on a table, his body naked as it had been before. But this time there was more of it. Considerably more, Thanatos noted as his gaze slipped to the youth's crotch. In the actual flesh, the lad's endowment was quite impressive.

His earlier encounter with Hippolytus had been with whatever it was the youth remembered of himself. He had to chuckle at that – dimensions did vary between actuality and memory.

'Are you sure Zeus didn't mark him for death out of sheer envy?' he asked Artemis, who, for her part, snorted and locked her gaze on Hippolytus's face. 'Interesting indeed,' Thanatos continued. 'I can see why Aphrodite was keen for this one. Maybe Poseidon wanted a tumble with him as well.'

'Uncle, please!' protested Artemis. 'Can we just get on with it?'

Thanatos chuckled but noticed it sounded more like a giggle and wondered again at his transformation. This was going to take getting used to. He studied Hippolytus a moment longer and decided he owed the youth much. He'd protect him from whatever ire Zeus could muster. Death might be a quiet god but, when moved to emotion, could be very dangerous.

After all, the Titans had died, hadn't they? He'd been there. And he knew Zeus still remembered what he had seen that day when Death had last been moved to emotion.

He reached into his pouch and removed the sphere of Hippolytus's soul. He studied it a moment and then placed it back into the youth. He bent forward and kissed him, just as Hippolytus took his first breath in more than a day.

When he saw who stood over him, Hippolytus smiled.

The Gift of Eros

Dominic Santi

I couldn't quite understand the guy's accent. He said his name was Eric or something like that. But, after I'd asked him to repeat it twice, I figured it would be rude to ask again. I mean, he was a trick in a hotel bar. It's not like we were setting up to be eternal lovers or anything. Besides, he was really odd. Sexy as anything, but, let's face it, I ask the guy what he does for a living, and he tells me he's a god!

More like he thinks he's God's gift to mankind, I thought to myself. Sure, he was gorgeous. OK, so he was perfect. Not too tall, about five-ten, probably a hundred and sixty pounds. Curly honey-blond hair. And bright green eyes – you know, the sparkly come-hither ones that make you feel like you've known the guy for ever the first time you meet him.

I guessed he was about my age – twenty-six or so. And he had a body like you usually only see in magazines. Dark little tips showed through his shirt where his nips were perked up against his white silk shirt – on perfect pecs, of course. Washboard abs. And a bulge in his pants that made my mouth water just to look at it. The trousers were your typical Wall Street grey wool, but the way they fit him said they were no off-the-rack cut. You could tell they'd been made to emphasise his assets – not vulgar, just flattering. And his assets had definitely caught my attention. About seven inches, and the way those suit trousers draped over him, I could tell he was uncut. I mean, the guy definitely wasn't wearing underwear.

I figured him for a model. Like me. Or maybe somebody in marketing. Though from the looks of his clothes, he was working a lot more regularly than I was. That made sense. I doubt he'd ever had a zit in his life, and I ate way too much sugar to have a perfect complexion without the help of make-up. This guy's face was all his own. And the way he was looking at me made me so hot the sweat started trickling down my back. I wanted him, and I wanted him bad.

I also noticed the ring – on his perfect finger. Shit, even his hands looked like they'd been sculpted by Michelangelo.

'You married?' I nodded towards the thin gold band on his third finger. Usually, I'm not that nosey. 'Straight' guys aren't all that uncommon here. Personally, I kind of like them – that's one of the reasons I cruise this particular hotel. It's near the convention centres, so there are lots of one-timers looking to get their rocks off while they're in town without the little lady. But most of them remember to pocket the hand collar before they come in the door.

After the 'god' comment, I figured old Eric's answer might be fun. He surprised me when he just smiled and nodded, holding his hand up so the light caught the gold.

'I've been married a long time.' At my raised eyebrows – I mean, twenty-six is not that old – he laughed out loud. 'Sherry understands my occasional need for a man. She doesn't mind.'

He slurred his wife's name, too. I really couldn't place his accent.

'She doesn't mind your cruising a gay bar?' I laughed. I know there was more than a twinge of sarcasm in my voice as I looked at him over the top of my drink, but let's get real here.

He seemed to find my scepticism amusing.

'No.' He smiled. 'She sent me with her blessings. She knows I'll come home to her.'

Well, at least I knew this one wasn't going to weird out on me and announce he'd found 'true love' in the morning. I hate it when that happens. Then I remembered there was a computer trade show in town this weekend. He looked smart enough to be one of those cyber whizzes, so I turned the conversation towards more interesting topics.

'Where you from – San Jose?'

He shocked me again when he shook his head. 'Greece.'

Now that got my attention! I'd always wanted to go to the home of butt-fucking love.

'Athens?' I asked excitedly. 'I've always wanted to see the old cities.'

'No.' For some reason, my answer seemed to amuse him. But when I raised my eyebrows he shook his head, grinning like what he'd heard was some sort of private joke. 'I'm from farther north, up in the mountains.' He muttered something about old cities – he was still laughing – and ordered us both another glass of wine.

He was drinking a white wine I'd never tasted before. I didn't recognise the label. But, then, I don't read Greek. The wine was good, though. Not too dry, not too sweet, with lots of flavour.

'I thought Greeks drank uzo.' I nodded towards his glass.

'No.' He smiled. 'At least not where I'm from. We prefer the wines.'

'High altitudes and wine, that makes sense, I guess. I've got some friends who go out west to the Rockies each year, hunting. You like hunting?'

He seemed to find that hilarious. I slapped his back until he'd stopped choking.

'Excuse me,' he choked. 'Yes, hunting has always been a favourite pastime of mine. Do you also use the bow and arrows?'

'Only this shaft, bud,' I said, and smiled as I hefted my crotch with one hand and took another drink. 'This is all I need to catch the prey I'm looking for.'

Again the laughter, though this time he didn't choke. I was starting to like old Eric. He was weird, but he was fun.

We were sitting at a table along the wall, near the door to the back dining room. As the waiter finished filling our glasses, Eric looked around. The place was getting full, and there was lots of eye candy in the room. I wasn't quite as impressed as he seemed to be. I knew most of the regulars, and the conventioneers changed each week anyway. So, while he was looking his fill, I took another glance at his clothes. His coat was expensive. Some sort of cashmere, though he had it draped casually over the back of the chair. It was his scarf that caught my eye. It looked almost like it was made of spun gold. I reached out to touch it, catching myself just in time.

I looked up to see him watching me.

'You mind?' I asked. I didn't want him to think I was a thief or anything. 'It's really beautiful. I've never seen another one like it.'

'It was a gift from my wife.' He smiled – a bit smugly, I thought. But hey, clothes like that are something to be proud of. 'Go ahead,' he motioned me towards it. 'It's the only one of its kind.'

He wasn't kidding. I could feel the tensile strength of the metal in the weave, but the wool itself was incredibly soft. This was not something one got at Macy's.

'She must really like you,' I said, rubbing my fingertips over the threads.

'Oh, yes.' He grinned. 'We love each other very much.' He took another drink and his eyes travelled over my body, flaring and darkening as they rested on my crotch. 'That love does not diminish my occasional need for a man.'

As he spoke he brushed his leg against mine, and I felt the heat shoot up my spine. Hey, if this guy's wife doesn't mind sharing, that's fine by me. He was hot, and the more I looked at him, the more I wanted him.

He seemed distracted though, especially as some of the guys filing into the dining room brushed against him on their way to the back tables.

'The men here . . .' He paused, hunting for the words. 'There's something . . . odd . . . about so many of them. A fuzziness in their blood. Something evil and brooding – something unhealthy. And it is not in you.'

He was looking at my friend, Sal, as he spoke. And, right away, I got pissed off. Yeah, there was something unhealthy in Sal's blood all right. And he was thin enough to show it. He'd damn near died last month. From a fucking cold! I didn't appreciate old Eric's attempt at humour.

'You mean the HIV?' I asked bitterly. 'Lots of guys have it. You one of those negative queens who can't love a man with AIDS?' Damn, things like that just piss me off. 'If that's your way of asking if I'm negative, pal, you can just get fucked.'

I was tempted to drop my drink in Eric's perfect crotch, except that he seemed genuinely surprised by my answer. And concerned.

'AIDS? What is that?'

I took a deep breath and regrouped. OK, so the guy was a foreigner. Maybe he just didn't know the right words in English.

'Maybe it's called SIDA where you're from,' I said lamely, rubbing my fingers over my eyebrows as I calmed down. Sometimes I get so tired of thinking about serostatus and worrying about my friends, and of being afraid every time I fuck.

I could tell I'd lost him. Shit.

'AIDS,' I said tiredly. 'You get it from fucking. You know, from sharing come.'

He looked at me like he'd just been gut-punched. 'You can die, from having sex?' He seemed truly horrified.

I shook my head at him, not really sure what to say. 'Man, I don't know how far out in the sticks your mountain is, but you are way the fuck out of touch with reality.'

I don't know what response I'd expected, but whatever it was, I didn't get it. Eric was so upset his hands were shaking. He looked absolutely stunned. I sighed and took his drink from him, setting it down before any more of the wine spilled on the tablecloth. I didn't know where the hell he'd been the last couple of decades, but I couldn't stay mad at him. I mean, how do you stay ticked at somebody who's just discovered AIDS?

Without even thinking, I leaned over and kissed him. His lips were full and soft, like he was hungry for the reassurance of a human touch. And he was so responsive. His breath caught just from that light contact. OK, so he was weird. He was still sexy. I pulled away and smiled at him. 'Don't worry, pal, we'll be careful.'

I don't think he heard me. He was shaking his head, looking

from face to face at all the guys partying and laughing around him, and he said very softly, 'We have been gone too long.'

I laughed and squeezed his knee suggestively. 'We haven't even left the bar yet. But I could be convinced.'

This time, he looked at me again, a Michelangelo look that made me feel naked under my clothes, in spite of the shadows in Eric's eyes. Then he gave me one of those melting, sultry smiles from beneath his incredible dark lashes, the kind of lashes that make eyes look mysterious and smoky and irresistible.

'Will you come upstairs with me?' he asked, moving sensually to his feet. 'I have a room here.'

'I'd like that,' I said, grabbing my plain, black wool coat as I stood up. 'Just keep in mind that I don't care if you are negative and a fucking god, we're still going to use a rubber.'

The room was classy. It was one of those theme rooms, designed like a hunting lodge with fur rugs on the floor and on the bed, and a fireplace blazing on the far wall. There was a large wine skin on the wooden nightstand, and I wasn't surprised to find it held the wine that he favoured. The glasses were crystal, though, and I watched the light play in the facets as I twirled the stem between my fingers.

'You come here often?' The room was so luxurious it was a bit overwhelming, so I figured I'd make some small talk.

'No.' He shook his head. 'I've never been here before. My wife knows my tastes, so she had it specially decorated for me.'

This time I was the one who choked, but Eric didn't seem to notice. He'd slipped off his shoes – he wasn't wearing socks – and he was curling his toes into the thick fur of the rug. He shivered at the sensation, closing his eyes and smiling, so I figured I'd try it, too. I could see why he liked it. It was like petting a long-haired cat with my feet. I shivered, too.

I kept my eyes closed as I said absently, 'She going to be joining you in a few days?'

His breath was hot on my neck as he answered: 'No. I will go home to her. This place is her gift to me, for my time among men.'

Then he was kissing me, and I didn't care if he had a whole

fucking harem back at home. His lips were soft and wet, and as my arms moved around him, my dick pressed up against his already firm erection. I opened my mouth and shivered as my cock filled against the hot, hard shaft trapped in his trousers.

Seeing how turned on I was, I was surprised at how much I wanted to go slowly – to make the evening last and really savour each minute. Let's face it, I don't have sex with a 'god' every day. We undressed each other slowly. Eric was trembling like a man who'd waited way too long for sex – denied himself far too long – but still couldn't give up the pleasure of unveiling his present.

He took off my clothes in a slow striptease, giving me a tongue bath as he peeled away each piece of clothing. And I mean he gave me a total tongue bath. The backs of my knuckles. The insides of my elbows. And when he reached my nipples, I thought I'd die.

He motioned me to lie back on the bed, but he still wouldn't let me touch him.

I can't say that I minded. I was so turned on I might have really embarrassed myself. My dick hadn't reacted that way to anything other than direct stimulation in years. And what he was doing to my ankles was making me squirm.

Besides, looking at him was a treat. He was on his knees at the foot of the bed, licking his way slowly down my feet. He looked like one of those Greek statues at the Museum of Fine Art. He had a perfect body. Defined muscles – not like he worked out specific muscle groups, more like he just used his body a lot. His arms were ropy, but not excessively so. And, where his fingers moved over me, I felt odd calluses. They seemed strange for a guy who probably plucked a keyboard all day in some fancy boardroom. But they felt good, especially each time he reached up and pinched my tits.

His pants hadn't lied, either. Eric's balls were perfect. Round, full spheres that hung down in a loose sac between his legs. Dark blond pubic hair. And his cock – it was even better than I'd imagined. I felt like Pavlov's dog, trying to swallow the saliva filling my mouth. Eric's foreskin completely covered the tip of the beautiful, veiny shaft. But, as he got harder, I could see the glistening, dark head peeking out of its cocoon like a wet butterfly being born.

When he finished sucking my toes, he didn't turn me over. Instead, he sat back on his heels, lifted my legs and slowly worked his way up to the backs of my thighs. A total tongue bath.

And he kept going. Pretty soon, his face was buried in my crack.

He inhaled deeply, nuzzling his face against my cheeks. Then he purred like a big blond cat and said, 'I have so missed the smell of a man.'

I groaned, guessing what was coming. But I still arched and cried out when his tongue first touched me. It felt like butterfly wings kissing my anus – soft and wet and fluttering. The pressure increased, and I could feel that he was really tonguing me, really tasting me. It was sort of embarrassing. But, damn, he was really getting into it, and it felt good.

'Mmmm.' Eric's slurping seemed loud in the quiet of the room. And he still wouldn't let me touch him. He pushed my legs further apart and hunkered down between them. He was stronger than he looked. I mean, I knew from looking at him he was muscular, but I was surprised at how truly strong he was. He reached under my hips and lifted my ass to his face like I didn't weigh anything at all.

Then he dug in and *ate* me. I mean he tongued me until I thought I was going to pass out. I couldn't believe how good it felt. He kissed me until my ass lips started twitching and kissing him back. I could feel it! He sucked and licked and stretched me until I was so loose and open and relaxed that my hole was his!

And the noise! Eric was not a quiet lover. He was moaning and telling me my ass juice was like wild honey, saying strange things like 'I can taste the flowers in you' and something about wishing he could 'sip the nectar of each of the bees that have visited' me. I couldn't understand all of it. And I couldn't make sense of most of what I did hear. He kept lapsing into his own language, though I understood his occasional laughter when I really jumped or groaned.

Then he slid his tongue into me, and I didn't even try to think any more. I mean, Eric tongue-fucked me. It was incredible. I felt like I was back in high school, having one of those wild, hot, hormone-driven make-out sessions down by the lake. Only this time, I was kissing my lover back with my ass lips. Eric's tongue was in me to the root – moving back and forth over my ass lips, wiggling around inside of me. I could hardly breathe, arching my butt towards him in a primal need to be fucked!

I was like some sort of human sacrifice on a fucking pagan altar. Each time Eric's tongue stabbed into me, I yelled and begged for more. I might as well have been screaming, 'Bring on the knife!' I was in heaven. I mean, it was ecstasy! My whole ass was alive and throbbing with pure naked want.

The next thing I knew, Eric had dropped my butt back on the bed, and there were at least three fingers where his tongue had been, only now they were pressing against my joy spot. Then he dove down on my dick and growled, 'Give me your nectar.'

And, man, I shot – just like that. I mean, I know I should have warned him so he could back off, or pushed his head away or something. But I couldn't help myself. It was like my will wasn't my own any more. My climax was spontaneous, totally uncontrolled, and it almost broke me in two. My dick started spurting and then I was coming and coming and coming. And I couldn't stop! The climax just went on and on and on. I know I was screaming, but I couldn't help myself. It was like Eric was pressing and sucking every ounce of juice right up out of the bottom of my balls. His throat moved over me as he swallowed, drawing my semen through me. I thought I'd died and gone to heaven. Finally, my nerves were so overstimulated I had to push him away. But my hand was shaking like a leaf and I couldn't catch my breath.

Eric lifted off carefully, but, instead of moving away, he held me tenderly in his hands. And then he very gently, very lovingly, pressed the last drop out of my tube. I shuddered so hard my teeth chattered. Then there was just the soft, sandpapery touch of his tongue as he licked the last bit of moisture from my slit.

I was totally blissed out. Totally wasted. Not very polite of me. I mean, the guy was hard as a rock against my thigh and I was so exhausted I couldn't even lift my hand to jerk him off. But he didn't seem to care. In fact, he seemed damned pleased with himself. All of a sudden, I had the oddest feeling the rim job had been for his benefit, not mine. He was licking his lips and smiling as he held my softening dick in his hand, playing with it gently as he watched it go limp in his fingers. I moved my shaking legs down on to the bed, but I kept them spread so he could keep his toy.

I sighed contentedly, and Eric grinned up me. I know it sounds strange, but I felt the warmth from his eyes travel all through me. It's hard to describe, especially the look on his face. It was open, not possessive like some tricks that get really weird on you. The only word I can think of is love, pure love – of me, the man sex, everything. It was strange.

There wasn't much time to think about it, though. Eric leaned forward and I jumped as he planted a quick kiss on the head of my dick. Then his tongue was bathing my belly again – slowly, like he was teasing the blood and warmth back down from my heart and into my pelvis. He moved further down and tenderly took my balls in his mouth, one at a time, then both of them, and sucked them until I was moaning. Man, that felt good. He rolled them back and forth with his tongue until they tingled. Then he cleaned my pubic hair and the edge of my thigh where my cock had been resting. He was laughing and slurping like the dried pre-come and the overflow of come he was drinking were the sweetest honey he'd ever tasted. I felt my cock stir just listening to how much he was enjoying himself. I wouldn't have believed it was possible. After a come like that, I should have been dead for at least a couple of hours. OK, probably until morning. But watching him smearing my juices around on his face made me smile. Married or not, this guy had been deprived.

When I could breathe again, and when Eric seemed satisfied that my skin was sufficiently clean, he moved up and kissed me. It was odd tasting my come on another man's lips. I mean, that's something you just don't *do* these days, you know? He had that tongue moving again, though. Tasting me. Like he wanted to take in every molecule of me he could get off my skin. I couldn't resist his kisses. His mouth was like the best candy I've ever had, and I'm a connoisseur of rock candy. He was sweet, but flavourful, so my tastebuds were really noticing him, really getting to know him. Getting addicted to him.

Then he was straddling my chest, his perfect balls resting on my chin. I licked them tentatively, taking first one, then the other, of those firm spheres into my mouth and sucking on his softly wrinkled skin. His taste was even more pronounced down there. I love that first lick when I lift a man's balls and bury my face in the musk that's trapped in his crotch. The close aroma made me crave his scent even more as I bathed the sweat and body oil from his perfect, creamy skin. There was a soft down of silky golden hair on his balls. It darkened and curled as my saliva wet it. And old Eric was every bit as responsive now as he'd been when he was eating me. He moaned and laughed. I mean, the guy was having a great time.

From that angle, his nipples were profiled against the soft glow from the firelight. I couldn't resist them. Yeah, they were perfect, too. Velvety brown and pointy – I don't care if he was 'straight', those were not virgin nipples. I licked my fingers, and took his full, hard tips between my fingers. He threw his shoulders back and arched his chest towards me, groaning like he was in pain. I milked them until he was panting and a drop of his pre-come dripped on to my cheek.

Then he leaned forward until his cock was resting against my lips. With each breath, I inhaled his musk – I could feel his scent on my tastebuds. Then I groaned and opened my mouth, taking in that glistening prize. As he slid in, my lips pushed his foreskin back the rest of the way and released the tangy peppertree honey trapped there. In all my life, I'd never tasted anything as good as Eric's pre-come. It tingled with his energy – his essence. It was better than any drug I'd ever tried.

Normally, I'd insist on a rubber for somebody who leaked that much. I don't know why I didn't. Well, OK, I do know. I was so hungry for the taste of a man – that particular man. And I know it was stupid, but I figured he probably wasn't very high-risk, what with being married and all and living some place where an educated man like him hadn't even heard of AIDS. And, after what he'd done to me, I admit it, I really wanted to give the guy something back – give him what he wanted. It was like some corny celebration of free love or something. I felt like a fucking pagan, worshipping at the temple of lust.

And worship him I did. When his cock was all the way in my mouth, I started sucking. Man, did he go crazy. He was louder than shit! His primal *unh, uh, uh*s seemed like they were being torn out of his gut each time he surged forwards and into my throat. Hell, I was glad he was having a good time. It was getting me hard again.

But I didn't want him to come too soon. So, after a while, I grabbed his hips and held him in place so I could really work his glans. I kept my lips and tongue soft and gentle, but I still went to town on that slick, ultra-sensitive knob. He shook the way an uncut guy always does, like he almost couldn't stand the pain and stimulation, but he couldn't quite bring himself to make me stop.

I gotta admit it, Eric was gorgeous. And, the more turned on he got, the hotter he looked. I felt like I was staring up at a statue when he grabbed my head and started fucking my mouth. The perfect lines of his abs, each well-defined muscle shivering with delight. His skin looked like marble in the firelight, yet it was wonderfully warm and alive. And his cries told me how much he was truly enjoying the feel of my hot, wet mouth pussy. He was gulping in air and I could feel every muscle in his body tightening – he had my hair in a death grip.

Then he shot. I wasn't ready. I mean, most guys will warn you. But old Eric just let loose, his hose spurting down my open throat. In retrospect, he probably was telling me he was going to come, but I don't speak Greek or whatever the hell he was yelling. One minute, his cock was gliding in and out over my tongue, harder and hotter as he thrust his body forwards. Then his body stiffened and suddenly, he was flooding the back of my throat.

I know I should have pushed him away. But his whole body shook like it was breaking. I had my hands on his hips. While at some visceral level I knew I should have pulled away, instead I held him deep into my throat and just let him come, squeezing his butt as he cried out in total ecstasy.

When he was done, he sat back on my chest, sweat dripping down the side of his face and rolling down his chest as his softening cock slipped over my lips and landed with a soft plop on my collarbone.

Eventually, he caught his breath and looked down at me. His smile lit his face.

'Thank you,' he said softly.

'You're welcome.' I couldn't help smiling back. But I reached up and flipped my finger over that beautiful, limp cock that was so tantalisingly close.

'But we have got to talk, buddy. We shouldn't have done that, and I'm hoping like hell you really are negative. But if we're going to do anything else, we are *going* to use a rubber. You got that?'

He looked so confused, I finally sighed and rolled him on to his side. Isolated or not, Eric had some major things to learn. I reached over the edge of the bed and grabbed my trousers from the floor, pulling the three-pack of rubbers from my back pocket.

'We're going to use these, pal. Capishe?'

Eric looked totally bewildered. 'What are they?' he asked, reaching out his hand and curiously fingering the wrapper.

Shit, I'll buy a lot of things, but these days everybody knows what a condom is. Well, OK, apparently, everybody but Eric.

I tore open one of the wrappers. 'This is a condom – one each, latex. See?'

The thin sheath wasn't lubed, and it glowed like marble in the soft light. Eric picked it up, turning it around in his hands. He put it over the tip of his finger and started to unroll it, and suddenly I could see the light bulb going on in his brain. He looked at me, shocked.

'This goes over your –' He motioned towards his crotch, apparently at a loss for words.

'That's right, bud. Right over the old dick, just like this.' I had gotten really hard from sucking him, but I took advantage of the situation and slid the rubber on myself. Hell, I should go to work for the health clinic doing demos, you know? 'See? It keeps my come from getting in you, so I can't give you AIDS.' I reached over and touched the tip of his perfect dick. It had retreated into his foreskin, but he wasn't all the way soft by a long shot. I could tell the evening was far from over. 'And, if you're thinking of putting your pecker up my ass, you better believe it's going to be wearing one of these little latex raincoats.'

'But how –' He stopped, running his fingers over the smooth surface of the taut latex. 'How do you touch?'

I tried to smile at him, but I couldn't quite make it. The question hit way too close to home.

'That's the million-dollar question, isn't it, pal?' I reached up and smoothed away the wrinkle of concern – of pain, maybe – that had appeared on his forehead when he'd realised what the condom was for. 'We touch through the latex. That is, if we want to stay alive. Otherwise, we end up like Sal. And I got too many plans for that. I intend to be around for the wild fuck party that's going to happen once a cure or a vaccine or whatever the hell they're gonna come up with gets here.' I kept stroking Eric's face, tracing down his cheek over the faintest light shadows of bristles that let me know where his beard would be come morning. 'If you're going to have sex with anybody but your wife, you better learn to make friends with these babies. Now.'

He said something in Greek, but his voice was all thick. I looked at his beautiful, sparkling green eyes and realised there was a tear running down his cheek.

'Aw, come on, man. It's not that bad! We can still fuck, you know?'

Shit. I didn't know what to do. I mean, nothing like this had ever happened to me before. I don't play with virgins. Not that Eric was a virgin, but he was so damned innocent. Me, I'm one of the wild party crowd. A different guy every night and two on Saturday. I'd figured out condoms in junior high and never looked back. Shit.

I lay down next to Eric and took him in my arms and held him, feeling his hot tears run down my neck and on to the sheets. I swear, it was like he'd just beamed in from another planet. Or maybe his mountains in Greece really were that isolated. So I just lay there and held him. I mean, it didn't feel strange or anything. He wasn't weak or whining. He just was so incredibly sad. Well, shit, sometimes AIDS made me sad, too. I let him cry it out on my shoulder.

And, when he'd calmed down, I started kissing him. You

know, to help him feel better. Not a come-on or anything. I kissed his hair and his forehead, then I lifted his face and moved my lips over his damp eyelids and down the line of his face, kissing away the last salty signs of his tears. He held on to me like he was drowning, his arms and legs all tangled up with mine.

Then our swelling cocks were touching, and he was kissing me back. And his kisses tasted good. The condom had slipped off while we'd been holding each other, so now our naked bodies were touching everywhere, elbows and knees and tits and the incredible heat rising from his torso.

Eric rolled over on to his belly and spread his legs. His perfect butt looked even more rounded like that. So open and so vulnerable. He wanted me to fuck him so badly.

I couldn't resist one little kiss. Right on his pucker. OK, then one more. And one more. Pretty soon my tongue was licking him and he was moaning into the sheets, grabbing handfuls of them. He loosened to my tongue and he was so hot inside. I never thought I'd ever see a perfect asshole, you know? But this guy's was a perfect dark rose, even in the dying firelight, and it wrinkled right up around my tongue. I covered him with my spit. I mean, I slobbered him with spit.

Then I moved up over him. I had another rubber in my hand, you know? And it wasn't like he'd asked me to do anything I didn't want to. But he just needed to be touched so badly – man-touched, you know? He needed it. So, I said 'what the fuck' and tossed the rubber. I put my cock against his hot, spit-wet hole and I slid into him like a knife into butter.

I don't know what I'd expected from him. Maybe that he'd yell at me for going in bareback or bitch about my just going in too fast, or something. Instead, he gasped and cried out something in his language, then he rose up on his elbows and his whole body stiffened, like he was mesmerised. This beatific smile covered his face and his asshole snugged up around me like the tightest, most form-fitting kid glove I could ever have imagined. I mean, this guy was in heaven, and his bare skin felt so good on my dick that I was shaking with pleasure. My hips twitched with wanting to thrust into him.

After a moment, he dropped his head down, breathing hard.

'Your condom,' he said, rolling the unfamiliar word around on his tongue. 'You do not want to use it?'

'Do you?' I asked. I was having trouble keeping still as I held myself over him.

'No!' He shook his head vehemently.

'Then shut up and enjoy this. Because I'm no doubt really going to regret this in the morning.'

He didn't say another word. Just nodded his head slowly, and then he arched up to meet me. And, man, Eric knew how to fuck! He did the old clamp and clench like his asshole had been born for my cock to fuck it. And he was hot as a volcano inside.

'Take it easy, guy,' I gasped, holding his hips hard to slow him down. 'That's one helluva talented ass you have, and I don't want to shoot yet.'

'I would like to roll over,' he gasped, 'so I can see you when I come.'

Again the accent. But I just nodded, afraid that if I so much as spoke I'd shoot before we got a chance to change positions. For some reason, I knew he really needed to come while a hard cock was fucking him, and I didn't have much self-control left.

I don't know how in hell he did it, but he swivelled his legs around and rolled over with my dick still in him, then his legs were on my shoulders. I grabbed his ankles and pushed them way back, then I leaned forward and I really started fucking him. His jizz was leaking out of his dick, and my cock felt like it was fucking hot, wet, living velvet. It was perfect. I leaned over until just the tip of my dick was still in him, and I licked a slick, clear droplet off that perfect slit. His gasp made my skin crawl as even more blood rushed into my full-to-splitting shaft. I don't know that I've ever had someone want me so badly.

And I don't know that I've ever wanted anyone as badly as I wanted Eric. I couldn't get enough of him. I wanted to shove myself so deep up his ass that I could feel his heart beating. I wanted to make him feel so good he would scream like he was dying when he came.

He was getting close. His head was thrashing on the bed, soaked with sweat, and even his nipples were hard. He was crying out with each thrust.

Suddenly he roared out, '*Fuck* me!'

I couldn't believe the power in his command. That sure as shit wasn't Greek. It sounded like he was yelling right into my head! Like my muscles were obeying him, not me. I couldn't have resisted him if I'd wanted to.

Fortunately, I didn't want to resist. I slammed into him, as hard and as deep as I knew how. And I kept it slow, so he felt every micro-inch of my dick stretching his asshole. Fucking him. But his ass was pulling the come through my dick, and I couldn't stop that either.

'I'm going to have to pull out, buddy,' I gasped. 'I'm going to come . . .'

'No!' He commanded. 'Stay!' His ass clamped down on me like a vice. I had to obey him. Then he shuddered, like he was drawing on some supreme effort of will, and he said more softly, 'Please, stay!' The power was gone from his voice, and there was only an overwhelming need left as he looked into my eyes and choked out. 'Come in me! Please!'

Well, shit. What's a guy to do? I thrust a couple more times, figuring I'd pull out at the last minute anyway. By then, Eric was crying out in his native language. His asshole spasmed around me and his whole body went stiff. Then he clamped down and his cock was shooting. All over his chest and belly. From the amount, I could tell I was pushing it right up out of his joy spot. His voice filled my ears and he kept coming and coming – surge after surge of glistening white man milk pulsing out of his perfect cock.

I couldn't help myself. I leaned over and licked it up, my dick still in him. The taste of his come, oh God, the taste – and then I didn't have any choice about pulling out. I was past the point of no return. The semen boiled up out of my balls and poured into Eric's asshole. I shoved myself deep and just let it happen. I'd never done that before. Not in my whole life. Not even once.

It was the most incredible thing I'd ever felt. I mean, fucking's always good. But this touching was exquisite. Shit, it took so much out of me, all of a sudden I felt like I was going to cry.

I blinked back that crazy response fast. And, when my eyes were clear again, I looked down and I couldn't believe what I saw. Eric was getting hard again. He was smiling up at me, with

237

that beautifully perfect face of his gifting me with pure love and passion. This time, his finger was playing with my asshole, and I knew what he wanted. And I couldn't say no to him. I rolled on to my back and pulled my knees up and back and opened myself to him.

I must have looked as scared as I felt. But the look he gave me held such love. His hands were magic as they teased my sphincter open. He drooled saliva on to his finger and stuffed it up me. His spit was more slippery than any lube I've ever felt. Then that perfect, naked dick of his was sliding up my hungry hole. A flash of pain burned through me as I tightened in fear. Then he was in me, and it was heaven.

He fucked me long and slow. I could feel my asshole sliding over his dick, feel him feeling me. He fucked me until I wasn't afraid any more, then until I couldn't think. My whole world was where we were joined, with our naked nerves feeding pleasure off of each other until I'd almost lost my mind. Incoherent sound rose out of my throat, loud and wanting and needing.

Then he leaned over and took my dick in his mouth and sucked me into his throat. I wouldn't have thought I had another drop in me, but, when he started pulsing against my prostate, when I felt his hot come filling my ass and his thick surging cock sliding over his cream, I shot again. It felt like Eric was sucking his own come through me and out my dick. I screamed and screamed and screamed until I passed out.

I don't remember much of the rest of the night. I know we slept together for a while. I had the oddest dreams. All kinds of strange shit like lofty mountains and hunting live prey – animal types – with a bow and arrows and seeing the fuck lust in the eyes of every person I saw. Yet I felt surprisingly well rested when I woke up just before dawn. Eric was dressing to leave.

He reached over and touched his hand to the side of my face.

'Thank you for your gift of love,' he said, and smiled.

I grinned back up at him, still feeling blissfully sleepy and sated.

'You're welcome, I think. I just hope you really are negative, pal, or I'm screwed.' The joke seemed funny to me and I laughed, though I figured groggily that, by morning, my sense of humour would probably have worn off, along with the languor.

Eric was stroking my hair. It was incredibly relaxing, like my bones were melting away. I tried to stay awake, but I couldn't. As I drifted off again, his voice sounded really far away as he said the weirdest thing: 'In return, I give you my own gift of love. The gift of immunity.'

Now, I must have been more tired than I thought. You know, the accent thing. Because what he said sure didn't make sense. Suddenly, I couldn't keep my eyes open. And then there was this horrific pain in my left pec, almost over my heart. It felt like something hard and sharp had sliced into me, burying itself deep in my skin. I yelled as my mind filled with colours and music and lust! Then there was only blackness.

When I woke in the morning, Eric was gone. There was a continental breakfast on the nightstand – hard, crusty bread; a soft round tangy cheese I'd never tasted before; and the last of the wine from the night before. I was ravenous, so I ate it all. I hadn't really been expecting a note, and there wasn't one. Just a copy of the hotel card, propped against our empty glasses from last night, with 'checkout time at 11:00' circled. It was ten thirty. I left the dishes on the stand, then I got dressed and left.

I felt great, and, surprisingly, not as worried about my serostatus as I'd expected, though I resolutely headed down to the health clinic for another baseline test. I figured it was going to be a long few months of waiting. The doctor asked about the bruise and the small slitlike cut next to my left nipple. But, when I said I didn't know where it was from, she just shook her head and told me to keep it clean until it healed. It was already scabbed, so I left it alone.

Ever since then, I've been a walking libido. I mean, all I can think about is fucking. I'm so horny all the time, I'm afraid I'm going to lose my job. I'm fucking in the stockroom between coffee breaks. I'm sucking guys off in the john at lunchtime. I'm picking up two and three guys a night from the bars – every night. I want every man in NYC, and I want him now!

And I only want him once. It's fucking bizarre. Ever since that night with Eric, I feel like my skin is crawling with sex and lust. I want to fuck every guy I see.

But that's not the real problem. The real problem is that I can't keep a condom on. I mean, the damn things come off; they break; they tear. My semen seems to want to get into every guy I meet and the latex is just no fucking barrier!

Even Sal got pissed at me. We've always fucked a lot, but he's really careful about his health, what with his immune system being compromised and all. So when the rubber broke just as I came, he decked me. Well, shit, I was using a Trojan extra strength. I felt like I was fucking in a shower curtain the damn thing was so thick. Those things are *not* supposed to break.

I think most of it was still up his ass when he threw me out the door with my clothes behind me. We made up last week, though. Sal's in too good a mood these days to stay pissed at anybody. When he went to the doctor to see if I'd given him any new or different diseases, he had T-cells coming out his ears and they couldn't find a single trace of HIV in his blood. That's happening to a lot of guys I know, and to their friends. The lady on the news said some bigwigs are even coming in from Atlanta to try to figure out what the hell's going on around here. They're saying something about a mutation that might be the key to a cure or even a vaccine.

That would be so fucking great. So fucking cool if the party's finally here. Especially now that I'm a walking libido and everybody's after my ass.

I just hope that wherever Eric is, he gets a chance to come to the party.

IDOL NEW BOOKS

Information correct at time of printing. For up-to-date availability,
please check www.idol-books.co.uk

WORDS MADE FLESH

Published in November 2000   Thom Wolf

Best-selling novelist Glenn Holden has an appreciation for the rougher side of sex. But
when a handsome stranger breaks into his house claiming to be a character from one of
Glenn's own thrillers, the author is suddenly thrust into a surreal sexual adventure that
goes further than the concoctions of his own dirty mind – a bizarre world full of mysterious
men and even wilder sex.

£8.99/$10.95   ISBN 0 352 33544 0

DIVINE MEAT

Published in January 2001   Edited by David MacMillan

An Idol short-story collection. Gods pleasure themselves with male flesh and vice versa in
this astonishing array of tales of human/divine homoeroticism. From Ganymede and Zeus
to lustful voodoo deities, sacred genies and the Cerne Abbas giant himself, these stories are
hot, horny and (well) hung. *Divine Meat*: where man meets his maker. In more ways than
one.

£8.99/$10.95   ISBN 0 352 33587 4

MAN ON!

Published in March 2001   Turner Kane

Greg Williams of Middleton United is young, talented and handsome, a favourite with
both fans and players alike. But when he signs his new football contract with Weston City,
and when he starts sleeping with his soon-to-be-wed best friend Matt, things start hotting
up, both on and off the pitch.

£8.99/$10.95   ISBN 0 352 33613 7

Also published:

DARK RIDER

Jack Gordon

While the rulers of a remote Scottish island play bizarre games of sexual dominance with
the Argentinian Angelo, his friend Robert – consumed with jealous longing for his coffee-
skinned companion – assuages his desires with the willing locals.

£6.99/$9.95   ISBN 0 352 33243 3

TO SERVE TWO MASTERS
Gordon Neale

In the isolated land of Ilyria men are bought and sold as slaves. Rock, brought up to expect to be treated as mere 'livestock', yearns to be sold to the beautiful youth Dorian. But Dorian's brother is as cruel as he is handsome, and if Rock is bought by one brother he will be owned by both.

£6.99/$9.95 ISBN 0 352 33245 X

CUSTOMS OF THE COUNTRY
Rupert Thomas

James Cardell has left school and is looking forward to going to Oxford. That summer of 1924, however, he will spend with his cousins in a tiny village in rural Kent. There he finds he can pursue his love of painting – and begin to explore his obsession with the male physique.

£6.99/$9.95 ISBN 0 352 33246 8

DOCTOR REYNARD'S EXPERIMENT
Robert Black

A dark world of secret brothels, dungeons and sexual cabarets exists behind the respectable façade of Victorian London. The degenerate Lord Spearman introduces Dr Richard Reynard, dashing bachelor, to this hidden world.

£6.99/$9.95 ISBN 0 352 33252 2

CODE OF SUBMISSION
Paul C. Alexander

Having uncovered and defeated a slave ring operating in London's leather scene, journalist Nathan Dexter had hoped to enjoy a peaceful life with his boyfriend Scott. But when it becomes clear that the perverted slave trade has started again, Nathan has no choice but to travel across Europe and America in his bid to stop it. Second in the trilogy.

£6.99/$9.95 ISBN 0 352 33272 7

SLAVES OF TARNE
Gordon Neale

Pascal willingly follows the mysterious and alluring Casper to Tarne, a community of men enslaved to men. Tarne is everything that Pascal has ever fantasised about, but he begins to sense a sinister aspect to Casper's magnetism. Pascal has to choose between the pleasures of submission and acting to save the people he loves.

£6.99/$9.95 ISBN 0 352 33273 5

ROUGH WITH THE SMOOTH
Dominic Arrow

Amid the crime, violence and unemployment of North London, the young men who attend Jonathan Carey's drop-in centre have few choices. One of the young men, Stewart, finds himself torn between the increasingly intimate horseplay of his fellows and the perverse allure of the criminal underworld. Can Jonathan save Stewart from the bullies on the streets and behind bars?

£6.99/$9.95 ISBN 0 352 33292 1

CONVICT CHAINS
Philip Markham

Peter Warren, printer's apprentice in the London of the 1830s, discovers his sexuality and taste for submission at the hands of Richard Barkworth. Thus begins a downward spiral of degradation, of which transportation to the Australian colonies is only the beginning.

£6.99/$9.95　　　　　　　　　　　　　　　　　　　　　ISBN 0 352 33300 6

SHAME
Raydon Pelham

On holiday in West Hollywood, Briton Martyn Townsend meets and falls in love with the daredevil Scott. When Scott is murdered, Martyn's hunt for the truth and for the mysterious Peter, Scott's ex-lover, leads him to the clubs of London and Ibiza.

£6.99/$9.95　　　　　　　　　　　　　　　　　　　　　ISBN 0 352 33302 2

HMS SUBMISSION
Jack Gordon

Under the command of Josiah Rock, a man of cruel passions, HMS *Impregnable* sails to the colonies. Christopher, Viscount Fitzgibbons, is a reluctant officer; Mick Savage part of the wretched cargo. They are on a voyage to a shared destiny.

£6.99/$9.95　　　　　　　　　　　　　　　　　　　　　ISBN 0 352 33301 4

THE FINAL RESTRAINT
Paul C. Alexander

The trilogy that began with *Chains of Deceit* and continued in *Code of Submission* concludes in this powerfully erotic novel. From the dungeons and saunas of London to the deepest jungles of South America, Nathan Dexter is forced to play the ultimate chess game with evil Adrian Delancey – with people as sexual pawns.

£6.99/$9.95　　　　　　　　　　　　　　　　　　　　　ISBN 0 352 33303 0

HARD TIME
Robert Black

HMP Cairncrow prison is a corrupt and cruel institution, but also a sexual minefield. Three new inmates must find their niche in this brutish environment – as sexual victims or lovers, predators or protectors. This is the story of how they find love, sex and redemption behind prison walls.

£6.99/$9.95　　　　　　　　　　　　　　　　　　　　　ISBN 0 352 33304 9

ROMAN GAMES
Tasker Dean

When Sam visits the island of Skate, he is taught how to submit to other men, acting out an elaborate fantasy in which young men become wrestling slaves – just as in ancient Rome. Indeed, if he is to have his beautiful prize – the wrestler, Robert – he must learn how the Romans played their games.

£6.99/$9.95　　　　　　　　　　　　　　　　　　　　　ISBN 0 352 33322 7

VENETIAN TRADE
Richard Davis

From the deck of the ship that carries him into Venice, Rob Weaver catches his first glimpse of a beautiful but corrupt city where the dark alleys and misty canals hide debauchery and decadence. Here, he must learn to survive among men who would make him a plaything and a slave.

£6.99/$9.95   ISBN 0 352 33323 5

THE LOVE OF OLD EGYPT
Philip Markham

It's 1925 and the deluxe cruiser carrying the young gigolo Jeremy Hessling has docked at Luxor. Jeremy dreams of being dominated by the Pharaohs of old, but quickly becomes involved with someone more accessible – Khalid, a young man of exceptional beauty.

£6.99/$9.95   ISBN 0 352 33354 5

THE BLACK CHAMBER
Jack Gordon

Educated at the court of George II, Calum Monroe finds his native Scotland a dull, damp place. He relieves his boredom by donning a mask and holding up coaches in the guise of the Fox – a dashing highwayman. Chance throws him and neighbouring farmer Fergie McGregor together with Calum's sinister, perverse guardian, James Black.

£6.99/$9.95   ISBN 0 352 33373 1

BOOTY BOYS
Jay Russell

Hard-bodied black British detective Alton Davies can't believe his eyes or his luck when he finds muscular African-American gangsta rapper Banji-B lounging in his office early one morning. Alton's disbelief – and his excitement – mounts as Banji-B asks him to track down a stolen videotape of a post-gig orgy.

£7.99/$10.95   ISBN 0 352 33446 0

EASY MONEY
Bob Condron

One day an ad appears in the popular music press. Its aim: to enlist members for a new boyband. Young, working-class Mitch starts out as a raw recruit, but soon he becomes embroiled in the sexual tension that threatens to engulf the entire group. As the band soars meteorically to pop success, the atmosphere is quickly reaching fever pitch.

£7.99/$10.95   ISBN 0 352 33442 8

SUREFORCE
Phil Votel

Not knowing what to do with his life once he's been thrown out of the army, Matt takes a job with the security firm Sureforce. Little does he know that the job is the ultimate mix of business and pleasure, and it's not long before Matt's hanging with the beefiest, meanest, hardest lads in town.

£7.99/$10.95   ISBN 0 352 33444 4